The Hamlin Park Irregulars:

boom-BOOM!

By

Wally Duff

www.HamlinParkIrregulars.com

For permission requests, write to the publisher at:

Attention: Wallace Duff
c/o K, M & N Publishers, Inc.
Hamlin Park Irregulars, A Nebraska Limited Liability Co.
Suite 100, 12829 West Dodge Road
Omaha, NE 68154

Visit the author's website: www.HamlinParkIrregulars.com

First Edition

ISBN-13: 9781548686109
ISBN-10: 1548686107

To Gracie, you were there at the beginning.

Rocky, you were there in the middle.

And little Bentley, you're here at the end.

Many of today's at-home mothers, having worked for a while, are used to having colleagues around for gossip or lunch — and they miss that at home. Without bosses to provide the atta-girls they learned to crave, they look to other women. The question is, how to find them?

Christina Duff: *Wall Street Journal*

Part 1

Arlington, Virginia

8 a.m.

Tuesday, July 3

1

My heart pounded so fast I found it hard to breathe. I called FBI Special Agent Scott J. Wiles. "He's here!"

"Who is this?" Wiles' voice was annoyingly calm. "And who's where?"

"It's Tina Edwards, and the bomber I warned you about yesterday just walked into the surgery entrance of the Arlington Women's Clinic."

"Oh, really?"

"He's disguised as a deliveryman."

"Ms. Edwards, are you sure you're not overreacting?" He paused. "Again."

Jerk.

I grabbed my backpack and jumped out of my car. "He's pushing a laundry cart and the bomb is in it!"

"Are you certain he took the device into the building?"

I sucked in a deep breath before I answered. "Not exactly. No."

Wiles didn't say anything.

"He is *not* the regular laundry deliveryman, and he's *here* on the wrong day!"

"I will send an agent to investigate," he said.

"With D.C. traffic, your agent will be lucky to be here by noon."

Forget this damn story.

I shouldered my backpack. "Wiles, I'm going in there to stop him."

"Ms. Edwards, do not go into that building!"

I hung up on him and slammed my car door.

My next call was 911. I told them about the bomber and gave them the clinic's address.

Jamming the phone into my backpack, I turned my jog into an all-out sprint. There were several abortion protesters on the other side of the street from the clinic's front door. They saw me coming and began chanting anti-abortion protests as I roared past them.

"Bomb!" I shouted, pointing at the clinic. "Run!"

I didn't stop to see what they were going to do. I ran through the clinic's front door and skidded to a stop in the middle of the waiting room. There were about half a dozen young women sitting with their heads down, looking at their cell phone screens. A couple wore ear buds. Two female staff personnel sat at a glass-enclosed desk. They worked on their computers.

"There's a bomb in this building! Get out of here!"

One young woman looked up at me. The rest continued to stare at their cell phone screens, oblivious to what I'd said.

"Stop looking at your damn cell phones!" I yelled again, this time stomping my foot. "I'm a reporter, and you're all going to be blown up!"

No one moved.

They might die because of their stupid cell phones.

One staff member picked up a phone. If she called their security, help might be on the way. But I didn't have time to wait. I had to find the bomber and stop him before he blew up the building and all of us inside.

2

The door to the surgery area was to my left.

He might be in there.

As I stepped into the hallway, the odors of cleaning solvents and medications washed over me. The frigid air being spewed out by the building's overly enthusiastic cooling system instantly gave me goose bumps.

Twenty feet in front of me, the men's bathroom door flew open. The laundry deliveryman walked out. He turned to his right and moved toward the exit door into the parking lot.

Where is his laundry basket?

Did he plant the bomb in the bathroom?

Adrenaline surged through my blood stream. I reached into my backpack and grabbed a Glock 19. It was a departing gift from the Marines I'd been embedded with while doing stories in Afghanistan.

Throwing down my backpack, I jacked a bullet into the chamber. The click-clack noise echoed off the white walls and the green tile floor of the hallway.

The laundryman's head snapped up.

Now you know I have a gun.

He stopped and turned toward me. I held the Glock in front of me with both hands, my right index finger on the trigger guard. He reached into his white jacket pocket with his right hand and pulled out a flip-phone.

You can use it to detonate the bomb.

I motioned with the gun. "Put the phone down and step away."

He ignored my command and shuffled backward toward the exit.

You don't think I'll pull the trigger.

Turning on my gun's internal laser sight, I pointed the narrow red beam at the center of his chest. I wanted to prove to him that I would shoot.

But will I?

He continued to back up. I walked toward him. With each stride, the laser beam moved back and forth across his chest. My ASICS squeaked on the tile floor.

The surgery entrance door opened behind him. A slender young woman entered the hallway. The dazzling morning sunlight from the open door backlit her stringy blond hair. She stopped when she reached the man.

"Excuse me," she said. "I'm looking for pre-op registration."

The bomber grabbed her around the neck and twisted her toward me, using her body as a shield.

I don't have a clear shot!

She twisted and turned, struggling to break free. "Let go of me, you creep!"

Her screams became muffled as he tightened the pressure on her throat.

I stopped walking. Assuming a shooter's stance, I slid my index finger onto the trigger. The girl's eyes widened when she saw me aiming the gun in her direction. She broke loose from the bomber's grasp and dived to the floor.

He pushed a number on his flip-phone.

"Baby killers!" he screamed.

I heard a phone ring in the men's bathroom.

Shoot him!

The bathroom phone rang a second time.

I fired two shots at his center mass.

A blinding flash of light...

A thunderous *BOOM!*

Acrid smoke and dust... Chemical odors... My body thrust upwards... Pressure in my ears... My chest slamming into a wall... Searing pain in my ribs... My head bouncing off the floor... A shower of lights behind my eyelids... An explosion inside my head...

And darkness...

Part 2

Chicago, Illinois

9 a.m.

Saturday, June 24th

Almost five years later

3

Arlie Wickstrom fingered the sparse, white hairs on her upper lip. "Tell me again, why are you here?"

Because I was canned from my last reporting job and this is the only one I can find.

Saturday morning, I sat with Mrs. Wickstrom in the living room of her 1920s red brick home in Lakeview, an upscale neighborhood on Chicago's North Side. The elderly lady sat with her ankles crossed, her hands in her lap, and her slightly bowed spine about six inches from the back of her padded Queen Anne chair. Her overpowering, lilac-scented perfume hung in the air.

"As I mentioned to you on the phone, I write a monthly column for the *Lakeview Times*," I said.

She stared at me, and her eyes seemed to defocus.

"It's a free weekly newspaper sponsored by our local merchants," I continued. "My pieces are published once a month. I would like to feature a story about your collection of Sunbeam Mixmasters in the July twenty-eighth issue."

I waited for her to say something.

She didn't.

Blink so I'll know you're still alive.

"All righty then, let's move along," I said, opening my pocket-size spiral notebook and hoping she would realize that an interview meant she should answer my questions. "There must be an interesting story about why you began buying them."

"Not that I remember, dear."

My head began to throb.

"I understand your collection runs from 1935 to 1960 and includes one hundred thirty-four models."

"One hundred thirty-five. I recently purchased an exquisite, red, 1942 wartime mixer."

Finally! A response.

"And?"

"And what, dear?"

I did three weeks of background research prepping for this? Woodward and Bernstein couldn't make this story interesting. Am I trying to create fabulous stories out of banal neighborhood events?

Okay, I am, and it obviously isn't working.

I need to find a story to resurrect my career from the literary trash dump of discredited reporters.

And I have to do it soon.

4

An hour later, I stood in the mid-morning sun in front of Mrs. Wickstrom's home. I held my cell phone in one hand and my battered, brown leather briefcase in the other. I called my husband.

"Carter, I'm finally finished with Mrs. Wickstrom's interview," I said.

I began walking toward our home and tried to ignore the explosions from illegal fireworks that the neighborhood kids were shooting off as they warmed up for the Fourth of July.

"How'd it go?" he asked.

"It sucked. My well-planned, probing questions and her fading memory weren't a good fit."

Another blast rocked the neighborhood.

I hate this time of year.

On July third five years ago, I'd been blown up in a bombing at the Arlington Women's Clinic. The PTSD attacks began two weeks after I came home from the hospital. I had the symptoms under control except for this time of year.

Fireworks are overrated.

"Let me see your notes when you get here," he said. "Maybe I can give you a few suggestions about how to punch it up."

In D.C., we'd been investigative journalists at the *Washington Post*. Now, Carter is an assistant managing editor for local news at the *Chicago Tribune* and editing his reporters' stories is one of his main duties.

"Thanks for the offer, but Joseph Pulitzer couldn't help this story. What have you and Kerry been doing?"

Kerry is our two-year-old daughter.

"We made a finger painting picture for you, and now I'm taking her up for a much-needed bath."

I pictured a multicolored paint mess on the family room wood floor. My husband always forgets to use a drop cloth. And he mentioned bathing Kerry but nothing about any other cleanup.

Another job for mommy.

5

Our home is on the corner of West Melrose and North Paulina in Lakeview, ten blocks from Mrs. Wickstrom's residence. Like many houses in the neighborhood, it is three stories high, with all floors above the ground. It has atrocious gray siding, which makes the outside look grimy even in radiant sunlight.

I trudged up the nine steep steps to the main level and entered through the front door.

"Hey, Kerry," Carter called out from the family room. "Mommy's here."

Kerry roared down the polished hardwood floor of the hallway to greet me. "Momma, Momma, Momma!"

She skidded and slammed into my knees.

Socks? Guess Daddy forgot your shoes.

Stooping down, I scooped her into my arms and sniffed the scent of baby shampoo in her freshly washed hair.

"Kerry, you smell so good. Daddy said you made a finger painting for me. May I see it?"

She wiggled free from my grasp and rushed back into the family room, once again slipping and sliding but at least not falling.

I stood on my tiptoes and kissed my hubby. "I'm thinking shoes might help out."

"Our daughter declared she didn't want to wear them."

"The inmate is running the asylum."

"But I don't want her to remember me as a 'strict daddy' when she grows up."

"It could be worse. Kerry will think of me as a mother who writes boring stories."

"At least none of them are dangerous."

There it is: the "D" word.

He never lets me forget that I was severely injured after entering the clinic building when I shouldn't have. Or that was the FBI's conclusion, which ultimately got me fired from the *Post*.

But it had been almost five years ago. I wanted to scream that my brains were turning to mashed potatoes from lack of stimulation, and his consistent harping about looking for "safe stories" was making me crazy.

Honey, enough's enough.

Maybe spending the rest of the weekend with them was the perfect way to forget the mind-numbing interview with Mrs. Wickstrom. But I would go cuckoo if I didn't discover a story that was a lot more challenging to research and write about than Sunbeam Mixmasters.

6

On Monday morning, Carter stood at the kitchen counter making breakfast for Kerry. She sat on her booster seat in the kitchen nook with her two constant companions: a twelve-inch, baby-glop-stained, red Elmo and a pink-colored flannel blanket she'd named Ralph. Daddy would feed himself while Kerry ate. Elmo and Ralph would watch.

Kerry has inherited Carter's sandy hair, blue eyes, and strong angular face. He is a tick over six feet two, and she's at the top of the growth chart, proving she inherited her daddy's height DNA.

"I'm going out for my run," I said from the front hallway. "I love you."

"We love you," Carter called from behind me.

Unless there's a *Tribune* staff meeting or a breaking story, he doesn't have to be at work until ten. He spends most of the early morning with Kerry, which allows them time together and gives me the opportunity to do solo activities like running along the tree-lined streets of Lakeview.

My plan was to begin my six-mile run by going north on Paulina. The branches of the locust and maple trees on each side of our neighborhood streets touch and often intertwine, creating a feeling on a dark and windy day like I'm Ichabod Crane in Sleepy Hollow. The canopy of leaves provides much-needed shade on sunny days, and during fall, the colors are spectacular.

As I ran, I listened to the BoDeans in my ear buds. Running has helped to drive away the PTSD demons since the bomber blew me up in Arlington. The music helped blot out the repeated explosions from the fireworks being set off in the neighborhood.

Don't forget to journal while Kerry is napping.

Daily journaling is the other way I found to deal with the PTSD symptoms. I document my feelings and the events that happen in my life, hoping to eventually share them with my family.

Once I get into my running rhythm, I observe any activity going on around me, and if I discover a potential storyline, I try to find time to go back and check it out.

I need to find a great story.

Last night, I was in our kitchen nook comforting my stuffy-nosed toddler with a bottle of milk. All the books say this is wrong at her age, but the sage authors who have written this dandy advice were home sleeping soundly, and I had a miserable infant in my arms. Any sane mom would do the same thing. We both needed to get some sleep.

Kerry drank most of her bottle and then drifted off to sleep. Continuing to rock her, I glanced out the front windows and noticed a "Sold" sign had replaced the "For Sale" sign previously stuck into the front yard of a house on West Melrose, diagonally across the street from ours. That was not unusual, since homes in our neighborhood frequently go on and off the housing market. It was too dark to snap an iPhone picture, so I copied down the real estate information from the sign.

It was a good thing I did. During the beginning of my Monday morning run, I glanced at the house and the sign had already been taken down.

Why so fast?

I had to check it out, so at the end of my run, I sprinted down the street toward the house. A van from Cort Furniture Rental was double-parked on the street in front of it. Two men in blue work clothes manhandled a couch out of the van. I slowed down and jogged in place about one hundred yards from the truck.

Rental?

The property had to have sold in the high six figures, maybe even the low sevens. If my new neighbors could afford that price tag, why would they need anything from a rental company?

The workers carried the couch inside. Once they disappeared through the open front door, I put my cell phone on camera and jogged toward the back of the truck.

I held the phone like I was pretending to change tunes but, instead, rotated it toward the truck and began snapping pictures. To avoid appearing like I was a snoop, I didn't stare into the vehicle.

Sounds of footsteps came toward me from the house.

Get outta here!

7

I sprinted toward our house, keeping the truck between the workers and me. Glancing up at the house next to our home, I saw our elderly neighbor, Lyndell Newens, staring down at me from her front window. She beckoned for me to join her. I turned to my right and hustled up her front stairs.

Lyndell has advanced arthritis in her knees making her mobility painful and limited. To keep her from struggling to get out of her chair and let me in, I punched in her security code and used her front door key, both of which she'd given me for emergencies.

She is a longtime widow who lost her husband to the evils of smoking, a vice he picked up in the Second World War. She delights in keeping me informed about the ebb and flow of the activity in our neighborhood, spending most of her days sitting in a motorized recliner chair that not only tilts backward but also has enough power to push her forward and upright into a semi-standing position. Her computer sits on a table next to her.

Lyndell's daily uniform is a mid-calf-length dress with a floral pattern. Because of her joint problems she wears white support hose and sensible shoes. Her hair is completely white and tightly curled. Her large black glasses magnify her ice-blue eyes.

And she doesn't spray on clouds of cloying perfume like Mrs. Wickstrom.

I sat down next to her.

"I see we have new neighbors," she said.

"We do. But why did they take down the 'Sold' sign after only one day, and why are they renting furnishings when they just bought an expensive house?"

"A good question. Let's have a look at the pictures you just took."

You caught me spying.

I hoped the new home owners hadn't been as observant. I opened the pictures on my phone. A chrome kitchen table and four metal chairs, one table, two stuffed chairs, three floor lamps, four mattresses, four dressers, and several boxes marked "kitchen" sat in the van.

"Basic," I said.

She nodded toward her computer. "Would you like me to record everything that's delivered?" She fancies herself as Chicago's version of Miss Jane Marple, spying on the world through her front window.

"Absolutely. It'll save me time and help me decide if there's a story here. Have you seen the owners?"

"No, and I'm not sure I've ever seen that in this neighborhood before. It certainly didn't happen with you and Carter."

"No kidding. When we first moved to our new home from D.C., I supervised the movers and all the installers day and night."

"It certainly made it easier for me to meet you."

Lyndell's arthritis wasn't as severe then, and she'd walked up our steps to welcome Carter and me to the neighborhood with fresh chocolate chip cookies.

"Why don't you bake a batch of cookies and take them over from both of us to see if the neighbors have an interesting story you can write?" she asked.

8

An hour later, Carter had left for work. I was in the kitchen with Kerry and slid the dough for her favorite M&M sugar cookies into the oven. At the same time, I helped her make "cookies" with her Play-Doh baking set.

"Kerry, while the cookies are baking, let's try to use the potty and then get out of your jammies and pick a nice dress for you to wear to meet our new neighbors. We'll take the cookies to them and see if they have any kids for you to play with."

"Okay, Momma."

After five minutes, we gave up on the potty training, and I helped Kerry get dressed. I smelled the aroma of freshly baked cookies and rushed down to the kitchen — with her in my arms — to remove them from the oven before they were carbonized into hockey pucks.

Once we were back in the kitchen, she helped me put the lid on the three Play-Doh cans we had used while making her "cookies." I piled my cookie-making mess in the sink and wrapped up a dozen of the still-warm treats and stashed them in my backpack.

Slipping the backpack over my shoulders, I held the front door for Kerry, and we walked out onto the porch. I reached back into the hallway, pulled out her stroller, and shut the door. I hauled her and the stroller down the steps and strapped her in.

"Let's go meet our new neighbors."

"Okay, Momma. Elmo and 'Walph' go?"

She has a tiny problem with her "R's." I grabbed her two companions out of the backpack and handed them to her.

"Meet new friends, Elmo!" Kerry said to the red guy.

I hesitated when another blast of fireworks in the neighborhood bombarded my ears.

Relax. Breathe.

After slowly sucking in a deep breath, I pushed the stroller across Melrose and turned left to approach the house. We entered the front gate.

"Kerry, let's see if the new owners are home."

Setting the brake, I stopped at the foot of the stairs leading up to the main level of the house. The front door was open. I set my backpack on the sidewalk and shifted the cookies to my left hand.

"Hello?"

There was no response.

"Hello?" I called louder.

A man stepped from the shadows into the sunlit foyer. I was startled by his unexpected appearance, and my heart rate accelerated. He glared down at me. I stared back.

He had brown skin, short black hair, and a receding hairline. His closely trimmed black beard had a sprinkling of gray. He wore a black T-shirt, black jeans, and well-worn, brown leather sandals. Even from ten feet away, I could detect the stink of cigarette smoke drifting toward us.

"Hi," I said, holding out my cookies. "I'm Tina Thomas, your neighbor, and I wanted to wel-"

Without a word, he stepped back into the foyer and slammed the door. The unexpected loud noise startled me. My head began to pound.

No!

9

My brain had been sensitized by the neighborhood kids blowing off their fireworks. Until this moment, I'd been able to ignore those explosions. But not this unexpected loud sound so close to my ears.

I dropped the cookies on the sidewalk and shut my eyes. A full-blown PTSD attack slammed into my head. Behind my eyelids, I saw a brilliant flash of light, followed by the sound of an exploding bomb.

Breathe slowly. It'll pass.

Within thirty seconds, it did. Kerry stared up at the terrified look on my face that she'd never seen before. She began to whimper.

"Don't cry, Honey. Mommy's okay."

Heat rose in my neck. I stepped forward to tell the man what I thought about his rude behavior, but bumping into Kerry's stroller made me stop. A confrontation with a man I didn't know didn't meet Carter's definition of avoiding potentially risky situations, especially with Kerry at my side.

My eyes are always blurry after a PTSD attack. I blinked several times to clear my vision. Unlocking the brake, I grabbed my backpack, turned the stroller around, and stomped away, leaving the cookie mess on the sidewalk.

You're right, Carter. It's not about me anymore.

I pushed the stroller through our front gate and glanced back at the house. As I unbuckled Kerry, I heard a voice in my head:

Who are you? Why did you come to the door if you didn't want to talk to me? Or eat my cookies? Is there more here than you being, for whatever reason, a first-class, antisocial dickhead?

Without realizing it, my reporter's instincts had kicked in.

Maybe I finally have a story.

Or was I still trying too hard?

I knew how to answer this.

"Kerry, let's go inside and have a snack, and then you can take your nap."

While she slept, I would employ the best weapon available to me: I would go online and research his background.

And he would never know I was doing it.

10

Kerry and I went back into the kitchen. While I cleaned up the cookie-making mess I'd left in the sink, I continued to watch the man's house. Kerry played on the kitchen floor with wooden blocks, a birthday gift from Carter's parents.

"Kerry, what would you like for a snack?" I asked.

"Dinkel's donuts!" Kerry exclaimed.

Figures.

"How about sliced apples with peanut butter instead?"

The corners of her mouth turned down. "Okay, Momma."

After she ate, we walked upstairs to her room on the third floor and read a book before she went down for her morning nap.

I rushed down to our first floor office to check out the rude neighbor online. Sitting down at my computer, I turned on the baby monitor. A call on my landline interrupted me.

"Tina, what happened?" Lyndell asked.

I sat down and related my dismal experience with the man.

"And he didn't say a word?" she asked, after I finished.

"*Nada.*"

"What now?"

"I'm about to go online and research him."

"Good plan."

"And I really need your help to watch the house."

"I'll be happy to." She paused. "I noticed you didn't set your security system when you left with Kerry."

"Thanks for reminding me."

Again. For God's sake, we just went across the street.

She'd first noticed my security system whoopsie when I began toting Kerry and all of her gear out our front door and down the stairs to the sidewalk. Our neighborhood was safe and Lyndell constantly watched our house. I saw no need to climb back up the stairs with Kerry in my arms while I activated the system.

What can happen?

I hung up and turned on my computer to begin a background check on the man. The *Washington Post* had paid a computer jock a bushel-basket load of money to teach me online sleuthing skills, which I had used on all the investigative stories I'd written.

I entered the information from the "Sold" sign, logged onto the realtor's website, and backtracked into the Chicago bank involved with the financing of the man's house. What came up grabbed my attention: The Arun Corporation, an import/export business registered in Delaware, but with a Singapore mailing address, owned the home.

Strange.

My new neighbor might work for the Arun Corporation and the house might be an expensive perk of his employment contract.

But there are other possibilities, which is always what makes doing research on compelling stories challenging.

I began a file on him: Rude Neighbor. I would add to it, but I needed to uncover the missing financial links to flesh out his story. Except for Carter at the *Tribune*, I no longer had access to any high-level journalistic help. And I couldn't ask Carter for assistance without admitting why I needed him. Lacking that expert help, I might not be able to proceed with my story.

11

Monday afternoon, Lyndell called again.

"At noon, a black Mercedes with tinted windows turned into the alley behind the man's house," she said. "I haven't seen that car before."

"Could you read the license plate number?"

"No. Even with binoculars, my eyesight isn't what it used to be."

She sounded frustrated.

"That's okay. Keep watching."

"That's why I called. Five minutes ago, an unmarked white van pulled into the alley. I couldn't read that plate either."

"Thanks. I'm on it."

I disconnected and woke Kerry from her afternoon nap. While she tried to use the potty, I dug out my old camera, a Canon 5D Mark II. It has a 24-105mm lens. I needed the zoom lens to spy on, and then photograph, any happenings in the alley. I shoved the camera into my backpack.

Our detached garage sits at a right angle to our home and faces North Paulina instead of our alley. I strapped Kerry into the car seat of our mommy van — a two-year-old, blue Honda

Odyssey. Backing out onto Paulina, I drove north, moving slowly past the neighbor's alley on the west side of the street.

All of the houses on each side of the alley have small, fenced-in yards and detached garages opening into the alley. To my left, I saw a white van parked next to the open garage door of the fourth house on the south side of the alley.

It's his house.

Two men unloaded boxes from the back of the van. When one man began to turn toward me, I sped up and drove to the next street, West School. I circled around back to our garage, dialing our regular babysitter, Mrs. Alicia Sanchez, as I drove.

"Alicia, hi, this is Tina. Can you watch Kerry for a few minutes?"

"Sure. I'm in the back yard."

"Perfect. See you in two minutes."

12

I pulled back into our garage and took Kerry out of her car seat. I shouldered my backpack and ran with her in my arms across Melrose to Alicia's house located on the opposite corner from our home.

"Kerry, Mrs. Sanchez is going to play with you for a few minutes," I said, as I ran.

Rushing through Alicia's side gate into her back yard, I handed Kerry and her two friends to her.

"Thanks so much," I said.

"No problem," Alicia said. "Kerry, would you and Elmo and Ralph like apple juice?"

"Yes, pweaze."

Running out the same gate, I crossed Paulina, walked north, and then turned to my right, entering the east side of the alley. I slipped behind two trash cans on the north side to have a better angle to see the truck.

I sniffed.

Yuck.

The stench of the garbage in the trash cans began to nauseate me. I breathed through my mouth and glanced around the side of the can closest to the alley. When I saw the two men face the white truck, I pulled out my camera and rested it on top of the can.

Through the camera's viewfinder, I spied the rear end of a black car on the side of the garage closest to me. I refocused the lens: a Mercedes.

Bingo.

The men stacked boxes from the floor to the ceiling on the other side of the garage. As they worked, they scanned the alley, which forced me to pop up and down to avoid being spotted.

A layer of clouds hid the sun, providing uniform light for the photos. I snapped several pictures of their faces and the boxes in the garage and in the truck. The sun broke through the clouds just as the second man turned toward me. The unexpected bright light reflected off the camera's lens directly into his eyes.

Damn!

I squatted down with the camera in my hands. I took two deep breaths and peeked around the side of the can. The man walked toward me. He had his hand in his warm up jacket pocket.

A gun?

Sweat poured off my forehead. I needed a car or truck to drive past me on North Paulina and shield my escape through the gate behind me and into that backyard.

Glancing around the side of the can, I saw the man was two strides from the street.

I need cover now! Where's Chicago traffic when I need it?

There was the rumble of an engine from my left. A truck appeared. I would have only one chance. As the hood of the truck blocked the man's vision, I opened the latch into the home's back yard. In less than ten seconds, I ran through the gate and into the yard.

But did the man see me?

13

Fifteen minutes later, Kerry and I were in the lower level office of our home. She played on the floor with a puzzle. I downloaded the photos of the truck onto my computer and put them up on the screen.

The two men were young and fit with short black hair, beards, and dark skin. They were dressed like the man who had slammed the door on me. I needed facial recognition software, but I didn't have it.

There were ten boxes labeled "computer screens" stacked in the empty side of the garage. There were ten more boxes with electronic labels, likely the hard drives and other gear to run the computers. Several boxes had letters printed on them. I saw the letters "S.A." on one box, but the rest of the letters were obscured.

I emailed the pictures to Lyndell because I knew she'd seen me drive around the block, come home, go to Alicia's house, and return.

Two minutes later, she called me. "Do you think the two men live there?" she asked.

"Four mattresses were delivered, but until one of us sees them going in and out of the house on a regular basis, the number of people living there would only be a guess, and I don't write stories based on that."

"They're young and look a little like the man I saw confront you. They could be his sons."

"But if three or four people live there, why do they need ten computer screens?"

"How are you going to proceed?"

I told her about the Arun Corporation.

"Is this a perk of his employment?"

"It could be. I tried to hack into the Arun Corporation's hard drive, but I don't have the computer savvy to do it."

"How about your friend Linda Misle? She's a computer whiz who helps me when I have technical difficulties."

"I know, but except for you, I always work alone."

"Young lady, I strongly suggest you expand your team. Linda is the solution."

If she has the time and wants to help me.

14

The next morning, after Carter left and I'd cleaned up the kitchen, I called Linda Misle, my best friend in Chicago.

"I need legal advice," I said. "How about you and Sandra meeting us at Dinkel's for a snack?"

"In my state, I never pass up Dinkel's. See you there in fifteen minutes."

Dinkel's Bakery is three blocks from our front door. The mouth-watering aroma of freshly baked chocolate chip butter cookies, powdered sugar stollen, strudels, muffins, and a variety of chocolate and vanilla cupcakes slathered with multiple flavors of frosting bombarded us when we entered. All beckoned to us from glass cases. To the right of the front door in similar cases were bear claws, long johns, and multiple varieties of their famous donuts.

I bought Kerry and Sandra — Linda's daughter — each a carton of milk, got bottled waters for Linda and me, and filled my tray with more than enough selections of goodies for all four of us. While carrying the tray in one hand, I pushed Kerry in her stroller through a doorway to the right of the last glass case where we entered into a second bay about 1500 square feet in size.

Sound reverberated through the minimally decorated room making conversation difficult, especially when kids began crying. I selected a four-top table in the corner hoping it wouldn't be too noisy. I needed to talk to Linda.

Setting the tray on the table, I secured Kerry in a booster chair. I sat down as Linda walked in. She pushed Sandra — a toddler the same age as Kerry — in a stroller.

I'd met Linda at Hamlin Park a little over a year ago. A University of Chicago-trained attorney, with an undergraduate degree in accounting and computer science from the same institution, she worked at defending people accused of white-collar computer crime before she went on a stay-at-home-mommy hiatus.

She is a woman who is comfortable in a black power suit, black pumps, and a high neck, white blouse, carrying a designer briefcase into a courtroom. Now in the middle trimester of her second pregnancy, she wore a shapeless, green maternity top and white shorts. She looked like a plump olive stuck on a long toothpick.

"I need your expertise with the financial research on a potential story," I said, diving right into the reason we were there.

Kerry and Sandra munched on their donuts and drank their milk.

Linda took a yellow legal pad and pen out of her backpack and put the items on the table. And then she stopped.

"A problem?" I asked.

"A tiny one. What does this pay?"

"Pay?"

"Yes, as in billable hours. I usually charge seven hundred fifty dollars an hour. Because you're my best friend, I'll discount the fee to five hundred dollars an hour."

"You have to be kidding."

She swept her shoulder-length hair behind both ears. "I never kid about billable hours."

15

I pulled out two eleven-inch metal knitting needles, a ball of yarn, and Kerry's partially finished baby blanket from my backpack.

Linda stared at my knitting. "Oh my God! Tina, you're pregnant! I'm so happy for you!"

"What are you talking about?"

"In your March article, you wrote how — when Kerry was born — your mother expected you to bring your new baby home from the hospital in a blanket you'd knitted. You're knitting. There's only one logical conclusion."

"Yeah, about that. I bought Kerry's blanket on Amazon. It even had her name added to the border. But don't tell my mother that the next time you see her."

"Then you're not pregnant?"

"Nope, but Carter wishes I were. He wants a son, but I'm not ready to have a baby."

"Why not?"

"Good question. Not sure."

She pointed at the needles in my hands. "Then why are you knitting?"

"It relaxes me."

"Is our discussion causing you to feel stressed?"

"A little. I can't afford your fee, and I'm worried you won't help me."

"If you want me to work *pro bono*, what's in it for me?"

"How about being part of a fabulous story? Won't that be enough?"

"*Please*. This is billable hours you're talking about." She tapped her pen on the legal pad. "I assume this for your local column."

"It might be."

"But could it be for a real newspaper?"

"Maybe, but researching and writing it would take an enormous amount of my time."

She doodled on the pad. "What about book or film rights?"

Every lawyer I know is an aspiring author or screenwriter.

"If the story turns out to be the real deal, it could be a fabulous book or a movie."

"I would be interested in that."

"Okay. If a newspaper wants to publish my story, I'll make sure to retain film and book rights. If you do this research for me, I'll give them to you for free. But only if you hire me to write the book or screenplay."

"I can work with that. I'll retain the ownership and give you a percentage of the profits instead of a fee for writing the manuscript or screen play."

I knew my friend and didn't need to ask if she was talking about gross or net profits. It would be net, the much smaller amount.

"Great."

"I'll type up a contract for you to sign." She made a note on her yellow legal pad and then raised her head. "Give me a dollar."

"Why?"

"Just do it."

I reached in my backpack and pulled out a dollar. I handed it to her.

"I'm now your lawyer of record. What we discuss about this case is a privileged communication."

"Meaning you can't tell anyone about it without my permission."

"You got it."

16

"Since we're talking about money, what do you get paid by the *Lakeview Times*?" Linda asked.

"One hundred dollars for each published story," I said.

"That's all?" She made a note on her pad. "I wouldn't turn my computer on for that. Why bother?"

"After not being in a newsroom for almost five years, I realized writing is who I am. Being a mommy and a wife is fabulous, but if I can't write stories, there's a huge hole in my life."

"I get that. I lived for depositions when I kicked ass. I also miss the money."

Kerry began to fidget. "Honey, would you like to do a coloring book?" I asked.

"Uh-huh, Momma."

I pulled out a Dora the Explorer coloring book and crayons from my backpack and put them on the table in front of her. Before Sandra began complaining, Linda did the same thing with a Curious George sticker book.

"Where were we?" She glanced at her yellow pad. "Okay, here it is. Why are you working for the *Lakeview Times*?"

"It was the only job I could find."

"That's hard to believe. When I first met you, I researched you online. You were nominated for two Pulitzer Prizes."

"My stories were critically acclaimed, but Carter won the Pulitzer."

"I saw that too. But that doesn't explain why you would ever work for one hundred dollars a story. It's insulting."

"Because of what happened in Arlington, the Suits at the *Post* canned me."

Linda and Lyndell were my only Chicago friends who knew about my debacle in Arlington, but I hadn't told her this part.

"You were fired for being blown up? That's preposterous. I should have been your lawyer for that one. When I'd finished with them, we would have been rich."

"In D.C. the FBI carries a lot of weight. The FBI agent told me not to go into the abortion clinic, but I did anyway. The agent claimed that when the bomber saw me he prematurely detonated the bomb."

I didn't tell her that I'd hesitated when I had the chance to shoot the bomber, giving him time to grab the girl and then blow the device. My surgery scars were a constant reminder I should have pulled the trigger when I had a clear shot.

If I ever get a chance like that again, I won't hesitate.

"The entire newspaper industry knew what had happened to me," I continued. "I quit writing, but not to have a baby or write a book. The bosses at the *Post* threw me out because I made a mistake chasing a story. And then I had Kerry and was content until I met you in the park last year and decided to write about it."

She tapped her pen on the yellow pad. "Redemption."

"What?"

"You want to write this story, or one like it, to redeem yourself in the industry."

"I guess I never thought about it like that, but you're right. I want to prove I still have it, and they made a mistake firing me."

"Then let's get to work. But give me another donut first. I'm pregnant. I can't think with low blood sugar."

17

Linda munched on a glazed donut.

"For starters, I need the details about the finances of a corporation listed as the owner of a residential house," I said.

Beginning with the address of my newest neighbor's house, I told her what I'd discovered about the Arun Corporation in Delaware.

"But I don't know his name and how to hack into the company's computers to follow the money trail," I continued.

Linda furrowed her brow. "Do you think you're trying too hard to find a story here?"

Hate to admit it but she might be right.

"I hope not, but I really need a real story."

"What else do you have?"

"Ten boxes of computer screens and other electronic gear were delivered to his garage."

"Now, that is interesting." She tapped her pen on the pad. "He could be into online fraud or credit card theft. Or gambling, either online or old-fashioned bookmaking. Or drugs, street or prescription, but in our neighborhood most likely prescription. Could be a bookie, and there's an outside chance he's handling online prostitution."

"Best guess?"

"Computer fraud." She checked her notes and then looked up. "As your lawyer, I have to advise you that he's likely computer savvy, and he won't like us snooping into his files."

"Are you suggesting this could be dangerous?"

"I am, especially if it involves sizable sums of money. If he discovers what I'm doing, I'll quit. It isn't worth the risk."

"If I were paying you seven hundred fifty dollars per hour, would you still say that to me?"

"Of course not. But I would demand a sizable upfront cash retainer."

Gotta love Linda.

18

On Wednesday morning, I was about three miles into my run when my cell phone rang. I pulled out the ear buds and put the phone on speaker, allowing me to keep running.

"Tina, this is Gayle."

Oh, boy.

I stopped running.

Gayle Nystrom is the publisher and sole editor of the *Lakeview Times*. She has never worked on any newspaper with a circulation bigger than her college daily. And her job there involved the money side of publishing, not the editorial content. Initially, my writing experience had awed her, but she wasn't intimidated any longer. From the icy tone of her voice, there was only one reason she'd called me.

Earlier that morning, before Kerry and Carter were awake, I'd emailed her the Mixmaster story for my column even though it wasn't due until July fourteenth. I had submitted it because I didn't have any more creative ideas about what I could do to fix it. I hated the piece and wanted it out of my sight. I hadn't even considered asking Carter to read the final version, which I usually did.

"Did you like it?" I asked, hoping she saw something in it I'd missed.

"It's worse than your karaoke story, which I reluctantly printed. I'm completely underwhelmed."

"Were there specific parts that bothered you?"

The line was silent a few seconds. "It lacked the warm emotions you displayed in the marvelous baby blanket column in March," she said. "Your voice in this article is almost detached."

Because it bored me to tears.

"And you turned in the story before your deadline," she continued. "Does this mean you feel it's finished?"

"I do."

"Then, I'm sorry, but I won't print your July column."

Gayle hadn't liked any of the stories I'd written since the knitting baby blankets story in March. She'd published my April column, which she had called "lackluster," but she didn't run the May story about women who played bridge in Lakeview.

"I expect more from a writer with your experience."

She is pissed.

"Work with me here."

I remained silent.

"If you can't come up with better stories, I'll terminate your contract."

She disconnected before I could defend myself. If I didn't find a first-rate story before my August eleventh deadline, I would be canned from the only writing job I could find.

I called Linda and told her what had happened.

"She can't fire you," she said. "I won't let her." She began talking faster. "When I get done with her, she won't even have a newspaper."

"Might want to back off on that right now. What I need is a story, and the sooner the better."

"It would be more fun to sue her, but I'll start working on it this afternoon."

19

I started to run again and called Lyndell on speaker phone. I didn't mention Gayle Nystrom's threat to fire me because it was embarrassing. Telling Linda was different. She was my BFF and now my lawyer.

"Any new information on the neighbor?" I asked, hoping to push the story forward.

"He doesn't leave through the front door of the house," she said. "I saw the black Mercedes drive in and out of his alley early in the morning, at noon, and then, again, later in the afternoon. The car's windows are dark so I can't see who is driving. And I still can't read the license plate."

"What about the white van?"

"I haven't seen it again."

"You are so sweet to do this. Keep it up. It's exactly what I need."

As I ran home, I began scoping out cars whizzing by me. Running south on Paulina toward our house, a black Mercedes sedan with tinted windows passed by me and turned into the alley behind the new neighbor's house.

Is it his car?

Jogging in place on the north side of the alley's entrance, I peeked around the corner and watched as the Mercedes pulled into the garage of the fourth house on the left.

His house!

If I could snag his license plate number, I was in business. I would run a DMV search for his name and follow that with a background investigation on him.

I waited to see if the driver exited into the alley or the garage's side door behind the fence. When the garage door began to go down, I had my answer. He'd gone in through the side door, and because of the fence, he couldn't see what I was about to do.

Sprinting down the alley, I screeched to a halt in front of his garage.

Security cameras?

I didn't have time to do more than a cursory scan of the eaves on the garage and didn't see any cameras.

Go for it!

Grabbing the trash can next to me, I shoved it under the door. When the bottom of the door hit the top of the can, the door stopped closing and creaked back up. There were two vehicles: the black Mercedes I'd seen and a black Range Rover. There were still several boxes stacked against the sidewalls of the garage next to the Range Rover.

Pulling out my cell phone, I snapped a picture of the rear license plate on each vehicle and the boxes and slid the can back into its original position. As I did, I heard the back door of the house open and then close.

Run!

I made a mad dash toward the end of the alley, sprinting on my toes to dampen the sound of my footfalls. When I whipped around the corner of the alley toward our house, a car engine fired up behind me.

Yikes!

Lowering my head, I pumped my arms harder, racing at full speed past the front of our home and into our alley. I hid behind our trash cans for ten minutes.

If the man thought he forgot to push the switch to lower his garage door, he wouldn't be troubled when he climbed into his car and discovered the open door. If not, or if he'd seen me on a security camera I hadn't spotted, I might have a problem.

20

Thursday morning, I finally found time to go down to the office and boot up my computer while Kerry took her morning nap.

I downloaded the pictures I'd taken of the vehicles and boxes in the garage. The Range Rover blocked the writing printed on the boxes.

No help there.

I entered the plate numbers on the Illinois DMV website. In thirty seconds, I had the registrations for the Mercedes and the Range Rover on the screen in front of me. The Arun Corporation owned both vehicles. I called Linda.

"Are you going to spinning class?" I asked.

"I am."

"We need to talk. See you there."

After Kerry woke up, I took her and her two friends and headed for the eleven o'clock spinning class at XSport Fitness, our neighborhood exercise club. It's on North Ashland, two blocks east of our front door. It has all the gear a fitness junkie could want, advertising more exercise equipment per square foot than any other club in the North Side of Chicago. There is the added benefit of cheap and reliable childcare for Kerry while I work out.

Linda and I walked to the back of the packed spinning room. The irritating odor of cleaning products and hand sanitizer collided with the pleasant smell of hair sprays and colognes brought in by the riders, the majority of whom were female. Our spinning instructor, Cassandra Olson, wanted the room temperature frigid. The goose bumps on my arms proved she got what she wanted.

I'd met Cas at Hamlin Park shortly after my first encounter there with Linda. She is about six inches shorter than my five feet eight. She has minimal body fat and chiseled muscles, especially her legs and shoulders. With her dark-brown eyes, black hair, and olive skin she resembles Eva Longoria on steroids.

Before I could tell Linda about the two vehicles in the neighbor's garage, '90s rock music blasted out of the speakers in the front of the room and class began. We did a relatively slow warm-up, but it didn't last long. Cas doesn't like slow.

She announced the start of the ride in her typical fashion.

"Go! Go! *EMPUJAR!*" she screamed into her headset microphone.

We began peddling. I kept my head down hoping Cas wouldn't catch me talking to Linda. But when I turned my head to tell her my news, Cas interrupted me by yelling into her microphone.

"I can see you two gossiping in the back. If you can talk, you're not working hard enough."

She has the personality of a pissed-off pit bull when she is teaching one of her classes — especially kickboxing — or when one of our friends, usually Linda, disagrees with her when we have our play group discussions.

Cas stared directly at us. "One more full turn and out of the seat!" she bellowed.

21

Fifty minutes later, spinning class ended. The stink of sweat was now the predominant odor in the room. After we finished stretching, I wiped my bike down and told Linda about the registration of the two vehicles.

"What do you think?" I asked after I finished.

"A lot of money is being funneled from the Arun Corporation to your neighbor," she said.

"I need to know where those funds are coming from."

"I'll try to hack into the Arun Corporation's computers, but it'll have to wait until after the Fourth. We're going to visit Howard's parents in New York City. It'll be our last flight there before the baby comes."

"Let me know what you find out. The guy pissed me off, and I want to know why he's such a jerk."

Droplets of sweat covered the floor around me. As I wiped them up with a towel, Sammy Simmons and Corky Gibson, two stunning twenty-somethings, waved at Linda and me as they slid off their bikes and hurried toward the exit, most likely to another class.

I gazed in admiration at their trim bodies and cellulite-free legs. They never wore makeup, but then, they didn't need to. And they were total men magnets. A young California surfer type tagged along with them, smiling widely and laughing, probably throwing out his best hookup lines.

"Did we ever look that good?" I asked Linda.

"I'm not sure I ever did," she said. "But they should be buffed. They practically live here."

"You are so right." As I watched them leave, I noticed Sammy looked different. "Plastic surgery helps too."

"What are you talking about?"

"Check out Sammy's chest. She has new boobs."

"Are you sure?"

"Come on, I'll prove it to you."

Linda followed me to the body sculpting class where Sammy and Corky placed their equipment in the front row. The surfer dude stood between them. Sammy's fabulous body was even more perfect than the last time I saw her.

"Breasts that size only come out of a box," I said. "And if they did, I wonder where Sammy got the money to pay for them."

"Could be a story right here: Where to get breast augmentation surgery in Lakeview."

"Or better, what did Sammy do to earn the money to pay for the operation?"

Might have to keep my eye on her.

22

Friday, I spent my time running in the neighborhood seeking another possible story, playing with Kerry, and working on the computer. But I hadn't come up with any additional information involving my rude neighbor or any ideas for a new story.

Saturday afternoon, Carter came inside from working in his garden.

"Honey, one of the guys on my staff just called," he said. "They're going to Hamlin Park for a slow-pitch softball game. Do we have anything planned?"

"Nothing," I said. "I'll take Kerry to Whole Foods to shop for dinner tomorrow night."

I'd thrown a line in the water to tempt him to indulge in one of his favorite pastimes: cooking. If he did bite, I could watch him do it while I relaxed and played with Kerry.

"Any suggestions for our menu?" I continued.

"I would love to try that rub for ribs I read about in the New York Times Wednesday food section."

Hook, line, and sinker.

He printed the list of ingredients he needed from my computer and handed it to me before he left for Hamlin. I lugged my daughter and her two companions down the front steps and loaded them into the stroller. As I hoisted the backpack over my shoulders, I had a "Mommy Moment." I went through my mental checklist but came up blank.

The Lincoln-Belmont branch of the Chicago library system is on the corner east of our home. As I pushed Kerry in her stroller past it and toward Whole Foods, I heard Lyndell's voice in my head: "Tina, you always forget to set your security system."

Yep. Did it again.

As I continued pushing Kerry's stroller east past the library's free parking lot, I made a mental note to try and remember to do it next time. A second — public-pay — lot sat in the middle of the block. I noticed a shiny black Ranger Rover in the first row.

Huh?

Taking out my cell phone, I scrolled down to the photos I'd snapped of the neighbor's license plates. It was his SUV. In that picture, there were still a few boxes in his garage. Maybe the two guys in the white van had returned and delivered more boxes. If they did, the man had to move the Rover while the boxes were temporarily stored before he unpacked and sifted through them.

Carter and I had done the same thing when we moved to Chicago. For the first three months, unpacked boxes filled one side of our two-car garage. Now, half of that side contains clothes and toys from Kerry's infancy, all of which are being stored in case I ever become pregnant again.

In the other half of that side of the garage, we have stacks of the hard print copies of all the articles Carter has ever written, even though each story can easily be found on the Internet. We'd argued about this because, in my judgment, it was a complete waste of space. He countered that my stash of writing equipment, which I'd stored while I took a break to heal from my wounds and then to have Kerry, took up unnecessary room.

My previous job as an investigative journalist often required tools other than a pen and notebook, binoculars, a camera, and a computer. When I worked for the *Washington Post*, I'd purchased a lock pick gun and torque wrench online. Several times they'd come in handy to break into offices or homes in pursuit of a story.

Was that legal? No, but I'd worried about breaking the law only after I had the facts I needed to complete the piece.

I also had electronic gear I used to bypass the phone lines and power sources of home and business security systems. I'd learned the technique from a man I had interviewed for a story about breaking and entering into homes. And I did it while he was jailed on a B&E charge.

The last item I'd purchased was a GPS tracker. It was expensive, and my bureau chief at the *Post* had yelled at me when the invoice appeared on my expense account. But he'd paid for it after I used it to help write a story discrediting the CEO of a major retail corporation.

I'd taken it with me when I was fired after the clinic bombing in Arlington. If I could find the GPS device and the software disc to record the data, I would be able to track the movements of at least one of the new neighbor's vehicles and then investigate each place he visited.

But I needed to find the GPS device in time to run back to the parking lot and tag the Rover before the man drove it away. Pawing through the boxes in our garage would take time I didn't have.

I had a Sunday afternoon project I didn't want Carter to know about, but I needed to do it.

23

Sunday afternoon, while Kerry napped, Carter prepped the ribs for the dinner he was going to make that evening for the three of us. During that time, I found all of my equipment in our garage.

And I discovered one other item I had previously purchased: an electronic scanning device. I had needed it in Afghanistan where I'd written a series documenting government corruption. The local powers had bugged my room hoping to find out what I'd uncovered before I finished the story. The black box had helped me find their bugs and finish my story without them busting me.

On Monday morning after Kerry's nap, she and her two companions rode in her stroller as I pushed them into the parking lot of Whole Foods to buy the groceries for Tuesday's Fourth of July holiday. But I put my plan on hold when a black Mercedes pulled in. I checked the license number in my cell phone. My target car parked thirty feet away from us.

Do it!

I waited for my cranky neighbor to enter the store before I made my move. Pushing Kerry in her stroller, I rushed up behind the car and took out the device. As I bent over to put it under the rear bumper, I heard the car's passenger side door open.

Dammit!

The Mercedes had tinted-black windows, and I hadn't seen a passenger inside. The harsh odor of cigarette smoke drifted in my direction, and I smelled the passenger before I heard him climb out.

I stood up with my back to him. "I know Momma dropped her keys in this parking lot," I said loudly to Kerry. "I guess I'll have to search under all of the cars out here."

Turning to him, we made eye contact. He resembled the two men I'd seen unloading boxes from the white van.

"I lost my car keys" I said to him. "Again."

The man threw down his cigarette but didn't reply.

"Would you be a dear and help me find them?"

He crossed his muscular arms over his chest but didn't move.

Time to play the empty-headed mommy card.

I yanked Elmo out of Kerry's hands. Her instant shrieks attracted the attention of several shoppers who looked over to see what had happened. He muttered to himself, climbed back into the Mercedes, and slammed the door.

No one came to my assistance as I pretended to look on the ground for my keys. Kerry continued to cry. Finally, a lady my mom's age walked over to me.

"Dear, what's wrong?" she asked.

Tears might work.

I cranked out a few. "I lost my car keys, again, and my husband will be furious," I sobbed, as Kerry continued to scream.

The tears worked.

"Where'd you drop them?" a white-haired man with the lady asked.

I waved around the lot. "Somewhere around here."

The two bystanders began searching the pavement and under cars. I handed Elmo back to Kerry, and she stopped crying.

The man sat in the Mercedes and couldn't see me below the level of his trunk.

Now!

I pulled out the device from my backpack and planted it under the right rear bumper. Then, I waited until the two people helping me had their backs turned and dropped my keys under the tire of the car behind me. A minute later, the white-haired man found them.

"You are such a dear," I said when he handed them to me. "Thank you so much."

After putting Kerry in her seat, I got back in the car and hurried home to activate the tracking software on my computer. I could shop for food later.

When I got to my computer, I downloaded the software for the GPS device I'd hidden on the Mercedes. It took me fifteen minutes to remember how the system worked, but once I did, the readout indicated the Mercedes was back at the man's house. I would wait a couple of days to let a pattern of travel develop.

24

Monday afternoon, all of my friends and their kids were out of town for the Fourth of July. Carter had been called into work. I asked Kerry what she wanted to do. Her vote was Hamlin Park, and I agreed.

The eight-acre park has activities for each member of the family. There are fields used for baseball, softball, soccer, and lacrosse, a free swimming pool, plus a playground. The scent of freshly mowed grass from the fields drifted over us as I pushed Kerry into the park. The sounds of splashing and yelling from the kids frolicking in the pool were mixed with the plunk of a metal bat striking a ball.

Kerry and I sat down in the shade to protect my little girl's pale skin from the intense Chicago sun. The playground was empty except for another woman I'd never seen before. She sat on a bench about fifteen feet away from me watching four kids play on the equipment.

My friends kid me about being the "Mayor of Hamlin Park" because they say I act like I'm campaigning for an elective office, constantly walking around introducing Kerry and myself to anyone new to the park.

I do it to find new storylines. But today I wanted to spend time with Kerry. I didn't feel the need to introduce myself and get her story.

Kerry sat at my feet piling up little mounds of loose wood chips to make pretend ice cream scoops and imitate the vanilla custard cone I had purchased for us at Scooter's on the way to the park. She began feeding wood chips to Elmo. Unexpectedly, she began cramming the woodchips into her own mouth.

"Spit, Kerry. It's yucky."

Kerry, having inherited her stubborn gene from Carter's side of the family, clamped her jaws shut. I picked her up and tried to pry open her mouth. She twisted and gagged.

Heimlich!

Turning her around, I tried to perform the maneuver.

It didn't work!

"Help!" I screamed. "Please, somebody, help! My baby is choking!"

25

911!

I reached into my backpack for my cell phone. Kerry thrashed in my arms, knocking it into the wood chips.

"Stop!" The lady on the bench said. "Give her to me!"

I don't know you.

The woman limped over to me.

You can't have her!

"I need to do a Heimlich maneuver!"

She tried to pull Kerry out of my arms.

I resisted.

She pulled harder.

I let go.

She turned Kerry around to face me, made her left hand into a fist, and placed it over my daughter's abdomen. She joined her hands together and yanked them upwards toward Kerry's chest.

Wood chips flew out of my daughter's mouth.

Once Kerry could breathe again, she began shrieking.

I reached out for her.

The woman turned away from me and nuzzled Kerry's neck. My daughter blinked and ceased wiggling and crying.

I reached out again.

The woman ignored my outstretched hands.

She softly sang to Kerry in a language that sounded like German. While she swayed back and forth in rhythm with her tune, she placed her ear on Kerry's chest and listened.

That's why she wouldn't give Kerry to me.

She nodded to herself and handed Kerry back to me.

"Thank you so much," I gushed. "You saved my daughter's life." I hugged Kerry. "This is the first time something like this has happened to her — to us — and I totally panicked."

The lady was shorter than me. Her dark hair was sprinkled with gray, and she wore a shapeless green cotton dress that did nothing to flatter her figure.

"This is your first child, yes?" she asked, glancing down at my toned runner's body.

"She is."

"A mother must be ever watchful with her child." Her voice was flat.

Jeez, no hug? Thanks for comforting me.

"I assume you've had medical training with how you took care of my daughter," I said.

She lowered her head and examined her hands. "I am a pediatrician," she said to the ground.

"I hope you practice in our neighborhood. Our daughter's pediatrician is in Lincoln Park, and it's a total pain to fight the traffic to drive there to see her."

"At this point in my life, I am not working."

"Welcome to the club."

The woman didn't respond.

"What I mean is, like me, there are several previously working women around here who are now primarily stay-at-home moms."

She continued to stare at the ground as I rocked Kerry.

Introduce yourself, Ms. Mayor of Hamlin Park.

"I'm Tina Thomas and this is my daughter, Kerry."

She lifted her head. "My name is Hannah Eisenberg." With her left hand, she pointed at two young girls climbing on the jungle gym. "Those are my daughters. Sara is six and Rachael is five." She nodded at the swings. "And there are my sons: Gerald, who is eight, and Jason, who is twelve."

"Did you recently move to this neighborhood?"

"Yes, we did."

This is turning into another Mixmaster interview.

"From Germany?"

She stared at me. "Why would you ask that?"

"The song you sang to Kerry sounded like German to me."

"It is a Yiddish song I learned from my husband's *Bubbe*. And to answer your question, we moved from Israel, first to a condo and finally to a home in this neighborhood."

My journalist's antennae shot up: a doctor/mom with four kids coming to a new country. Questions began whizzing through my brain. She was perfect for a story.

Start digging.

"Hannah, I write a monthly column for our local newspaper. The stories showcase people in the Lakeview area. I would love to feature you and your family. And if you ever decide to go back into practice, it would be a terrific opportunity to get your name out there."

"This is not possible. My husband would never allow it." She abruptly turned and beckoned to her children. "We have to leave."

Huh? What just went wrong here?

26

"Thanks again," I said, waving at Hannah's back. She had an abnormal gait, hobbling like her feet hurt from blisters or ill-fitting shoes. She limped toward the park's gate with a son supporting her on each side. With their other hand, each of the boys held the hand of one of their sisters.

I'd been rattled by Kerry's near-catastrophe, and I'd neglected to ask Hannah for her address or cell phone number. If I was interested in her personal story, my publisher Gayle Nystrom and my *Lakeview* readers might be too. When I returned home, I would go online to find out more about Dr. Hannah Eisenberg and follow that with an interview.

And working it won't take much time.

To my right, I heard a vehicle engine fire up. A black Cadillac Escalade pulled out of a parking place on West Barry, a one-way street like all the streets around Hamlin Park. The luxury SUV rolled to a stop at the playground gate where Hannah and her children stood.

A slender, bearded young man jumped out of the driver's side. He took one last drag on his cigarette before he flipped it onto the street and walked around to the passenger's side. He resembled the two men in the alley and the passenger in the Mercedes at Whole Foods, but I couldn't be sure if he was one of them.

Opening the front door, he assisted Hannah up into the passenger's seat. Jason, her oldest child, did the same thing with the rear door allowing his siblings to pile in. The two older kids climbed into the third row of seats. The man buckled the two youngest ones into their seats in the second row. He was quick and efficient, evidence he'd done it before.

He climbed into the driver's seat, and the SUV accelerated to the corner. He stopped at the stop sign and turned left, driving south.

License plate?

My cell phone sat in the wood chips. I picked it up to snap a picture, but the park's main building now obscured my view of the SUV. As I strapped Kerry into her stroller, I silently berated myself for my negligence with her and then for losing my reporter's focus on Hannah. Another car zoomed past on West Barry.

A one-way street.

I pushed Kerry and her stroller through the park's exit gate and sprinted east toward the corner of North Damen and West Barry. If Hannah lived in our neighborhood, the driver had the option of returning to her house by driving the SUV around the park on the one-way streets.

The only new neighbor I knew was the bad-mannered man across the street from us. Could he be Hannah's husband? Was the man at Whole Foods or either of the two men in the white truck one of her drivers?

Hurry up!

Nearing the corner, I saw the Escalade moving north along North Damen. He had driven around the park. I hid in the shadows of the trees as the SUV passed West Barry allowing me time to snap a picture of the SUV's rear plate. I now had a second way to research Hannah and find out if she lived across the street from me.

27

When we arrived home, the full impact of what had happened with Kerry hit me. I didn't want to put her down for her nap, instead choosing to hold her close to me where I could monitor her breathing.

After one book, she fell asleep in my arms. I carried her downstairs to our office and placed her in the pink portable bed on the floor next to my computer. Letting her sleep upstairs two floors away from me wasn't an option, even with the baby monitor.

Booting up my computer, I entered the license plate number of the Escalade. The DMV registration came up. The Hannah Eisenberg Trust at the Wells Fargo Bank in New York City owned the SUV, not the Arun Corporation.

Huh? Maybe she doesn't live across the street.

I needed Hannah's history. Using her name, her profession, the names of her children, and where they lived before moving to Chicago, I began digging. I discovered a link to her medical career and was able to backtrack into her life.

When I had it all, I called Linda who was in New York with Howard and Sandra visiting his family. I hated to bother her, but I needed to talk to my BFF. But I didn't tell her what had happened to Kerry at the park. I would never tell anyone about that.

"Sorry to bother you, but I met a woman at Hamlin," I said. "She just moved here and has four kids."

"So far that doesn't really grab my attention as a potential story," Linda said.

"I'm not sure about that."

"Okay, convince me."

"Her name is Hannah Eisenberg. She grew up in Manhattan, the only child of unfathomably wealthy parents. She went to Harvard as an undergrad. During her junior year, her parents died in a private jet crash, leaving her tub loads of money."

"Love that. Money always interests me. What else?"

"She graduated from Harvard Medical School and did a residency in pediatrics at Columbia. For one of her clinical rotations, she traveled to Israel, where she met — and then married — another physician named Micah Mittelman. After she finished her training, she joined a group medical practice in Tel Aviv."

"What about the children?"

"Two girls, five and six, and two boys, eight and twelve. She had the first three while she worked full-time. Two years before the birth of her last one, she stopped practicing."

"I thought you said she has lots of money."

"I did."

"Why didn't she hire a nanny or two and keep working?"

"No clue, but she has a driver."

"There or here?"

"I don't know about there, but she has one here. And he looks like he might be an Israeli."

"He could have come to the U.S. with her and her family," she said. "With her money, I'll bet he's a bodyguard too."

"In our neighborhood?" I asked.

"I traveled a lot in Israel. We always had a driver and a bodyguard. And my parents have one here too."

"Why?"

"In some parts of Chicago? Do I need to list the reasons?"

"Guess you're right, but nothing dangerous or exciting ever happens in our neighborhood."

"If it did, you wouldn't be writing a fluff column in the *Lakeview Times*."

28

"What about her husband?" Linda asked.

"Dr. Micah Mittelman is a native-born Israeli," I said. "He trained in England for his undergraduate, medical school, and an OB/GYN residency. He was at the top of his class at each level. After returning to Israel, he established a private practice in Tel Aviv, where he met and married Hannah, who is five years younger than he is."

"Smart guy, but a doctor in private practice? Boring."

"Initially, that was my take, too, until I read that seven years ago, at the same time Hannah hung up her stethoscope, he closed his practice and became chief of a huge IVF clinic in Tel Aviv."

"IVF is more interesting, but I'm still not buying into this story."

"His move to Chicago sixteen months ago coincided with the opening of a lab here where he's now doing research with three doctors at Northwestern."

"What kind of research?"

"Embryonic stem cell."

"Now, you got me. This could be interesting. What else do you have on him?"

"He has all the proper professional medical licenses to work in Illinois and a driver's license for our state," I said. "The same address is listed on his medical and driver's licenses, but it's in an industrial area about twenty minutes from our front door."

"Probably his lab," she said.

"That would be my guess because I can't find any listing of a purchase agreement for their residential house."

"Did you run her car plate?"

"Her Escalade is owned by the Hannah Eisenberg Trust at Wells Fargo."

"Do you think the man across the street is her husband?"

"I was kind of hoping so, but why would the Arun Corporation own the house and the two cars when her trust owns the Escalade? And where does she park it?"

"Hard to argue with that."

"Now you know why I called," I said. "I need your help to prove that she and her family are, or are not, in some way connected to the guy across the street."

"She goes by Eisenberg, not Mittelman, right?" she asked.

"Uh-huh, she used her maiden name when she practiced. Her medical license is still in that name."

"I'll begin with her trust fund."

"And I'll keep running in the neighborhood trying to somehow find her again."

29

July third is the fifth anniversary of my horrific event in Arlington Women's Clinic. If I had listened to FBI agent Wiles and not entered the building, I wouldn't have been blown up. But the good news was that Carter visited me daily in the hospital. When I was discharged, he acted as my support group of one to help me deal with my burgeoning PTSD attacks. That led to a few dinners, and months later, we fell in love, making that day an offbeat celebration for us.

Monday night, Carter had been late coming home after editing a breaking story, but we still had time to go to a movie. We then walked hand-in-hand to the Volo Restaurant and Wine Bar in Roscoe Village.

The restaurant is located on West Roscoe, close to North Damen. It has succulent food, and in the summer, we love sitting outside on the cabana patio. Carter ordered the three-glass Spanish red wine tasting flight to go with steak tartare. I asked for the *manchego, Montchevre* and *Grana Padano* cheese plate and a roasted beet salad. But when the heavenly smell of their famous b.m.g. flatbread with a rendered slab of Berkshire bacon, shiitake mushrooms, and goat cheese drifted over me, I ordered it, too, along with the same red wine flight.

"Do you want to talk about it?" he asked.

"The movie?"

He nodded.

The movie was a mesmerizing tale about reporters at the *Boston Globe* who collaborated on the Pulitzer Prize-winning series of stories about sexual abuse in the Catholic Church. It was an amazingly accurate portrayal of what it's like in the newsroom.

"It made me realize how much I miss working on a compelling story, especially with other reporters," I said.

He sipped his wine. "You know it's not always exciting. Most of the time here in Chicago it's just one shooting after another."

"But your reporters get to bounce ideas off each other and discuss the stories they're writing. I can't do that at home with a toddler."

"What we need to do is find a safe — but still challenging — story for you."

"I might have one, and I would like your advice about it," I said.

I recounted the same information I'd told Linda about Hannah, her husband Micah, his research, and their four children. Once again, I omitted the near-disaster with Kerry and the wood chips.

Carter stared at me a few seconds before he spoke. "Did you say his research involves embryonic stem cells?"

"I did."

"Do you know much about it?"

"Nothing more than it's very expensive, and Molly had IVF with her first child. Why?"

"I assume your female readers would prefer a column about a personal story rather than a dull scientific research piece. My take on this would be to focus on the doctor's wife and her transition in moving to Chicago and compare it to living in a country virtually at war all of the time."

"But Hannah wouldn't talk to me," I said. "She was pretty firm about not discussing any details of her life."

"That's never stopped you before," he said.

You're so right.

All I had to do was figure out a way to get her to talk to me.

30

On the Fourth of July, we picnicked at Hamlin Park and then hung out at the pool. Carter found a pickup softball game to join. That night, I told my hubby I was too exhausted to drive to Lake Michigan and watch the fireworks.

This was partly true, but my recent PTSD attack proved my trauma in Arlington still lingered below the surface of my psyche. After Kerry went to bed, we watched the DVDs of two of our favorite Fourth of July classics: James Cagney dancing in *Yankee Doodle Dandy* and the shark gobbling up people in *Jaws*.

Wednesday morning, our lives were back to normal. Before I could gather up Kerry and go down to the computer room to access the GPS data, my landline rang. One of Lyndell's sons, and his wife and two children, had come to stay at her home for the holiday. This was the first time she'd had an opportunity to call me.

I played with Kerry in the family room as I filled Lyndell in on the events she had missed. I began with my encounter with Hannah at Hamlin Park, but again, I avoided mentioning Kerry's near disaster with the wood chips.

We discussed Hannah and Micah as a possible story, but I saved the best for last: hiding the GPS transponder on the neighbor's Mercedes and the revelation that he had a passenger in the car with him.

"There's another man?" Lyndell asked. "Do you think he lives in the house too?"

"That's a possibility, and don't forget the two men I saw in the alley," I said. "They could live there too. But until one of us sees any of them enter or leave his house on a regular basis, it's only an assumption. I don't write my stories based on that."

"Did you recheck the pictures of those two men? Could either of them be the other man you saw?"

"I did, but I can't tell for sure."

"What have you found from the tracker?"

"I was going to download the information when you called. I'll let you know."

"Please do. In addition to watching the house, I'll keep an eye out for the two doctors and their kids." She paused. "And the leprechaun."

"Excuse me?"

"This morning, a man ran past my front window, and he bore a striking resemblance to a leprechaun. I think it would be a fabulous story for your column. I can see the headline now: 'A Leprechaun in Lakeview.' "

Aw, man.

"It does have a nice sound to it. I'll watch out for him too."

Lyndell was such a dear, sweet person. If nothing else came out of my recent story efforts, she enjoyed helping with the research. But maybe she was trying too hard to create a story, or — even worse — perhaps she was beginning to mentally slide downhill and I wouldn't be able to count on her.

"Oh, and did Cox Cable fix your problem?" she asked.

"We have a constant problem with Cox," I said. "Did you see them?"

"Him. While you were at Hamlin on the Fourth, a cute young man knocked on your front door and then walked around to your backyard."

"Thanks for letting me know Cox is on the job," I said.

And you are too.

Snooping is a big part of her life, even with family visiting her on a holiday. She is better than expensive security cameras.

Wait. Holiday?

Why would a Cox repairman be working on a holiday?

I spent the next two hours on the phone waiting to talk to a Cox representative about the visit and ran out of time to check on the GPS tracking data. And I never did speak to a human.

Was something else going on in our lives or, like Lyndell with her leprechaun, was I pushing too hard to invent a story about Cox and their man working on the holiday?

If I found time, I would call Cox again.

But is it worth it?

31

After breakfast on Thursday, Kerry and I went down to the computer room. I did a puzzle with her while I waited for the readout from the GPS recordings to be printed.

When the machine clicked off, I pulled the sheets from the tray. The evaluation didn't take long. Since Monday morning, the Mercedes had been driven to surprisingly few places, one of which I could have anticipated: Whole Foods.

"Kerry, Momma has to run an errand. Let's go for a ride."

"No!" she screamed. "Wanna pway with Elmo!"

Bribes usually work.

"Do you want to go to Scooter's first?"

"Yay! I wuv ice queam!"

Scooter's Frozen Custard Shop, one of our local favorites, is on the corner of West Belmont and North Paulina, a block from our home. Kerry held my hand as we walked there and shared a vanilla milk shake.

Fifteen minutes later, we went on a reconnaissance mission in our mommy van. I'd brought the read-out listing the addresses where the Mercedes had gone, as well as the dates and times of day.

Skipping Whole Foods, I drove to an address on North Greenview and pulled up in front of the North Side Mosque of

Lakeview. According to the tracking sheet, the car had arrived there around sunset on Monday, the day I attached the transponder to the Mercedes.

Tuesday at sunrise, at noon, and then once more at sunset, the car stopped there for over an hour each time. The neighbor might be a Middle Easterner and possibly a Muslim who attended services at the mosque. But I couldn't discount that he might be watching the mosque for more heinous reasons.

The mosque had security cameras scanning the neighborhood, and the readout indicated the car usually parked directly in front. If he planned to perform an evil act, he wasn't hiding his location while he scouted the premises.

I backtracked toward our neighborhood to check out two more addresses on the sheets: one on West Belmont and another on North Lincoln. Arriving at the first location, I found a hole-in-the-wall Middle Eastern restaurant. I drove to the second stop: another Middle Eastern restaurant, smaller than the first one.

One final address was twenty-five minutes south and east of Lakeview. The Mercedes was located there each night from around 9 p.m. until 2 a.m.

It might be where he works.

Hold it, Tina.

I was out of practice. A good investigative journalist never accepts assumptions as facts. I needed to gather all the data and go from there. Only a rookie reporter would make that mistake.

The mid-morning traffic was heavier than I had anticipated, and it took thirty-five minutes to get there. I stopped the van in the same place the Mercedes had been parked the night before. I found myself sitting in front of a freestanding, one-story, windowless building. Standing upright on the roof was a sign of a naked woman gyrating around a pole and the word "Twenties."

The sign was off.

It was a strip club.

A Muslim possibly connected to a strip club? Didn't see that one coming.

It was time for Kerry's morning nap. I drove home and called Lyndell with the news about the strip club.

"A what?" she asked.

"A strip club. You know, where women take off their clothes while dancing to music."

"Dear, I *know* what a strip club is. I'm not that out of touch with where men go. What are you going to do now?"

When I worked on stories in the past, I would have found a place to watch the club without being seen. I would have stayed in that location for as long as it took to push the story forward. At the abortion clinic, I'd parked on site daily for five weeks while I recorded the daily activities around the building.

But I am a mommy and that wouldn't be possible. There was only one thing I could do.

"I plan to visit the club," I said.

"Why don't you research it online first?" she asked. "It might be less dangerous."

Lyndell knew about my injuries and Carter's fears.

"I will, but I need to get a feel for the story, and I can't do it staring at a computer screen."

"Please be careful," she said.

"Don't worry. I have the perfect friend to go with me and cover my back."

32

It was a little after six on Thursday night. I walked into the kitchen. Kerry ate her dinner with Elmo, Ralph, and her daddy. "Cas is here. The seminar won't last long. I'll be home by nine at the latest."

From my daily GPS recordings, I knew the Mercedes arrived at the strip club around nine. Cas and I had to be out of there before then so my neighbor wouldn't catch me spying on him.

"I know you told me before, but I've already forgotten," he said. "What's it about again?"

"Exercise for young kids like Kerry."

"Right. That's exactly the type of story that should be perfect for your column. Mothers will love it."

I better have Cas give me background info on that kind of exercise, or I'll never be able to sneak out again.

"I love you," I said, kissing Carter on the lips and Kerry on the cheek.

Hurrying out the front door, I rushed down the stairs to Cas's silver Hummer H1, her version of a mommy van.

"Ready for an adventure?" I asked, stepping on the running board and pulling on the back of the seat with one hand and the top of the door with the other to climb up into the truck.

"I guess, but why are we going to a strip club at six o'clock on a Thursday night?" Cas asked.

"Like I said in my text, a man lives across the street from me, and he is connected to the club. There could be a story there."

"How did you figure this out?"

I told her about planting the GPS device on the Mercedes.

"Why not do the research online instead of going there?"

"Already did, but I need more," I said. "For me, a story is a visceral thing. I have to wrap my arms around it emotionally before I can commit to writing it. When I discovered the Twenties might be connected to the story, I wanted to get out there ASAP and do some recon. Oh, and take pictures with my iPhone."

"Why me and not Linda, or Molly?"

"If this goes upside down, you're my only friend fit and feisty enough to help me."

"Do you think it'll be dangerous?"

"Hope not. I looked online for police reports about the club. There's never been an incident, and there's supposed to be security onsite."

"Okay, I get all that, but why so early in the evening?"

"Yeah, about that…" I said. "The GPS recordings show his Mercedes shows up around nine. We have to be out of there by then."

"And if we aren't?"

"It could be big trouble for both of us."

33

The Thursday night traffic was even heavier than what I'd battled that morning, and it took forty-five minutes to get to the Twenties. Cas parked on the street close to where I'd previously stopped. As I'd hoped, the Mercedes wasn't there.

We walked into a dimly lit, high-ceilinged rectangular room. There were about fifty tables. Most were four-tops, but there were a few six-and eight-tops. The pounding music blasting from the surround-sound speakers made my chest vibrate. The stench of spilled beer and cheap whisky soaked the air.

"Welcome to the Twenties," the young woman at the hostess stand said. She had waist-length platinum blond hair. She wore a red micro-mini skirt and a lacy black top which didn't hide that she'd left her bra in the dressing room.

Cas usually wears color-coordinated exercise gear and matching high-tech training shoes. Tonight, she wore a black T-shirt, tight black jeans, and black Nikes. I had on a sleeveless blue top, white cotton pants, and flip-flops. I pulled a San Diego Padres baseball hat down to shield the upper part of my face in case there were security cameras. We had our hair in ponytails.

"Where do you guys wanna sit?" she asked.

"I think over there, don't you, Cas?" I asked, pointing at an empty table against the back wall.

The hostess led us there. Several of the male customers stared at us as we walked past them.

A young woman wearing a skimpy version of a sailor suit danced on a round stage in the center of the room. She did a contortionist routine around a stripper pole. An illuminated runway about ten feet long went from the stage and disappeared behind a black curtain at the other end of the room.

Patrons sat around the stage and both sides of the runway holding out money to the stripper. Two male bouncers — who looked like offensive tackles for the Bears — flanked the front door. There were a few couples in the room, but we were the only solo women.

We sat down and faced the stage. With my hat pulled down and my hand obscuring the lower part of my face, I scanned the room for security cameras. I counted six. Four rotated as they covered the room and front door. Two were fixed and directed at the bar, a computer behind the bar, and a cash register.

I palmed my iPhone and began taking pictures. The girl on stage had stripped down to a sailor's hat, a thong, and high heels. Her tanned, well-oiled skin glistened under the intense glare of the hot stage lights.

"I can't believe this," Cas said. "It's 6:45 on Thursday night, and this place is packed. Don't these guys have anything better to do with their time?"

I scanned the room. "Apparently not."

We watched the stripper throw her sailor's hat into the crowd. A young waitress wearing a white, lacy, see-through top and a black thong walked toward our table. As she moved closer, I saw that she had applied multiple hues of purple and green eye makeup which covered her lids from lash to brow.

"She looks like a raccoon," Cas whispered.

"Maybe she flunked Eye Makeup 101," I whispered back. "Her bra must be in the dressing room with the hostess's."

The waitress chomped on a wad of gum. "Guy over there…" she nodded toward a grossly obese man by the stage, "…wants to buy you two a drink," she said between chomps.

"That is so not happening," I said. "If we want a drink, we'll pay for it."

"Well, we got a two-drink minimum, and somebody's gotta pay for it."

"How about bottled water?" I asked.

"You wanna run a tab?"

"I think not," I said, handing her a twenty.

She kept her hand out. I gave her another twenty.

"Drinks seem kind of expensive here," I said.

"Guess you shoulda let the guy buy them," the girl said.

"Guess again, sweetie," Cas said.

"*Whatever.*" The waitress tottered away on her six-inch platform heels.

A new dancer strutted down the runway and stepped onto the stage. She wore a cop's uniform. I took her picture with my partially hidden iPhone.

Her face looked familiar. "I think I've seen that dancer before," I said.

"You have, and so have I. It's Donna Allen, the girl who works out with Corky and Sammy in my exercise classes at XSport Fitness."

"If Sammy's a stripper, too, maybe that's why she has breast implants, and how she's able to afford them," I said.

Donna stripped down to a thong, policeman's hat, and gun belt. The waitress returned with four bottles of water. I began to question her about that but then remembered the two-drink minimum. I took a sip and kept quiet.

A man entered the club. He stopped at the hostess desk and spoke to the blond woman who had seated us. They chatted and then he went behind the bar and logged on to a computer in the corner.

The manager?

I took his picture and then almost dropped the phone when I recognized who it was.

"Crap," I said, scrunching down in my chair and pulling my baseball hat lower.

"What's wrong?" Cas asked.

"It's my neighbor! He's early! We need to get outta here without him seeing me."

34

"We need a distraction," Cas said.

I kept my head down and my hands in front of my face, hoping my neighbor wouldn't recognize me.

"Any ideas?" I asked.

She looked around the room.

"Got it."

She waved at the server to come to our table. "Remember the guy who wanted to buy us drinks?"

"Yeah, Big Howie," she said. "Comes in all the time."

"Tell him we changed our minds. We want to party with him."

"You're kidding, right?" she asked. "He's kinda gross."

"Tell him it's his lucky night."

The server turned and walked toward the man. I grabbed Cas's arm. "What are you doing?"

"Distracting. Get up right now and go to the bathroom before he comes over here."

"But I don't have to go."

"Do you want to get out of here without your neighbor seeing you?"

"I do."

"Then get up right now," Cas said. "Act like you're going to the bathroom but, instead, hide in the hallway. When you see the big guy have a seizure, run to the Hummer. I'll meet you there."

"But..."

"Get going. He's coming."

The women's bathroom was in the hallway behind us. My neighbor was still on the computer behind the bar and had his back to me. I stood up and hugged the wall to avoid the security cameras. I crept into the hallway, stopped, and watched Cas from around the corner.

The man waddled up to our table. He pulled out a chair and plopped down. "Waitress said you want to party," he wheezed.

"You got that right, big boy. Let's have a few drinks and get it on."

Cas snuggled up to him and, at the same time, reached into her bag. He turned to wave at the server. When he did, she touched his leg and suddenly he began shaking. He knocked over our bottles of water and then fell out of the chair and had a full-blown seizure.

"Help!" Cas screamed. "Help this guy!"

The two bouncers and my neighbor rushed toward the quivering man. Several more people did too. Cas reached down to help the man and, within seconds, he had another seizure.

That was my cue.

Go!

I hurried out of the building without being noticed.

35

I stood in the steamy Chicago night air next to the Hummer and watched as Cas sprinted out of the Twenties. As she ran, she remotely unlocked the truck's doors. She jumped into the driver's seat, and I joined her on the passenger side. She fired up the engine and roared away before I'd securely fastened my seat belt.

"How did you make him have a seizure?" I asked as she screeched around the corner and I finished latching my seat belt.

"Let's get outta here first," she said.

She drove four blocks and pulled over. She opened her purse and took out a stubby black and yellow gun. "I used this."

"What is it?" I asked.

"A contact Taser."

"Why do you have it?"

"I worked in the ER. Drunks or people on drugs are impossible to control, but there we had male cops and security guards to help us. Now, when I'm alone, this Taser is my equalizer."

"It really looked like the guy was having a seizure."

"Oh, he had one, but I caused it."

"And thank God you did."

"Did you get what you wanted before we left?" she asked.

"My neighbor might be the owner, or at least he seems to run the place, but it isn't conclusive evidence. I need more."

While Cas drove, I texted Linda about the Twenties and then told Cas what I'd done.

"Is Linda helping you on this too?" she asked.

"She is. I did online research of the sale of that man's house. But I couldn't hack into the real house owner's bank, and I asked her to take over."

"What about me?"

"What about you?" I asked.

"I would really like to continue to help you with this."

"Why?"

"There are only so many ways I can try to make the spinners think they're riding an indoor stationary bike outdoors up a mountain road. I enjoyed doing this."

"What about your exercise classes? Can you take time away from them?"

"They don't pay me enough to cover my gas expenses driving back and forth to the club. I'll make the time."

"Okay, but what if we run into trouble?" I asked.

"It doesn't take much strength to pull the trigger on my Taser," she said. "What's our next step?"

"Carter doesn't want me doing dangerous stories. I told him we were at a seminar about exercise ideas for young kids. You need to tell me what I can say to convince him we were there."

She double-parked in front of my house and gave me the basics about kid's exercise classes.

"This is so cool," she said when she finished. "When we met at Hamlin Park and formed our playgroup, who knew it would lead to us helping you work on a story?"

"What about Molly helping us too?"

"Gotta think about that one. Molly's...well, Molly, you know?"

"I do."

She drummed her fingers on the steering wheel.

"A problem?" I asked.

"Kind of. Your neighbor's a Muslim, right?"

"He might be."

"When was the last time you heard or read about a Muslim man being in a business with naked dancing women?"

"Never."

"Then, why is your neighbor?"

36

Friday morning, Linda and I left Kerry and Sandra in the XSport Fitness daycare and walked to our usual seats in the back row of the spinning class. I scrubbed down the bike with antibacterial wipes before I adjusted the seat and handlebar.

"After I unpacked last night, I finally found time to hack into the Arun Corporation's accounts," Linda said, as she wiped down her bike.

"What did you find?"

"The corporation does its banking at the First Caribbean International Bank in the Cayman Islands."

"Would a shell corporation do that?" I asked.

She climbed on the bike and clipped in. "How much do you know about financial shenanigans like that?"

"Only the basics. The research into it was the breakthrough I needed in my first investigative story when I was a rookie reporter in Chicago. It involved Dr. Mick Doyle, who became famous as the 'Fat Doctor.' "

"I remember him. When I was in law school, all my girlfriends and I used his product, and it worked."

"It did, but my story proved it had dire side effects, and not only was it taken off the market, but he went to jail."

"What does this have to do with a shell company?"

"I discovered a shell corporation owned Doyle's business, homes, and cars. Ultimately, my friend — who was an experienced journalist on the economic beat at the Chicago bureau of the *Wall Street Journal* — discovered the profits he made from fat Americans were funneled to terrorist groups all over the world."

"Did you just call me fat?"

I felt my face flush. "Sorry, but he did make millions of dollars on people trying to lose weight using his product instead of dieting and exercising." I climbed on my bike and clipped in my bike shoes. "Did you find a shell corporation?"

"Not yet. It'll take a lot of time on my computer, and you need to know that doing it might not be exactly legal."

"As an officer of the court, how do you feel about that?" I asked.

"Do you want the information, or not?"

"Obviously, I do. I won't have a story without it."

Her lips compressed into a thin line. "Then, don't ask how I do it, okay?"

"Sure, no problem."

I didn't admit to her that I'd used a lock pick gun to break into places while chasing a story.

37

A funky grin crossed Linda's face, as we began to warm up.

"What?" I asked.

"I was still on the computer when I received your text that your neighbor might be associated with the Twenties. What do the patrons do there?"

"Watch women take off their clothes."

"What else?" she asked.

"Drink," I said.

"And to consume an alcoholic beverage at a strip club, the owner needs a liquor license. In order to jump through that legal hoop, the individual needs to provide a driver's license or a passport and have his fingerprints taken. And best of all, it's in the public record."

"How did you figure that out?"

"You have my husband to thank for this. Howard asked me what I was doing on the computer so late at night. One of his partners helps clients obtain liquor licenses in Chicago. Howard showed me the website. The Twenties has a new owner, and his name is Mohammad al-Turk. He's your new neighbor."

Yes!

"You rock!" I said. "Thank you, so much! This might be the breakthrough I need. I can't wait to get home and research al-Turk's history. Was there another man's name on the liquor license?"

"No. Why?"

I recounted the details about planting the GPS device on the Mercedes and my close call with the passenger.

"Al-Turk is the only person listed on the application," she said. "I didn't find a second man's name."

"But thanks to Howard, I have one."

"What about using two GPS trackers?"

"I don't want to spend money on a second device until I see if I need it. It depends on what I discover about al-Turk."

"Sound financial thinking, but if we proceed with the story, a second device will be mandatory."

"You might be right. We can talk about this after class."

Our friend Molly Cutchall walked into the class. She has straight, waist-length blond hair and a flawless face. Her to-die-for long legs make her nearly four inches taller than me. She usually isn't interested in any exercise more strenuous than carrying shopping bags full of designer clothes to her new silver Mercedes GL 550. Even though she has an aversion to working out and has given birth to four babies, she still has a fabulous figure.

She had arrived late, and there were no seats available except those being saved by riders already on their bikes. Sitting at the far end of the middle row was the surfer dude I'd seen talking to Corky and Sammy the last time I was in spinning class. He waved at Molly and pointed to a seat next to him he'd apparently been saving.

Giving up his buddy's bike.

Leave it to Molly to entice the buffed young man to do that. He leaped off his bike to help her adjust her handlebar and seat height. Once she sat down, he made sure her shoes were properly clipped in. The whole display was nauseating, but Molly had that effect on men, and this guy was no exception.

"Who's your new friend, Molly?" I asked.

She turned to him. "Jamie, say 'hi' to Tina and Linda."

He flashed a five-star smile at us. "What up?"

Cas cranked up the music and class began.

38

After class, Linda and I walked to the locker room. The cloying odor from hair sprays, colognes, and deodorants hung in the steamy air. Molly came in behind us. Cas remained in the spinning room to make sure all the bikes had been disinfected to her satisfaction. I sat down in front of my locker. Linda groaned her way down next to me.

"Thanks to your husband, we have one name and possible access to the man's fingerprints making our research easier," I said.

"And quicker," she added, as she wiped her face with a towel. "I'll go online and try to find the bank al-Turk uses. If it's also the First Caribbean, I might be able to use his account as a platform to uncover who is sending the money to him from that bank."

"If we have that, we might be on our way to figuring out what my neighbor is doing and if it's illegal."

I glanced at Molly, who stood with Sammy and Donna at the other end of the locker room. I couldn't hear what they were talking about, but what Molly did grabbed my attention.

"Check that out," I said, nodding toward Molly and the two younger girls.

We watched as Molly squeezed Sammy and Donna's breasts, and they did the same thing to her.

"I've never seen that in here," Linda said.

"Maybe it's the millennial replacement for mammograms."

"If it is, I think I'll pass." She threw her towel in the bin. "But breast implants would be, pardon the pun, a titillating story for your column. This proves it."

"And you wouldn't have to bill me for the research," I said. "I could do most of it sitting right here."

39

Molly joined us. "What are you guys talking about?"

"Linda's helping me with a story," I said. "So is Cas."

Linda's head snapped up. "She *is*? You didn't mention it in your text last night."

"Sorry. Cas went to the Twenties with me. I needed her to cover my back in case there was a problem."

"What's the Twenties?" Molly asked.

"A strip club," I said.

"Sounds like fun. Can I go with next time and help out too?"

"I didn't think you'd be interested in doing a story with me."

"Oh, I'm way interested. When I traveled around the world modeling, I used to do things like that for extra money."

"Things?" Linda asked.

"Greg was in the Marines and attached to our embassy in Rome. We met in a bar, and I, of course, looked hot. He hit on me, and we hooked up."

Silence.

"And...?" I prompted.

"Oh, and he saw how men were attracted to me and would talk to me," Molly said. "He contacted a couple of guys at the embassy, and they hired me to help them out. They had friends in other countries where I modeled. I helped them too. The extra money was great."

"Who were these men?" Linda asked.

"They said they were agricultural attachés, but they weren't."

"CIA?" I asked.

"Yep."

"You never mentioned you worked for them," I said.

"You never asked."

Got me there.

"Can you get information out of people?" Linda asked.

"I'm good at it. Men think I'm an airhead, so they tell me all kinds of secret stuff."

"What about women?" I asked, thinking about my problem with Hannah.

"Pretty much the same thing."

Molly retired from modeling when she was thirty. Her husband, Greg, is twelve years older than she is. She wanted to get pregnant as speedily as she could because she'd read in a fashion magazine his sperm might be getting too old to produce normal children.

They had trouble getting the job done, an issue that wasn't a problem for Carter and me. All he had to do was walk through the bedroom and I got pregnant with Kerry.

They sought medical help from a fertility specialist and selected *in vitro* fertilization. The result was Chase, who is five. Before she could resume IVF to try for a second child, her own reproductive apparatus shifted into high gear, and she had three more male babies, each one year apart.

Given her experience with IVF, she would be perfect to help me with Hannah's story. "I might have an assignment for you on another story I'm considering writing," I said. "Give me a couple of days to work it out."

"Sure, fine," Molly said.

Finally, I had a plan in motion to further flesh out Hannah and Micah's story. Molly could help me with it, and Cas and Linda could continue investigating Mr. al-Turk.

40

Okay, dude, who are you?

I stared at Mr. Mohammad al-Turk's face looking back at me on my computer screen.

Friday night, I'd finally found the time to sit down in front of my computer to meet my neighbor.

Carter was upstairs putting our daughter to bed.

Linda had emailed me the liquor license research, so I had a definable starting point. To operate a club in Chicago where alcohol would be served, a new owner like al-Turk had to obtain a tavern license. He'd needed to provide his personal history, a photo ID, a driver's license or passport, documentation of ownership of the Twenties, a financial disclosure form, and confirmation he had the necessary funds to acquire the business.

I called Linda with what was on the computer screen in front of me.

"Al-Turk is forty-two years old and unmarried," I said. "He was born in New York City where he graduated from NYU with a business degree. His credit rating is perfect. He has no lawsuits or complaints against him, and no skirmishes with law enforcement agencies in Chicago, New York, or anywhere else in the country."

"Sounds squeaky clean," Linda said. "I hope you found more than that."

"Oh, I did. Twelve years ago, he and two other men founded an import/export business specializing in products made in the Middle East. It's called Business Ventures."

"Bingo. That's the company we need to research."

"I tried, but I can't hack into any of the financial details."

"To use your baseball term, I'm in the batter's box," she said.

"I can't do much without that information."

"We need to know where he lived before he moved into your neighborhood."

"From my research on liquor licenses, I know it takes about forty days to obtain one. Al-Turk has to have been in Chicago at least that long."

"You work on that, and I'll tackle his businesses."

"Great."

She didn't respond.

"Linda?"

"There's a lot going on here. Do you want to continue working on it?"

"You mean the possibility of it being dangerous?"

"I do," she said.

"My gut tells me there's a story here, and I want to do it."

"What did your gut tell you about the abortion clinic bomber story?"

I fingered the scar on the side of my head. "That got me blown up, but this is different."

"Are you sure?"

A good question.

Am I?

41

Saturday morning, Carter prepared breakfast for Kerry while I went out for my run. Each morning since I met Hannah, I looked for new "Sold" signs, hoping one of them might be her recently purchased home. I searched the neighborhood and found six homes that had recently been purchased. The Hannah Eisenberg Trust didn't own any of them.

Twenty minutes into my run, I discovered a "Sold" sign in the front yard of an antique-red brick home on West Henderson Street, two blocks north of my front door. Stopping in the middle of the block, I jogged in place about twenty-five yards from the house. Attached to the eaves of the structure were rotating security cameras, scanning the street and the neighbors' homes on each side. I'd never seen equipment like that in our neighborhood.

Interesting. Anyone hungry for cookies?

I would bake a batch of cookies and welcome the owners of that house to the neighborhood. If Hannah answered the door, I'd accomplished my goal. If not, maybe I discovered a story about the new owners who needed security cameras to record continuous pictures of the neighborhood.

That meant they recorded me standing on the street spying on the house.

Uh-oh.

Turning around, I ran toward North Ravenswood. The only person on the street with me was a fellow runner who ran in the opposite direction, east on West Henderson toward the house with the security cameras. He slowed down and glanced at the home but then moved on.

I saw his pale face and red hair. He looked like a leprechaun.

Lyndell's leprechaun!

She had seen him. I needed a story, but her idea was about as exciting as folding laundry, and if I didn't like it, Gayle probably wouldn't, either. To keep my job, I needed an interesting and entertaining story for my readers. Not one about a leprechaun living in Lakeview.

Reinserting my ear buds, I ran home listening to Wilco's songs. If I did have Hannah's actual address, I had to do my research quickly to write a story for the August issue.

42

Saturday night, after Carter read two books to Kerry, he walked down to the family room. I went into her room and finished tucking her in for the night.

"Honey, I'm going downstairs to work on my story," I said when I joined him. "We can watch a DVD when I finish, okay?"

Carter sat on the couch, typing on his office laptop. "Great. How about *North by Northwest?*"

No. Not again.

We'd watched it way too many times, but I needed to get on my computer. "I'll get it out."

He went back to his laptop. I found the DVD and put it next to the machine before I hurried down to the lower level and threw in a load of laundry. While it ran, I went into the office to use my computer.

I had the address of the house on West Henderson Street I thought might belong to Hannah and Micah. Using that information and their individual names, I began an online search for the documents of the sale of the home.

After fifteen minutes, I found them. Employing the same technique I had used in an attempt to identify the new neighbor across the street, I tracked the real estate money backwards through the banking system. I discovered the Hannah Eisenberg Trust at the Wells Fargo Bank in New York City owned the home on West Henderson.

I needed help and texted Linda about our other project. She called me two minutes later.

"Is this about those two doctors?" Linda asked.

"It is," I said.

"Isn't one story enough?"

"It's taking forever. This is a fluff piece I can write quickly after I pull together all of their background information."

"Why not just interview them and be done with it?"

"Hannah's a little standoffish. She left the park before she would answer any of my questions."

"Strange."

"She told me her husband won't allow a story to be written about them."

"Allow?" she asked. "That's beyond strange."

"Her words, not mine," I said.

"Which is why you're now using the Internet."

"Trying to, but I have a problem. I'll email what I have."

I forwarded to her what little concrete information I had on Hannah and Micah's house and waited on the phone while she read it.

"It's the Wells Fargo trust fund again," she said when she finished.

"Can you do your magic and find out more?" I asked.

"I'll get right on it."

"And I'll chase down the personal side," I said.

I hung up and went back to my computer. I began an online search for Chicago's most expensive interior designers and added Hannah and Micah's names as possible clients. I didn't have to search for long. Leslie Berry, ASID, was a regular on Facebook, Twitter, his blog, and TV publicizing his decorating ideas for the homes and condos of Chicago's rich and famous.

My computer skills were competent enough that I could hack into Hannah's account at Berry's firm.

"Oh. My. God!" I whispered to myself when the numbers flashed on the screen.

The cost of decorating their house exceeded the purchase price of our home.

43

I called Linda and told her what I'd discovered.

"It's not surprising with what I have on the screen in front of me," she said. "To say her trust is filled to overflowing is an understatement. Her grandparents were among the original investors with Warren Buffett. The Berkshire Hathaway stock was passed on to her parents, and they subsequently bequeathed all of the remaining stock to her. It's in her trust account at Wells Fargo in New York City."

"What's the account worth?" I asked.

"At the market's closing yesterday, the value of her trust is a little over four hundred forty million dollars."

"Wow."

"The trust not only paid for all the interior decorating, it bought their home and two new vehicles, an Escalade and a Mercedes GLS. The trustee closed on their home on West Henderson Street in April."

"Hannah said they'd moved in about two weeks ago. I assume that time interval was necessary to furnish their home."

"That fits the timeline of their move," she said. "They came here on the first of April but apparently lived in Micah's luxury high-rise condo until the decorating was completed."

"What about Micah? Does he pay for any of this?"

"Nothing big. He moved to Chicago sixteen months ago and rented the condo near Northwestern Medical Center. The monthly rent came out of the trust."

"In that neighborhood, it had to be a big number."

"It was, but at the same time, twenty-five million dollars was wired from her trust fund to the Wells Fargo Bank here in Chicago. The account is separate from their joint account. The only signature on this new account is Micah's."

"What did he do with the money?"

"A portion of those funds went toward the purchase of an empty warehouse on the North Side. The rest went to an Illinois construction company that specializes in medical buildings. I found multiple local and state permits to build out the warehouse into a laboratory."

"Send me the address of that lab," I said.

She did. I checked my files. The address of the warehouse was the same as the ones listed on Micah's driver and medical licenses.

"What about the money to equip and run the lab and pay the staff?" I asked. "Where is that coming from?"

"I have no idea. If there's another account at Wells Fargo, I can't find it because I don't know the name of the lab. Do you know who the lab director is?"

"Why?"

"He might be signing the business checks out of a different account. If I have his name, I can find the account."

"Hold on a second. I have an idea."

I put Micah's file up on the screen. I found his scientific papers I'd put off reading.

"I'm sending you the names of three doctors Micah has written papers with," I said. "All are now at Northwestern. It's possible one or more of them are working with Micah at his lab and maybe one of them is the director."

"I'll chase them down," she said. "And I have a suggestion. Neither of us know squat about a medical lab. With her master's degree in nursing, Cas might be able to help us decipher this."

"Good idea. I already talked to Molly about Hannah. Adding Cas to research Micah's side of this might help me with my time-management problems."

"What about delivering her your welcome-to-the-neighborhood cookies?"

"That's my next move. I'll drop by their home with cookies and act like I didn't know she and her family lived there. If she invites Kerry and me in, great. If not, I'll at least have established contact with her."

"How about inviting her and her kids to our playgroup on Wednesday afternoon at Hamlin Park? That way all of us can work on her."

"That's a great idea. I'll do it Monday morning."

I shut down my computer and headed upstairs to watch the DVD of *North by Northwest*. I stopped in the kitchen and unloaded the dishwasher. As I put the plates away, I glanced at al-Turk's house.

Did one of his curtains move?

I shut off the kitchen lights and peeked out our front windows at the house.

Maybe he's watching me through his front windows.

Like I was with him.

44

"Kerry, would you like to go to Dinkel's and buy a donut for Daddy?" I asked. "He sure has been working hard in our garden."

Kerry jumped up and down. "Okay, Momma!"

No need for a bribe when a trip involves donuts.

Carter tended to the plants in our tiny garden, a chore he delights in doing but rarely has time for. After twenty minutes in the oppressive Chicago humidity, his gray White Sox T-shirt had become soaked with sweat, but he'd kept working.

I sat inside our air-conditioned home with Kerry who was busy pulling DVDs out of their jackets and joyfully flinging them around the family room. It was an activity she'd dreamed up on her own about two weeks before.

We buy, or I should say Carter buys, DVDs, especially classic movies like *Vertigo,* or new indie films like *Hank and Asha.* He loves owning them as much as he does keeping the print copies of all the articles he's ever written. I've tried to convince him that streaming movies would be cheaper, easier, and faster, but he won't change. That's the problem with marrying a man seven years older than me. Occasionally it seems like we grew up in different centuries.

And raising an active two-year-old means our house is always in a state of disarray. There are often multiple DVDs on the floor of the family room making it impossible to walk around without stepping on several of them. Before we departed for Dinkel's, I picked up the pile of glistening DVDs and slid them into the first empty jackets I found.

It is a system I devised for quickly cleaning up our daughter's mess, but Carter and I enjoy watching classic movies, and it makes finding our favorite films a challenge. The night before, I'd taken a DVD out of the *Vertigo* jacket and put it in the DVD player only to find out we were watching *Marathon Man*.

My stomach growled and I was more than happy to buy donuts. I saw it as a win-win errand for all three of us.

Come on, be honest.

The donut run had little to do with being hungry or being kind to Carter. I was stress-eating because I was frustrated. If I were still actively employed as a full-time investigative journalist, I would have had a new story totally outlined by now or at least an idea of whether there was even a story to write. But I didn't have time because I was busy doing mommy jobs like picking up DVDs and taking care of my sweet little girl.

Thank God my friends are helping. Otherwise I might eat all the donuts in Dinkel's.

After ten minutes, we could walk around without stepping on the DVDs. I secured Kerry in her car seat in the mommy van.

As I backed out of the garage, our alley appeared in the rearview mirror and an idea popped into my mind.

Driving north on Paulina, I crossed Melrose and took the next left west into the alley behind al-Turk's home. As I cruised by his property, I again scanned the garage and the back of the house on my left for security cameras.

Don't see any.

Pulling out the other end of the alley, I turned right and headed to Dinkel's. In Arlington, I'd sifted through trash to research the bomber's story. From the bills, I figured out that he wasn't the real laundryman. If al-Turk hasn't been too careful with his discards, they might be the key here too.

And I needed to find out if the second man in the Mercedes at Whole Foods lived with al-Turk. Or maybe even one or two of the other men I'd seen delivering boxes out of the white van. Discovering other fingerprints on the trash might be a way to do that. Any other details would be a bonus and might help me decide if I should pursue the story.

I had to make certain Carter didn't catch me doing research on a story that might be hazardous. The best way to begin was to have a stress-free family Sunday afternoon at Hamlin Park, including doing some knitting to relax.

I texted my trash plan to Linda.

She texted back: *Be careful.*

45

By midnight on Sunday, Carter snored heavily, thanks to the full bottle of Fourth Estate Pinot I'd made sure he finished while we watched the DVD of the original version of *The Magnificent Seven*.

Dressing in the bathroom with the door closed, I shoved my hair under a black stocking cap and put on a shapeless, black top and baggy, black slacks. I tiptoed down the stairs, out the back door, and ran to the end of the alley where al-Turk's house was located.

I slipped into the shadows opposite his garage. Trash cans stood next to the closed garage doors of each house. Standing statue-still in the humid night air, I scanned the eaves of his house and garage for security cameras.

No new ones.

After putting on latex gloves I'd purchased at Walgreen's, I crept across the alley. I was about seven feet from the trash cans when motion-detector floodlights in the eaves of the garage burst on.

Do it now!

I grabbed the can's lid and flipped it up.

The stench of the garbage bombarded me.

Reaching into the can, I grabbed the first trash bag my fingers touched. I turned to my left to sprint home the way I'd come but saw a car's headlights turning in to that end of the alley. The light bar on the roof flashed red and blue lights.

Cops!

The car screeched to a stop, blocking my escape.

Looking to my right, I saw another car's headlights appear in the far end of the alley. That vehicle slammed to a stop too.

Hide!

I retreated into the shadows behind me.

My new plan was to open the gate and hide in the back yard of that home, like I did when I photographed the two men unloading the boxes into the garage across from me.

I tried to lift the metal latch on the gate, but it wouldn't move. I jiggled the latch, but it still didn't budge.

Dammit!

When I reached over the top of the fence to open it from the inside, my latex gloves touched a locked deadbolt.

No! I'm trapped!

46

My blood pressure skyrocketed when I saw a man wearing the uniform of one of Chicago's finest climb out of a black and white at the left end of the alley where I'd entered a few minutes earlier.

The car's blue and red lights continued to flash.

Do something!

I pulled off my stocking cap, latex gloves, shoes, and socks. I threw them behind me.

Yanking the lid off of the garbage can standing next to the locked gate, I tossed in the trash bag I'd just stolen and lowered the lid.

The floodlights on al-Turk's garage blinked off.

The cop flipped on his tactical flashlight.

I shook my sweaty hair free and rushed into the center of the alley, keeping my back turned to the advancing cop.

"Harold! You come here this instant!" I began clapping my hands vigorously. "You naughty cat!"

Taking two more steps away from the approaching cop, I scanned the alley acting like I was looking for my cat. "Harold? Where are you, sweetie? Come to Momma."

The sound of the cop pulling a gun out of his holster grabbed my attention.

"Stop right where you are!" he shouted. "Hands on top of your head!"

That really got my attention.

I wheeled around. He pointed the gun at my chest and the light in my face.

"What?" I asked, holding up my right hand to shield my eyes from the intense beam.

"I said, 'Put your hands on top of your head!' "

I did.

"Turn around."

"But…"

"Turn around."

I complied. He patted me down.

"Okay, lower your hands," he commanded when he finished.

I did.

He put the gun in his holster and snapped off his flashlight. "What are you doing out here, lady?"

"We have a cat. Harold's his name. He loves to dig through the trash. Our new neighbor doesn't know the garbage system around here, and he leaves the lids off of his trash cans." I pointed at his can's lid that I'd partially pulled off. "Harold can't resist that. It's like trash can-nip for him."

The cop didn't laugh at my attempt at humor.

"But anyway, I was up going to the bathroom, and I realized Harold was still outside. When I saw the neighbor's security lights were on, I knew my bad boy was up to no good. I wanted to bring him back inside before he scattered the man's trash all over the alley."

The cop stared at me. He wasn't buying what I was selling.

"Your neighbor's security system has been going crazy tonight," he said. "According to that rent-a-cop at the far end of the alley, this is the second time it's gone off. That's why he radioed us. But it seems a little farfetched to me that a cat would do that."

I didn't correct him by telling him it had only gone off once and I had caused it.

"You don't know Harold. And the only things out here…" I waved my hand around, "…are trash cans full of, well, trash. In a neighborhood like this, it's not like we have a platoon of homeless people dumpster diving for meals in our cans."

"I need to see your cat to verify this story." He rested his hand on the butt of his gun.

"See, that's a problem. Harold's a typical male, out all night chasing around. If you just put the lid on that trash can, he won't be a problem. He'll come home when he gets hungry."

The officer stared at me and then slid the lid in place and pounded it down on the top of the trash can. He checked the other can's lid to make sure it was secure.

"Luke, radio the rent-a-cop that this lady's cat set off the alarm lights and to quit bothering us," he yelled at his partner. He turned back and faced me. He took in a breath but didn't say anything for a few seconds before he turned and walked to his cruiser.

"Goodnight, officer," I said to his back, as I shuffled toward the locked gate, pretending I was about to go into the backyard.

They drove off. The security guard at the other end of the alley did too. I grabbed the stolen trash bag out of the can next to the locked gate. Hoping to get out of there as fast as possible, I put on the shoes and carried my stocking cap, latex gloves, and socks in my hands. I checked around to see if I'd forgotten anything and ran home.

What else can go wrong?

47

I sprinted home from stealing the bag of al-Turk's trash and crept down to the laundry room, the one place Carter never went and where my loot would be safe. I put on another pair of latex gloves and opened the trash bag.

There were cigarette butts, empty carryout food cartons from Middle Eastern restaurants, soiled paper towels, used tea bags, coffee grounds, five empty boxes of Montblanc pen-and-pencil sets, six empty Crest toothpaste boxes, and four empty cartons for plastic mixing bowls.

Huh?

It all had to be checked for fingerprints, but other than that, who knew? Putting the trash back into the bag, I tucked it behind a box of Ultra Tide Free laundry soap and removed the gloves.

I planned to hide the sack in the garage in the morning before it began to stink up the room and Carter noticed the smell. Seeing the soap reminded me to put in a load of laundry as long as I was down there.

When I reached the top of the stairs, I ran face-first into Carter. He stood in the doorway and didn't look happy.

"What are you doing up at this time of night?" he demanded.

A reasonable question for which I had no plausible answer. Stepping back, I began to shift my weight from one foot to the other. It was a tick I had when I was about to tell a fib. Carter called it the "Tina-two-step," and if he caught me doing it now, he would know I was about to tell him a lie.

I was saved when the washer clicked into its agitation cycle.

Carter frowned. "Isn't it a little late to be doing laundry?" he asked.

Thank you, honey.

He'd given me a viable alibi, and there was no reason to contradict him.

"I couldn't sleep and came down here to get a couple of loads of wash done."

Sounds truthful to me.

"You're sweating, and you never do that when you're just doing laundry," he said, stepping back as I walked past him into the kitchen. "And you're not wearing your pajamas."

Got me there.

"I can come to only one conclusion," he continued.

Filling a glass with water, my hand shook as I gulped it down. "Oh?"

"You've been outside running."

Gotta keep this close to the truth.

"Outside, yes, but I wasn't exactly running."

"What were you doing?"

"When I was up checking on Kerry, I looked out our front windows and saw a police car parked at the end of the alley across the street. My reporter's instincts kicked in. I threw on clothes and ran over there to see what was going on. I didn't even take time to put on socks."

He opened his mouth to object, but I held up my hand to stop him.

"It wasn't dangerous, Honey. A neighbor's cat had set off the security lights of one of the homes by going through their trash. You can check it out when you get to work by accessing the police report."

He nodded, and I was positive that was exactly what he would do.

"Looks like we're both wide awake," he said.

A seductive smile crept across his face. I knew where this was headed, and I felt myself tense up. He is getting older and wants another baby, preferably a son. But I don't want to get pregnant. With a toddler and a new baby, I would never have time to write a great story that could resurrect my career.

But now my friends are helping me!

"You're right, Honey," I said. "I'm not sleepy. Let's go make a baby."

He arched his eyebrows. "You're not too tired?"

"The endorphin rush from interviewing the cop has me fired up. If you don't mind missing your sleep, I'm ready."

His smiled widened. "I'll go in late tomorrow."

Hand-in-hand, we walked upstairs to our bedroom. Maybe having another baby wasn't such a bad idea after all. If we succeeded tonight, I would still have nine months to complete the story about Mr. al-Turk.

Part 3

48

It was midmorning on Monday. Because of our nighttime lovemaking, Carter had gone in late, and I'd skipped my usual run. Instead, I baked up a double batch of M&M sugar cookies to deliver to Hannah's home. The trash samples might help, but I needed a story pronto, and Hannah was the only other one I had.

Kerry and I sampled them to make sure they were perfect and then headed off to Hannah's. There was only one front step at her home, which might have been one reason they bought that house: easy access for Hannah to go in and out. I ignored the security cameras as I rang the doorbell.

No answer.

I rang it again.

Still no answer.

Should I knock?

I did and waited.

The door finally opened. It was Jason, her oldest child.

"May I help you?" he asked. He wasn't smiling.

"Hi, Jason, right?"

"Uh-huh."

"Gosh, I didn't know you lived here. My daughter and I met you at Hamlin Park."

He stared at me and then his eyes flickered. "Yeah, I remember."

"Kerry and I always deliver cookies to our new neighbors to welcome them to the neighborhood."

He didn't respond.

I handed him the wrapped plate of cookies. "Here they are."

He took the goodies and started to shut the door.

"Ah... Jason, there's one other thing. My friends and I, and our kids, meet weekly, usually at Hamlin Park. Would you please tell your mom we'd love to have you join us there on Wednesday after lunch?"

"Okay."

He shut the door.

"Well, Kerry, that wasn't exactly what I'd planned, but at least we made contact."

I pushed her back toward our home. I was glad I'd added a note on top of the cookies with my contact information and the time and date of our playgroup.

Now if only Hannah will read it and show up.

My cell phone rang as I pushed Kerry and her two friends toward our home.

"What did you find in the trash?" Linda asked.

I reported the details to her.

"And your conclusion?" she asked when I finished.

"Al-Turk is going to write a novel, but only after eating leftovers of Middle Eastern food that he stores in plastic bowls. And he's concerned about his dental health even though he smokes way too much."

"Shouldn't you have the trash examined for fingerprints?"

"I'm going to call a Chicago cop I knew when I lived here fourteen years ago."

I didn't tell her that Carter wouldn't like me talking to that particular policeman: Tony Infantino, a hunk with whom I'd had a torrid affair.

"Is there something you're not telling me about this cop?" she asked.

"Me? No. Why?"

"Tina, I know you. I can feel you blushing."

My face began to burn. "We can talk about this some other time."

"Promise?"

"Only if you have a hot guy in your past."

I heard her sigh. "Only one, but he was amazing."

"Okay, then, after you stop breastfeeding, we'll go out for a drink. I'll show you mine if you show me yours."

"Done."

"But I still need a fabulous personal interest story for my August column. My deadline is Friday, August eleventh. Al-Turk's story is going to take way too long to be ready by then."

"Obviously the trash didn't help on this one," she said.

"Not yet. I don't know if it ever will."

"When are you going to call the cop?"

"Tonight. If he's off duty, he might have time to talk to me."

49

"Hi, um, may I speak to Tony, please?" I asked.

Monday night, I'd hustled around in the kitchen shooting baskets with Kerry on the Nerf basketball set my dad had given her and making a salad while we waited for a pizza delivery from Pizzeria Serio on West Belmont. The odor of anchovies I'd added to the salad hung in the air.

I didn't have Tony Infantino's current cell phone number, and I was too busy in the kitchen to go online to find it. I dialed the landline number he'd had when I moved to D.C. and he'd lived at his parent's home. When a woman answered, I recognized her voice.

"Who this?" the female voice asked. *She still has the trace of an Italian accent.*

"Mrs. Infantino?"

"Yeah."

"It's Tina Thomas. I used to be Tina Edwards, and..."

"I recognize you voice. What you want?"

"I would like to talk to Tony."

"Why?"

"I really need his help."

"Gimme you number."

I gave her my cell phone number.

Fourteen years earlier, when I was a cub reporter at the *Sun-Times*, Chicago Police Officer Tony Infantino and I had been an item. And who could blame me? He was a tall, athletic, movie-star-handsome, third-generation Italian-American in a tight-fitting Chicago PD uniform. As a single, twenty-two-year-old female in Chicago, I was into hot guys. At that point in my life, a man's I.Q. wasn't as important as his physical attributes.

The longer we were together, the harder it was for me to walk away, even though I suspected he would never be faithful to me. When I was offered a fabulous position in D.C. with the *Washington Post*, he rejected my suggestion to move there with me. He was a Chicago guy. His dad and grandfather had been on the Chicago police force, and he wasn't about to ditch that heritage and leave.

But I'd worked my butt off for the *Post* job and wouldn't pass it up, so I'd ended the affair and headed to D.C.

And I'd saved his ass by not reporting a mistake he made on the job. He owed me for that, and I was going to collect.

He quickly called my cell.

"I'm sorry to bother you at home, but I need your help with a potential story," I said.

"Meet me at Ann Sather, the one on West Belmont, at noon tomorrow," Tony whispered.

"Great."

He didn't respond.

"Tony?"

Still no response. I opened my mouth to say his name again, but I realized he'd already hung up. There was a noise behind me. I turned around with the phone still next to my ear. Kerry dropped her Nerf basketball.

"Daddy!" she yelped.

Uh oh!

Carter stood in the doorway, his eyebrows knitted together. Kerry ran to him.

"How's Daddy's girl?" He picked her up and gave her a kiss on the cheek. He turned to me. "Am I interrupting something?"

If you only knew.

I held up my free hand to keep him from asking questions I didn't want to answer.

"Thanks for the idea, Lyndell."

Push the off button.

I made it obvious that I was pushing it on the already disconnected phone.

"I'm sorry, honey." I turned and gave him a kiss. "I couldn't hear Lyndell with you talking. She called to tell me that a man who ran by her front window looked like a leprechaun. She's convinced he would be perfect for my column."

"Let me guess; she's already suggested the headline: 'A Leprechaun in Lakeview.' "

"She did. How did you know?"

"I'll need a glass of wine if we're going to have this discussion."

"Let me pour it for you."

Get him talking about something else.

Carter and I have a great relationship, but he is vulnerable in one area: my previous torrid affair with Tony. If Carter discovered I was doing an investigative piece on Mr. al-Turk and my former lover was going to help me, he would be crushed.

Out of respect for my husband, I would drop the investigation, and my rebooted investigative journalism career would be over before it had begun.

But if he doesn't find out, no harm, no foul, right?

50

Tuesday morning, as I was getting ready to step into the shower, Carter rushed into the bathroom. He had Kerry in his arms.

"I have to go in," he said. "Sorry."

He handed her to me and ran down the stairs.

Just freaking perfect.

My plan had been to shower after my morning run while Carter fed Kerry. I would shave my legs, curl my hair, and put on enough big-girl makeup to show Tony Infantino what he'd lost out on when he'd refused to move with me to D.C.

Exactly what any of us would do when we're going to meet a former lover.

Not gonna happen now.

Kerry was in her PJs and had yogurt and blueberries all over her face. I had to take care of her, leaving me no time to fix my hair or to slap on even a smidge of makeup.

"Well, Kerry, let's clean you up and then we can go for a ride, okay?"

I would be meeting Tony — my buffed and always immaculately groomed former lover — with atrocious hair that needed a cut, dark circles under my eyes, and lugging my two-year-old daughter in my arms.

At least I've lost all my pregnancy weight.

By the time I tried, and failed, to get Kerry to go potty, dressed her in one of the many cute outfits my mother had given her, hoisted her gear into the van, and secured her in her car seat, I was way past late. My armpits were sweaty, and I began to panic because my deodorant sat untouched in my medicine cabinet.

Kerry jabbered with Elmo as I turned east on Belmont and headed toward Ann Sather. The traffic was backed up, putting me further behind schedule. When I finally arrived, I drove around hunting for a parking place near the restaurant. It took fifteen minutes to find a spot three blocks away from the restaurant.

Grabbing my backpack, I plucked Kerry out of her car seat and sprinted toward Ann Sather.

She immediately began screaming, "Momma!"

Forgot Elmo and Ralph.

I'd left them behind in my rush to meet Tony. I ran back to the van and shoved them into her tiny hands.

When I finally made it to the restaurant's front door, sweat poured off my forehead and the moisture from my armpits extended to my waist. I looked like a sweaty bag lady with bad hair and no makeup, carrying a toddler who had a red stuffed animal and a "blankie" in her arms, with a stained backpack — rather than a designer purse — slung over her shoulder.

Tony's gonna really be impressed.

51

I walked into Ann Sather's industrial-strength air-conditioning and saw Tony sitting in the back at our favorite corner table. He read a newspaper.

Famous for its homemade cinnamon rolls and Swedish pancakes, the restaurant has been a Chicago landmark for over sixty years and a favorite haunt for Tony and me. My face flushed as I remembered the late Sunday morning breakfasts we had shared there after a long Saturday night of take-no-prisoners sex.

My mouth began to water as the unforgettable aroma of the freshly baked cinnamon rolls drifted over me. I glanced at his table, hoping he'd already ordered one for me, but only a single cup of coffee sat in front of him.

Tony wore beige slacks and a white silk T-shirt under a blue silk blazer. He glanced up. His smile was blinding, confirmation he'd made a recent trip or two to his cosmetic dentist. The brilliant white contrasted perfectly with his glowing tan. I walked to his table with Kerry in my arms.

He stood up as I approached, as much — I suspected — to show off his impeccably attired physique as to be polite.

"You look great," I said, before I could control my mouth.

He could be on the front cover of GQ.

"Think so?" Tony asked. "Blazer isn't too loose?"

"No, Tony, your clothes are perfect, like always."

"Good." He opened his coat to show me a shoulder rig on his left side. "I want to wear my gun without ruining how the material hangs."

I wasn't sure what I should say about that, so I kept quiet. He didn't notice.

"This is even better," he continued.

He pulled up his right pant leg and showed me an ankle holster and gun. "Smith and Wesson 442 .38 special. Holds five rounds. Internal hammer so it won't snag on the material. Never know it's there. My tailor does a fantastic job."

Notice anything about me, like the little girl I'm holding?

I thought I'd help him. "This is my daughter, Kerry. Honey, say 'hi' to Tony."

She smiled from ear to ear and reached for him. He held up his hands and lurched backward when he saw her fingers were sticky from the apple juice she'd been sipping on the way there.

"Watch out for the threads here, kid. You got the grubby paws thing goin' on."

"She's a baby. Her hands are always covered with some kind of glop."

"Whatever." He turned and walked out of the restaurant.

Kerry and I followed. This was not going the way I'd planned.

52

Tony and I stood in the stifling heat outside Ann Sather's restaurant. He slipped on designer sunglasses and faced me. "I'm on a tight schedule and gotta get rolling. Whaddya need?"

"To have trash samples analyzed for fingerprints."

He scanned the street, giving it the cop once-over. "Why?"

"For a story I'm working on."

"Can't do it. Would be breaking regulations."

"What's your problem? Have things changed this much in the department? Patrolmen bend the rules all the time."

"I'm a homicide detective. Didn't get my gold shield by screwing the system."

"I need this, Tony." I paused. "And you owe me big time. You wouldn't have that gold shield if I hadn't covered up that horrific mistake you made."

His jaw muscles twitched. "If I do it, then we're even, okay?"

"Done."

Fourteen years ago, I prevented the bosses from firing him, and by helping me now, he admitted it. It killed him.

I saw that look in his eyes.

You need to puff up your wounded ego.

"Maybe we can work out some form of tit-for-tat compensation for my time."

He put the emphasis on "tit."

"You'll never change," I said.

He continued to stare at my breasts. I looked at his forehead until he elevated his eyes.

His cop interrogation voice surfaced. "Keep me informed about everything, and I mean everything, you find."

"You know I have to keep my informants confidential, but other than that, I'll keep you in the loop, if you do the same with me."

"Okay, where's the stuff you want checked out?"

I struggled to clutch Kerry, Elmo, and Ralph while I slipped off my backpack. He crossed his arms over his chest, preferring to let me flounder rather than offering to hold my daughter and her companions.

When I finally unzipped the backpack, I handed him a sack with a few items from the trash I'd stolen. I hadn't brought all of it because I couldn't trust he would help me. When Kerry began to fuss, I pulled out the sippy cup of unfinished apple juice from the backpack and gave it to her.

"Your prints aren't on the contents, are they?" he asked.

"You know I'm smarter than that. I wore latex gloves; any prints you find are the ones I need you to run."

"Okay, prints it is. That all you want?"

"You're the detective. Detect a little here. What else should I look for?

"How about street or prescription drugs?"

"I considered computer fraud, or online gambling, but I guess it could involve drug trafficking."

"Or drug manufacturing."

"Okay, fingerprints plus a chemical analysis."

"Don't expect quick results. Lab's always backed up."

Kerry began squirming, and her face turned red.

Tony sniffed the air. "What stinks?" He glanced down at my running shoes. "You step in dog shit or something?"

I glanced at my daughter. She had a wide, relieved smile on her face.

"Jeez, get over it," I said. "She's still in diapers."

He waved his hand in front of his nose. "I'm outta here."

Sprinting down the street to his car, he hopped into a white BMW 650i Coupe. It was one of Carter's dream cars, but we could never afford the one hundred thousand dollar price.

How can Tony?

The reporter in me was intrigued, but police corruption wasn't anything new. I didn't have time to chase a story any reporter with a laptop could write. The stolen trash I'd given Tony might give me what I needed: the names of other people living with al-Turk.

But first I had to find a changing station for Kerry.

53

Tuesday afternoon, Kerry and I played in her sandbox in our back yard. Linda called me.

"I have info about Micah's financing," she said.

Yes!

"I began by hunting down the three doctors you said worked with Micah," she said. "There was one winner: Dr. Bruce Loring. He's a PhD in human molecular biology and is listed as the director of Micah's lab."

"Did you find the lab's name?"

"The Lakeview Center for Medical Research."

"Generic."

"Ya' think? Loring also works at Northwestern."

"Busy boy."

"You have no idea. His hand must cramp up from all the checks he's writing for the lab's operating expenses."

"How much has he spent?"

"Up to this point, over one hundred fifty million dollars. And the spending's been escalating dramatically in the past two months."

"How did you find this out?"

"He has an account at the Texas Capital Bank in Dallas. I hacked into it."

"Really? Not a Chicago bank?"

"No, and there's a reason. Have you heard of Sherman Krevolin?"

"Isn't he the ultra-conservative lawyer from Texas?"

"Dallas, actually, and behind the scenes, he's the single most powerful and influential fund raiser for the guy living in the White House. Krevolin also owns controlling interest in the Texas Capital Bank."

"Where Loring has his checking account."

"It is, and by hacking into Loring's Dallas bank account, I uncovered a complicated series of transactions where several of Krevolin's companies were funneling money into Loring's account."

"Is it possible Hannah doesn't know the money to run Micah's lab isn't coming from her trust fund?"

"Unless she monitors her statements, she probably assumes all the funds come from her trust."

"But they don't."

"No, they don't."

"This makes absolutely no sense. Hannah has enough money to pay for this."

"And why would Krevolin provide funds to run Micah's lab where he does embryonic stem cell research, an issue Krevolin and his friend the president are on record as opposing?"

"I need to interview Hannah and, hopefully through her, Micah. Without that, this story is dead."

54

On Wednesday afternoon, we had our weekly playgroup at Hamlin Park. After Linda's discovery about Micah's murky financing, talking to Hannah was my number one priority, so I prayed that Hannah had read the note I'd added to the cookies and was going to join all of us at the park. It would have been easier to call her, but I still didn't have her contact information.

Linda and I pushed our daughters on the park's swings. Cas and her two kids, Luis and Angelique, scampered around on the jungle gym. Molly was late again.

My reporter's focus intensified when a black Escalade drove up and stopped next to the park's gate.

Yes! She's here!

The driver climbed out and helped Hannah step down from the passenger side. She waited while he opened the back door and let her kids out.

I nodded toward Hannah. "There's your basic four hundred forty million dollar woman."

Linda eyed Hannah's simple, blue summer outfit. "She doesn't dress like it."

"I noticed that when I first met her. Fashion doesn't seem to be her thing."

The driver parked half way down the block and climbed out. He leaned on the front fender, lit a cigarette, and watched as Hannah ushered her kids through the gate into the park. I waved. Hannah waved back.

"Since Molly's late, you'll have to help me learn more about Hannah," I said to Linda.

"Why not just talk to her?"

"Like I told you before, the first time I met her here, I said I was interested in doing a column on her and her family. She immediately became standoffish, and now I'm worried she'll shut down, if I start asking personal questions."

"Okay, I'll help."

"Probably best not to mention her money."

"Hard for me not to, but I'll try."

When Hannah accelerated her pace, her stride toward us became an obvious limp, and she needed the support of her sons. Her daughters skipped along in front of them.

Hannah joined us. "Tina, so nice of you to invite us to meet all of you. The cookies were delicious." Turning to her children, she motioned toward the jungle gym. "Go on and play. I will be here with Mrs. Thomas."

"I want you to meet my friends," I said.

Linda introduced herself and her daughter. Cas noticed what was going on and joined us with her two kids. As in my previous encounter with Hannah, she had trouble elevating her right arm to shake hands with Linda and Cas.

Molly arrived. When she saw us with a woman she didn't know, she switched to her model walk, which wasn't easy because she pushed her two younger sons, Stevie and Cory, in a double stroller. Her two older boys ran to the jungle gym and began going head-first down the slides.

I introduced Molly to Hannah. "Hannah and her family recently moved to our neighborhood from Israel," I said, praying Molly would remember what I wanted her to do.

"Do you live close to Hamlin Park?" Molly asked.

"Our home is on West Henderson," Hannah said.

"Is it the house on the south side that just sold?"

"It is."

"Sweet. We're one block north of you on West Roscoe. Tina lives two blocks south on West Melrose so, see, we're all neighbors."

"Where did you live in Israel?" Linda joined in. "I traveled there several times."

"First, we lived in Tel Aviv and then, more recently, in Jerusalem," Hannah said.

"How do you like it here?" Linda asked.

"It is delightful — or will be, once the children adjust."

"I can so relate," Molly said. "When we moved here, Chase and Rex, my two older kids, were totally bored before I joined the playgroup."

"You mentioned the group in your note, Tina," Hannah said. "Tell me more about it."

I explained to her about the playgroup and how it started, but I didn't include that I'd begun writing again because of it.

"It sounds interesting," Hannah said.

"Would you like to join our playgroup?" Molly asked.

Hannah glanced down at her hands. "I will have to speak with my husband. He makes all the decisions in our family."

55

I'd told Linda about Micah not wanting me to interview Hannah, and she didn't say anything.

But Cas clenched her jaw muscles. "Your husband makes *all* the decisions?" she asked. "How interesting. What does he do?"

"Micah is a physician," Hannah said.

"And Hannah's a physician too," I interjected. "A pediatrician."

"But I am no longer practicing," Hannah said.

"What's your husband's specialty?" Cas asked.

"Obstetrics and gynecology."

"Super," Molly said.

Labor and delivery is one of her areas of expertise; in her view, having had IVF for her first pregnancy and three more natural child births in four years qualifies her as an authority.

"With all the young families around here, I bet he's super busy delivering babies," Molly continued.

"Micah does not see patients. He is presently devoting his life to medical research. "

"What's he working on?" Cas asked.

"It is extremely technical. You probably would not be interested."

Wanna bet on that, sweetie?

Molly winked at me. "Tina, why don't you write a story about Hannah and her family? I'll even try and read it, as long as it isn't too long."

"Hannah, I think Molly's spot on," Linda said. "Having visited Israel and experienced what it's like to be exposed to war-like conditions, I can say most of us would be fascinated to read about your transition from Israel to Chicago."

"For once, I agree with Linda," Cas said. "I can't imagine what you must be going through moving here with four kids. They must be in culture shock."

"And see, when you talk to Tina, we'll get to know each other better," Molly said. "That would be totally awesome."

"Works for me," I said. "The scope of the story would be personal, not science."

Hannah hesitated. "I will discuss it with Micah."

Judging from the flat tone of her voice and her dour facial expression, it was a long shot at best.

Molly seemed to pick up on that. "Hey, guys, I have a great idea," she said. "Why don't we have a welcome-to-the-neighborhood dinner party at Tina's house on Saturday night? Micah can meet all of us, and we can convince him to let you join our playgroup."

Hannah smiled for the first time. "If he agrees, a week from Saturday would work better for us."

Eight people? For dinner? Yikes!

"Let's exchange phone numbers," I said. "You can call me and let me know for sure."

I sure hope Carter will help.

56

On Thursday morning, I called Linda. "How about asking Molly to help us with al-Turk's story too?"

"I like it," she said. "I was impressed with how she talked to Hannah yesterday."

"Let's invite her to lunch at the Wishbone, and we can talk to her about it."

At 11:55 a.m., I pushed Kerry to the front door of the Wishbone, a southern comfort restaurant in a brick building at the corner of North Lincoln and West School Street, catty corner from Dinkel's.

Molly walked up behind me as I opened the door.

"Where are your troops?" I asked.

"The last time we ate here, Stevie and Cory had a meltdown, and the manager suggested they might want to 'take vacation' for a while."

"Like being put in the penalty box."

"Exactly, so I dropped my gang off with Hannah."

What?

"Will that work with eight kids?" I asked.

"No problem," she said. "She has a manny."

"A what?"

"A guy helping her instead of a woman."

"Good to know," I said. "How did you find this out?"

"I called her this morning to talk and mentioned you'd asked me to lunch, but I didn't have a babysitter. She said she'd do it and it wouldn't be a problem because she has a full-time manny."

"I saw a man driving her and the kids in a black Escalade. Is this manny young and fit?"

"You got it, and he changes diapers."

"Did he move with them from Israel?" I asked.

"Don't know. Hannah said that when they arrived in April, it took a couple of weeks for Micah to figure out she needed lots more help with the kids. He assigned a guy who works in the lab to stay at their condo and now at their house."

We walked into the Wishbone.

"Over here," Linda called out, waving Molly, Kerry, and me to her table in the back of the restaurant.

As I pushed Kerry's stroller toward the table, the aroma of spices and deep-fried foods from the chef's southern reconstructive style of cooking made my stomach growl.

"Where's Sandra?" I asked, as I secured Kerry into her booster chair.

"There's a luncheon at my mother's country club, and she wanted to show off the new designer outfit she bought for her only grandchild," Linda said. "Where's Cas?"

"She's teaching a class at XSport," I said.

Kerry loves eating at the Wishbone. She always wants the original mac n' cheese, even for breakfast. I ordered buttermilk-fried chicken. Linda ordered the Carolina crab cakes. Molly had the Wishbone's famous "Riverboat Tilapia."

"Linda and I want to include you in another story, Molly, but you have to keep it a secret."

"Will do. Tell me."

I did.

"You need to tag al-Turk's Range Rover," Molly said, after I told her about the GPS device I'd planted on his Mercedes.

"I don't want to spend the money," I replied. "Those things are expensive."

"Tell me," Molly said. "That's why I kept a couple I never returned to the farmers. We can use one of them."

"Do you have the software too?" Linda asked.

"Yep," Molly answered.

"Once the second device is put on his Range Rover, I'll follow both GPS systems," Linda said. "I'll email both of you a summary each day."

"And I'll handle tagging his Rover," Molly said. "Give me the plate number and where to look for it."

"His Mercedes is at the Twenties most of the time," I said. "I don't know about the Rover."

Molly smiled. My bet was she might visit the Twenties to look for al-Turk's SUV.

57

On Friday morning, I sang along with Macy Gray as I ran past our alley to reach West Belmont. An unexpected honk from a car horn blasted through my ear buds and jolted me out of my reverie. I stopped and turned to see what idiot had done it.

Tony!

"You almost gave me a freaking heart attack," I said, hoping the loud sound wouldn't trigger a PTSD attack.

He climbed out of the driver's side. "Wasn't sure if you wanted your husband to know we're hanging out again so I parked in the alley."

"We are not 'hanging out.' You're doing an old friend a favor."

"Gimme a break. I got what you need."

Seriously?

"Not happening. I'm happily married."

"What's that got to do with anything?" he asked, a puzzled look on his face.

"Not interested."

His face was flat. "Whatever."

"Why are you here?" I asked.

"Got the lab reports," he said. "There were four sets of prints on the trash you stole. Lab ran them through CODIS and IAFIS."

"And?"

"One hit. Guy named Mohammad al-Turk."

"No other names?"

"None."

"What about the other things you were going to test for?"

He raised his eyebrows. "What other things?"

"You mentioned drugs," I said.

"None found." He put his sunglasses back on and smiled. "By the way, where did this trash come from?"

"Why do you need to know about a story that's a dead-end?"

"Sweets, I gave you what you wanted. I just paid my debt to you. Now, how about you helping me out here?"

His smile widened.

Something's not right.

Without answering, I whirled around and began sprinting toward Belmont. Until I figured out why he was lying to me, I wasn't telling him anything else.

"Goddamnit, Tina! Come back here!"

He had al-Turk's name. He could chase that clue down. I wasn't going to do his detective work for him. I continued running and called Linda on my speaker phone.

"I have the report about the trash I stole," I said. "Al-Turk's prints were confirmed, but there were three other sets of prints that weren't in any system my cop used."

"At least we now know there are three other men living there," Linda said.

"No, we don't," I said. "All we know for certain is al-Turk lives there. The other sets of prints could have come from visitors."

"What about drugs?" she asked.

"He said they didn't find any, but I'm not sure he's telling me the truth."

"Your cop doesn't seem too reliable."

"He's the only source I have, but I'll keep working on him. How about the GPS data?"

"There was one anomaly," she said. "Al-Turk's Mercedes went out to O'Hare and then came right back. Maybe someone was either being taken to a flight or picked up."

"I'll tell Lyndell," I said. "She can look for a different person going in and out of the house."

"Or a different car. If she sees one, maybe Molly can tag it too."

"Until we find that out, all we can do is follow the GPS reports," I said.

"What else we can do?" Linda asked.

58

On Saturday, I put off doing laundry and cleaning. Instead, Carter and I took our little girl to Lake Michigan to play in the water and watch the boats. On Sunday, with what little available time I had after doing my household chores and playing with Kerry, I went online to research both stories. I didn't make any progress on either one.

On Monday, Linda called me. "A question."

"Fire away."

"What about al-Turk's religious beliefs and his connection to a business involving nearly-naked women?"

"Cas wondered the same thing after we left the Twenties. I didn't have an answer for her. What do you think?"

"That his financial footprints at the Twenties would be invisible because no one would suspect a Muslim being connected with a business like that."

"You are so right. It makes the Twenties the perfect front for him to launder money."

"I used that as a platform and started with al-Turk here in Chicago," she said. "He lived here for a year and a half in an apartment on the North Side before moving to this neighborhood. Shortly before he moved here, he sold his interest in Business

Ventures, a company in New York. He deposited $254,373 into the BMO Harris Bank here in Chicago, which on the surface appeared to be his proceeds from the sale."

"But they weren't?" I asked.

"No, that money came to BMO Harris via a wire transfer from the First Caribbean International Bank in the Cayman Islands, not from the Doha Bank in New York where Business Ventures had its corporate account."

"Is that where the money trail stops?"

"No, those funds actually came to the First Caribbean from JDL and Associates, a merchant bank in Luxembourg."

"Interesting. The First Caribbean is the same bank the Arun Corporation uses."

"And the Arun Corporation and its accounts are entwined with JDL and Associates too."

"Wow."

"This is just the beginning," she said. "Using al-Turk's account at BMO Harris, I hacked into the First Caribbean International Bank's computers long enough to find out that a little over nine thousand dollars a month flows into his BMO Harris account."

"That amount is low enough to avoid any federal scrutiny."

"It is."

"How much did al-Turk pay for the Twenties?"

"A little north of eight million dollars, which is more than it's worth, in my opinion."

"When did he close on the sale of the club?" I asked.

"April first."

"Did he finance the purchase?"

"He did. The Gupta Fund in Panama provided 100 percent of the purchase price."

"Is that legal? Doesn't the buyer have to put up his own money as a down payment?"

"For U.S. banks he would, but it was a private foreign transaction without a registered U.S. broker. The purchase details are hidden in cyberspace. But guess who owns the Gupta Fund?"

"JDL and Associates?"

"And you would be correct."

"I wish you could figure out who owns JDL and Associates," I said.

"I'm going to try and find out, but with the murky international banking laws, I might not be able to accomplish it."

59

Tuesday night, my landline rang while I was in the kitchen preparing dinner. Kerry played on the floor with several mixing bowls.

"Mrs. Thomas, I need to speak with you about Lyndell Newens," a deep male voice said on my answering machine. "Please call or text me at..."

I picked up the phone before he finished. "Hi, this is Tina Thomas."

"This is Tim Newens, Lyndell's son."

A bad feeling washed over me. "Is she okay?"

"Not exactly. Mom hasn't been getting around like she wants to. Last Friday we met with her rheumatologist. After telling Mom he had nothing more to offer her, he recommended she see an orthopedic surgeon. The orthopod recommended a total knee replacement — both of them, actually."

"I'm so sorry to hear that, but she has been having an agonizing time going up and down her stairs. When's her surgery?"

"You know my mom. She insisted the procedure be done as soon as possible or she would find another surgeon. She's having it done tomorrow. I would have called you before this, but it's been kind of a whirlwind getting her life organized."

"I totally understand. Which hospital will she go to?"

"The new one, MidAmerica Hospital."

"No kidding. My friend Linda is going there to have her baby. Would it be okay if I visit your mom there?"

"You'll have to hurry. Mom will be discharged on Saturday."

"Isn't that kind of a short stay?"

"It's these damn new Medicare rules. But because she's having both knees done, they'll pay for a rehab facility for six weeks."

"I'll visit her there. Which one is it?"

"The Brookstone Center on North Damen."

"Do you need my help? What about her house?"

"That's been an ongoing dilemma. My brother Nick and I want her to sell it, but she's adamant about keeping it. We came up with a compromise. She's going to rent it out until she can prove to us she can negotiate the steps."

"What's your timeline for that?"

"About three months. She'll live with one of us after she is discharged from the nursing home. But she understands the surgery might not help her enough to go up and down her front and back steps. If that happens, she assures us she'll sell."

"Is her house going to sit empty all that time?"

"No, the orthopod knew a dentist who wanted to rent a place immediately while he's establishing his practice in Lakeview.

Mom signed a month-to-month lease with him this morning. She's staying with me and my wife, Susan, until she goes into the hospital early tomorrow."

"Wow, that's certainly speedy."

"Like I said, Mom wants the surgery done pronto. In fact, the dentist moved in about four hours ago."

"I didn't see any moving trucks."

"You won't. He rented the house from Mom completely furnished."

A column here?

I needed a story for my looming August eleventh deadline. "Tell me about my new neighbor."

"His name is Dr. Greg Lorenz. He's from San Francisco, divorced, and no kids. He's rented space in the office building behind Starbucks."

"On North Paulina?" I asked.

"Yes, close to the corner at West Roscoe. He'll begin seeing patients on Friday."

"Please tell your mom how much I'll miss her, and I'll be sure and make cookies to welcome him to the neighborhood."

"It's already been handled. She insisted I help her make cookies to give him when he came over this morning to meet her and sign the lease."

"That is so like Lyndell. I'll be sure and drop by and visit her at Brookstone."

"Give it at least ten days. She doesn't want any visitors until she can get her hair done and be able to dress properly."

"If you have time, will you call and let me know how her surgery goes?"

"I sure will. Thanks."

I hung up and glanced out my side window at Lyndell's house.

Now who's gonna help me watch al-Turk's house?

60

The next morning, Kerry and I were doing a puzzle on the kitchen table. I glanced at al-Turk's house across and remembered what Linda had reported about the Mercedes's trip to the airport.

Is there another car involved?

"Kerry, let's go for a ride and then stop at Whole Foods for a healthy lunch, okay?"

She clapped her hands. "I wuv to go on wides!"

That is true most of the time but lately only if there is a bribe being offered. Otherwise, I would never be able to work on either of my stories.

It took forty minutes in the early lunch hour traffic to reach the Twenties. It was a long shot, but if I discovered a different, expensive, new car or SUV parked in front, there might be another player in the game. I would snap a picture of the license plate number for more DMV research.

I drove past the building but didn't see any new vehicles that attracted my attention.

Might as well recon the neighborhood.

Turning right, I spotted a one-story building without any signage across the street from the Twenties. I drove forward and, at the opposite end of the block, discovered a modern, four-story apartment building. I took cell phone pictures of both buildings.

It had been a wasted journey, but as long as Kerry and I were in the van, I drove in the opposite direction, north, to research my other story. It took another fifty minutes to locate Dr. Mittelman's laboratory, a two-story, windowless, gray, cement building. A ten-foot-tall chain link fence surrounded the lot, which was about half the size of a typical Chicago city block. There were no signs to indicate what type of business was inside. A guard gate was the only entrance. I took a picture of that building too.

Twenty-five million dollars doesn't buy much these days.

I was going nowhere with the story. "Kerry, remember what Uncle Jimmy does all the time?"

My brother, Jimmy Edwards is a starting pitcher for the San Diego Padres. He hasn't gotten a hit for the past two years, claiming he's paid to pitch, not hit.

"Stwike out!"

"I did too. Let's go to Whole Foods and buy our healthy lunch."

61

Late Thursday afternoon, I was in the kitchen starting dinner and glanced out the front windows. A man walked down the stairs from Lyndell's home and went past our house. He was a pale, pudgy, six-footer with greased-back black hair and white skin. He looked like a vampire but in the daylight.

Dr. Lorenz, I presume.

Putting my dinner preparations on hold, I carried my daughter down to our computer room. Kerry played with Elmo while I did an online search on my newest neighbor, Gregory Lorenz, DDS.

Obtaining the information on Lorenz wouldn't be a challenge. As a starting point, I had his name, new office address, and phone number, which was already up on social media. In six minutes, I had his entire life history: where he grew up, his parents' and siblings' names, his ex-wife's name, their address in San Francisco, when they were married, his various schools and degrees, and even his dog's name when he was a little boy.

This is way too easy.

Tony said the lab didn't find any drugs on the trash, but what if he'd lied to me? He wanted to know where the trash came from, but there was no reason he needed that information unless there was more to the story.

What if there were traces of drugs on the trash and, as Linda had originally suggested, al-Turk was a dealer? If that were the case, the local police, maybe with the DEA, would be all over this. All of Lorenz's credentials proved he was a dentist, but maybe he was actually a cop or DEA agent posing as a tooth guy so he could spy on al-Turk.

62

On Friday afternoon, I watched the dentist stroll past our front windows toward Lyndell's house. And he wasn't alone. A striking young lady walked with him. It was Donna Allen. Cas and I had seen her stripping at The Twenties. She also worked out with us at XSport Fitness.

Through the side kitchen window facing Lyndell's home, I watched them ascend the stairs up to the front door. I called Molly. "Have you been to the Twenties yet?"

"Greg and I went there last night," she said. "He loves watching me have a lap dance."

Not gonna ask about that.

"Did you see a guy who looks like a vampire?" I asked.

"You mean Dr. Greg Lorenz?"

"You know him?"

"Yep. He just opened a dental practice right behind Starbucks."

"How did you meet him?"

"My hubby went to the bathroom. I, of course, looked hot, and Lorenz came up and hit on me."

Big surprise.

"Did you work on Lorenz?"

"Didn't have to," she said. "He did it for me."

"How?" I asked.

"He was super friendly. Said he's trying to build up his practice and gave me a card for a free dental exam. And I saw him give cards to all the strippers."

"Did he try to hook up with any of them?"

"Uh-huh. He was all over Donna Allen, the girl who works out with us."

"Lorenz lives next door to me. Five minutes ago, Donna went into his home with him."

"Like I said, it looked like they were hooking up."

"Guess they did."

"Oh, and the Rover was parked in front of the Twenties. I put the GPS thingy under the back bumper."

"Did your husband wonder what you were doing?" I asked.

"He was busy lighting his cigar, and he didn't notice," she said.

I hung up and called Linda. "Molly planted the GPS transponder last night."

"Great," she said. "She showed it to me when she brought me the software. It's expensive equipment, better than yours."

"At least our taxes are being put to good use."

63

Saturday morning, Carter took Kerry to Hamlin Park. I was one block away from my front door as I finished my run. Donna Allen walked down the front steps of Lorenz's house. She wore the same clothes she'd had on Friday afternoon

Walk of shame. Been there, done that, sweetie.

I flashed back to my times with Tony when I'd returned to my Lincoln Park apartment on West Roslyn Place wearing the same clothes I'd had on the night before. Laurie Zoob, my roommate, would welcome me home with a wide smile and her "walk of shame" comment.

A taxi stopped in front of Lorenz's house, and Donna climbed in. The cab pulled away. A few seconds later, Lorenz exited down his front steps, but he wore different clothes and walked toward his office.

Saturday morning office hours? Maybe you really are a dentist opening a new office.

How did Donna the stripper fit into this? Before Carter and Kerry returned home, I needed go online and run Donna's name and recheck Lorenz's information. There were too many missing elements to this new story.

I'd already decided not to tell Carter about Lyndell's surgery and our new neighbor Lorenz. My husband knew her, but he rarely asked about her. If I told him about Lorenz, he might suspect I was working on a story. I didn't want to have to lie to him more than I already had to cover-up my interest in al-Turk and the Twenties.

At home, I grabbed a bottle of water and went down to the office. I began online with Donna. She grew up in Spirit Lake, Iowa, raised by a single mom. Donna had been a cheerleader and had won several local and then regional beauty contests, which led her to the bright lights and big city of Chicago before she finished high school.

She was twenty-four, with no apparent high school degree or GED. Until she was hired at the Twenties, her career had been on a downward spiral of low-paying, entry-level restaurant or bar jobs. She probably wanted to find a guy who would be her way out of the stripping business and into a normal life with a husband, a home with a yard, two kids, and a dog.

Going over Lorenz's background didn't result in any new discoveries. He might be okay, but if he weren't, whoever had created his online persona had done a perfect job. I tried all my research tricks, but his story was incontestable.

Or was it?

64

Saturday night, I was in the kitchen helping Carter prep the salad plates for our dinner to welcome Hannah and Micah to the neighborhood. The scent from his cooking lamb made my mouth water.

"Honey, I am so grateful that you're doing this for me," I said.

"I love helping you out," Carter said. "And I really wanted to try to prepare the lamb with the Joule *sous vide* I just purchased on Amazon."

My hubby loves his cooking gadgets.

That was why, during our Friday night movie and dinner date, I'd asked him to help me with the dinner party. He could not resist, and I'd gladly stepped to the side while he took over.

He had created his version of a classic Waldorf salad to which he'd added fresh strawberries and an ultra-tangy mayonnaise. It would be served after his first course, a tiny cup of tomato bisque with a dollop of crème fraîche and a pinch of caviar.

Our front doorbell rang. I opened the door and held out my hand. "Micah, I'm happy to finally meet you."

Micah Mittelman stood on the porch, supporting his wife's right forearm with his left hand. He was about Molly's height, and his light-brown skin tone complemented his black eyes and hair. He wore a short-sleeved, multicolored silk shirt that clearly hadn't come off the rack at Kohl's.

Micah shook my hand. "And I am pleased to meet you."

He had a mellow bass voice with the trace of a British accent. If any normal woman were to hear it in a bar, the tone would melt her thong.

Micah assisted Hannah into our front hallway. She wore a billowing, white silk designer dress that could only be purchased in finer stores. For the first time since we'd met, she had on jewelry. Her marquise-cut diamond wedding ring went knuckle to knuckle. A smaller, oval-cut, yellow diamond adorned her right ring finger. A pear-shaped diamond hung from her neck. Either of her solitaire diamond earrings could have been made into a spectacular engagement ring.

Amazing.

I introduced them to Carter who was still in the kitchen. His eyes widened when he saw her jewels. "Tina has told me a lot about you, Hannah," he said. "Your family's move to Chicago from Israel sounds fascinating."

"I am not sure Hannah would use that term to describe arriving here with four children," Micah interjected.

Hannah and Micah followed me into the family room where the rest of our group already sat chatting and sipping cocktails and wine. Micah continued to support Hannah's arm.

"Oh, my," Hannah said, as she scanned the room.

"What's wrong?" I asked.

"I am embarrassed. We are overdressed."

"It's my fault. I should have mentioned we're casual around here. But you look lovely."

"I will remember next time."

Kerry played upstairs in her room with a babysitter, Liv, one of Mrs. Sanchez's daughters. I went up and gave Kerry a kiss goodnight and then returned to the party.

65

Linda and I watched Hannah and Micah work the room.

"The doctors have done this before," I said.

"With all the money in her family, she had to have been raised attending society functions where she learned to socialize with all the guests," Linda said.

Like Hannah, Linda came from inherited wealth from both of her parents. She'd been raised the same way as Hannah.

Both members of the lucky sperm club.

"Watch how Micah supports her arm and then puts his hand in the small of her back as he leads her around the room," I said.

"It's like he's her human crutch," Linda observed.

"Hannah either leans against a table or sits on the edge of the couch until they move on."

"And they immediately hone in on what is being discussed, and then they take an interest in it too," she said. "I've seen my parents do this many, many times at their parties; once at our embassy in Israel."

"The doctors are practiced at it."

"Can you use any of this for their story?"

"I'm not sure, but I'm trying to eavesdrop on their conversations."

For appetizers, Carter had made smoked salmon crostini, a cheese tray with the proper accoutrements, and prosciutto-wrapped melons. At my suggestion, we'd placed the appetizers on the bar so I wouldn't be stuck serving them. For the guests, he had opened his favorite wines, a Fourth Estate Pinot and a Fourth Estate Chardonnay.

Our tradition for dinner party seating has always been to alternate man-woman, and couples don't sit next to one another. Or at least that was my original plan. As we approached the table, Micah placed Hannah next to my seat at the near end of the table. He sat next to her, and the rest of our guests plopped down wherever they wanted to, except for Carter and me. We sat at each end of the table where we could get up and down to serve each course.

Okay gang, keep drinking. I need to hear more than dinner conversation. I have a story to write.

66

"It was delightful and, at the same time, terrifying," Micah said. "Wouldn't you agree, Hannah?"

"I would, indeed," she said. "Especially with four children to protect."

Linda had related her experiences with a suicide bombing in Jerusalem when she traveled there with her parents. Hannah hadn't sampled her first course, the tomato bisque. During the chat in the family room, she hadn't touched her wine glass. I'd assumed she might not drink, but I was wrong. She didn't have the strength to lift the wine glass with one hand without spilling its contents. And I was sure she'd avoided the tomato soup course because she was fearful of dribbling the liquid on her gorgeous white dress.

As Hannah continued to talk to Linda, Micah slipped out of his chair. I watched him walk into the kitchen. When he didn't come back, I joined him. Carter added the finishing touches on the salads. With a knife and fork, Micah chopped a Waldorf salad into tiny pieces.

Now your wife can eat it without the embarrassment of being unable to slice the pieces into portions she can manage.

"Honey, are you ready for me to help you serve the salads?" I asked.

"I am," Carter said.

Micah looked up. "I will take care of Hannah's plates for the rest of the evening."

I picked up two of the salad plates. "Thanks for the help."

"I enjoy doing this for the woman who is the love of my life. I will do anything for her." He glared at me. "And for my children."

A shiver ran down my spine. Was he threatening me that if I ever did anything to hurt Hannah, there might be consequences? Or was he simply giving me insight about their personal lives?

Or was I overreacting?

Whichever, I might have uncovered another element to their story.

67

The dinner conversation covered many subjects. As the wine flowed and the chatter became louder, I kept listening, hoping the fellowship we were developing as a group would convince Micah and Hannah to let me proceed with their story.

"The lamb was perfectly prepared," Micah said when he finished the main course. "My compliments to the chef and his able assistant."

"Here, here," Hannah seconded. "A toast to Carter and to Tina: Thank you for a terrific dinner."

They raised their glasses toward my husband and me.

"And I would like to thank my husband who did all the work," I said.

"Thank God, he did," Cas said. "You would have burned the lamb to a crisp."

The group laughed and sipped their wine.

Hannah placed both hands under her wine glass, but before she could attempt to lift it, Micah reached over and gently placed his left hand under hers. His support allowed her to continue the toast without spilling her wine.

It was an instinctive move, one that had become part of their lives. And duplicating what he'd done with her salad, he had cut her lamb into bite-sized pieces. He'd done the same thing with the side dishes of roasted asparagus with a honey and balsamic drizzle and potato gratin.

Hannah whispered to Micah. He stood up.

"I am sorry, but Hannah and I must leave before dessert," he said. "I am about to begin Phase I trials, and I have to be at the lab early in the morning."

"On Sunday?" Molly asked. "Doc, I'm glad I don't work for you."

"Devastating diseases do not get the weekend off. If I am going to the change the future of medicine, I cannot miss even one day in the lab."

Micah scooted Hannah's chair back and helped her up.

"I'll show you out," I said, hoping to apply a little pressure for a future interview before they departed.

Micah continued with effusive praise about the events of the evening until we were outside on the front porch. Hannah hadn't said a word, either because Micah dominated the moment, or she was too exhausted to speak.

Micah turned to me. "Once again, we both thank you for this delightful time together."

"It was great fun, and I would like to continue it by interviewing both of you for my monthly column."

His face darkened. "Hannah and I are private people. We do not do interviews."

What about the hundreds of public interviews you'll have to give if your medical research changes the world?

Without another word, they left. He supported her arm as they descended our front stairs. Their driver pulled up in the black Escalade and stopped. He popped out and opened the rear door. Micah helped Hannah inside and then joined her. The SUV drove off into the Chicago night.

Along with my story.

My story deadline was the second Friday in August. I needed to interview them before that.

How am I going to do it?

68

In our darkened bedroom, I snuggled in Carter's arms.

"Did you catch Micah's comment about the Phase I trials of his work?" I asked.

"I did," he said.

"I don't know much about that. Do you?"

"A little. Northwestern and the University of Chicago frequently run ads in our paper announcing Phase I trials. They advertise for volunteer patients with the disease they are studying."

"I get that, but what's a Phase I trial do?"

"It tests a new drug or treatment on a limited number of patients. The doctors evaluate the safety profile, determine a safe dosage range, and identify any side effects."

"I assume there are other phases."

"Two more. Phase II involves more patients to determine the effectiveness while continuing to monitor side effects. Phase III involves an even larger group of patients but this time comparing the results with other existing treatments."

"Do the patients get paid?"

"They do, and it's one reason why these trials are expensive."

"Are the medicines free?"

"Yes, they are, and the patients also receive free medical exams during the trial."

"What if there are side effects of the drugs or treatment?"

"The patients have to sign release papers acknowledging those risks."

There's definitely a story here.

"Can you alert your ad guys to see if Micah's name comes up in requests for Phase I participants?" I asked.

"I'll do it tomorrow, but there's only one problem: Neither of us knows what disease he's treating."

"I made a computer file of all the scientific papers written by Micah in the past couple of years. I'll send them to Cas. Maybe she can figure it out."

"Let me know what she says."

"I will, but not tonight. I'm feeling that baby urge. Hope you're not too sleepy."

Silly question. He's a man.

69

Sunday morning, I ran and then went to Whole Foods. Carter took care of Kerry while I shopped for dinner items. In the produce aisle, the young lady pushing the cart toward me looked familiar.

She halted in front of me. "Oh hi, Mrs. Thomas."

"Corky? I didn't recognize you."

"I look way different when I'm not at XSport because there I don't wear makeup, or curl my hair."

I studied her. "But there's something else."

She arched her back allowing her breasts to stand out. "I have bigger boobs. I had them put in on the fourteenth. That's why I haven't been in class. The surgeon wouldn't let me work out."

Her breasts looked about the same size as her two exercise partners. "Like Sammy and Donna," I said.

"Exactly. They had their surgery on the Monday before I had mine done." She looked around. "But please don't tell anyone, okay?"

"Wouldn't think of it."

But I am curious why you said that.

"Speaking of Donna, may I ask you a question?" I asked.

"Sure," she said.

"Late Friday afternoon, she was walking in our neighborhood with Dr. Lorenz, the dentist who lives next door to me. She went inside with him. Are they hanging out?"

"Kind of."

"Is he your dentist?"

"For sure."

"Why did you choose him?"

"He's free."

"Each visit?"

"No, only the first one. But if other stuff needs to be done, he will give us a discount."

"Us?"

"Donna and Sammy and I work at the Twenties. He came there Thursday night and gave out his card for one free exam and cleaning."

"I might have to try him."

"He gave a card to your friend Molly. He said he was new and trying to build up his practice. Donna and I went in Friday morning. She went back Friday afternoon."

The dentist is sniffing around, but why?

There was one way to find out, and it couldn't be worse than the five pelvic exams I'd subjected myself to in order to get inside information for the Arlington clinic story.

Of course, doing it had almost gotten me killed.

70

Monday afternoon, Cas watched Kerry for me. I walked three blocks north of our home to Dr. Lorenz's office. I'd made the appointment using Linda's name, cell phone number, and her address in Lakeview. I had her driver's license, her black American Express card, and her dental insurance card.

I had been leaving our home, including for my morning run, through our back door. I didn't want Lorenz to see me, but if he did, Linda and I looked enough alike in the tiny picture on her driver's license that I felt sure I could pull off the switch.

Linda's pregnancy? Easy to handle. That morning I'd rented a third trimester padded pregnancy belly at a costume store I'd used in Lincoln Park when I was single. If he ran into the real Linda elsewhere in the neighborhood, he would see a pregnant brown-haired woman pushing a stroller.

Cheap reproductions of famous paintings hung on the walls, and baby diarrhea-colored linoleum covered the floor in his office. New magazines and brochures for expensive dental procedures were scattered on the top of the only table. Lined up against the wall were four metal chairs covered with light blue vinyl. The odor of fresh paint hung in the air. I hadn't seen a receptionist when I'd entered. I sat down to wait.

An inner door opened, and Dr. Lorenz stepped into his office waiting room. "Mrs. Misle?" he asked.

Lorenz had a mortician's voice, soft and atonal. He wore a short, white, lab coat with a yellow dress shirt and blue tie. His ample neck strained against the top button of his shirt.

"Yes, that's who I am, Linda Misle." My speech was pressured, and I sounded like a kid breathing helium from a balloon at a birthday party.

"Please, come in," he said, as he held the inner door for me.

I entered and followed him toward an exam room to my left. He led me to a dental exam chair. Sitting down, I glanced around and saw his dental school diploma prominently displayed on the wall in front of me. The odor of mint mouthwash and hand-sanitizer filled the room. His dental instruments sat lined up on a tray next to the chair.

Maybe you are a dentist and I'm wrong about you.

He handed me a pen and a clipboard covered with papers. "Please fill these out," he said.

"Do you need my dental insurance card too?" I asked.

"That would be helpful," he said. "I'll make a copy of it while you finish the papers."

I handed him Linda's dental card, her driver's license, and credit card. I heard his copy machine fire up while I finished the paperwork.

He came back into the exam room and handed Linda's cards back to me.

"Now, what seems to be the problem?" he asked, as he tilted the chair backwards.

71

"Problem?" I asked.

"Yes, I assume you have a dental issue," Lorenz said.

"Oh, right. Teeth. I just need a routine exam to make sure my teeth are okay.

"A good plan."

"But I'm a little nervous. I've had the same dentist since I was a child, and he died, poor thing, and I have to find a new one."

"It's possible I knew him. What's his name?"

"Name?"

"Your dentist. His name."

"Right. Thomsen. Allen Thomsen."

"Was his office in this neighborhood?"

"No, I grew up in Lincoln Park."

"Your driver's license shows you live on West Roscoe."

You did check me out.

"I do, with my husband, Howard, and our daughter, Sandra."

"Not too far from me. I'll do an x-ray first and go from there."

After he took my dental x-rays, he turned on his computer and went over them in detail. The dental exam followed and was thorough and painless. But it was accompanied by an interview about our neighborhood.

He began with softball questions, inquiring about shopping and my restaurant recommendations. That was followed with more detailed questions about our neighbors. The transition was subtle. He would go back and forth between inquiries about my favorite foods and people I had seen in the neighborhood.

The questions he tossed at me were the same ones I would have asked if I were working on a story about potentially strange happenings going on in the neighborhood. He was a pro at it. He took his time, and when he'd mined my brain for all the information he could obtain, my exam was over.

But I was a pro too. I avoided asking him any questions or giving away any facts that might reveal my true identity. Alerting him that I was a journalist would be the stupidest move I could make.

He finished the exam. "In summary, your teeth are perfect, and you need to keep them that way."

He followed that with a mini-lecture on how to brush and floss. He gave me a free toothbrush and a small sample of toothpaste.

"When should I come back?" I asked.

"I should have front office help soon. I'll have them call you."

He was a real dentist, but was there a reason he chose to live next door to me?

Did it have to do with al-Turk?

I have to know.

I couldn't be sure that stealing his trash would give me the answer. Breaking into his home while he was at work might.

What else can I do?

72

Tuesday afternoon, the torrid heat had disappeared, and the temperature, at least for one day, was delightful, in the mid 70's. It was a no-brainer to move our playgroup from Linda's home to Hamlin Park. I was late. The rest of the moms and their kids had arrived before me.

I'd spent my free time that morning planning how I would break into the dentist's house. From memory, I'd drawn up the floor plan of Lyndell's home and made an "X" on the room that had been her office, assuming that since Lorenz had rented all of her furniture, he would use that room for the same purpose.

Lorenz's home security system was my next hurdle. Even though I knew Lyndell's code for her system, I had to assume he'd changed it and her front door lock and key. From the boxes in the garage, I already had found the equipment to bypass the system. And the door lock wouldn't be an issue; I had my lock pick gun and torque wrench.

None of my friends needed to know about my plans to break into Lorenz's house. At least not yet.

"Sorry, I'm late," I said. "I was grinding away on the computer."

"What were you working on?" Linda asked.

"The Phase I trial Micah mentioned it at the dinner party," I said.

"What did you find?"

"Not enough. I need an expert."

"That would be me," Cas said. "I participated in several of those clinical trials, and let me tell you, they're a pain for the nursing staff."

"Why?" I asked. "I haven't found any mention of that online."

"And you won't. The doctors get all the glory if the treatment works, but the staff members who do all the real work rarely get mentioned."

"I don't get what you mean," Molly said.

"It's the amount of computer work. Each entry must be confirmed for accuracy and then backed-up. Any screw-ups and the FDA will pull the study and the funding."

"Is this why it's so expensive to do?" Linda asked.

"It could easily take four or five years before a drug is finally released and makes any money, and by then, the research teams could have blown through two hundred to three hundred million dollars."

"What if the drug is a spectacular success in the first trial or even the second one?" I asked. "The FDA can't let sick people die while the doctors are forced to go through all three trials."

"That happens way too frequently. But it's not the same in Europe and other countries. They find a drug or treatment that works and they release it."

"What about unknown side effects?" Linda asked.

"It's a risk a dying patient in the U.S. might want to take. They'll fly to one of those countries and pay whatever it costs to be treated."

"Can't the FDA fast track a drug that will obviously save lives?" I asked.

"If they do, it'll still take a minimum of two years before that happens."

"Micah is gonna be a busy boy for the next few years," Molly said.

"Did you notice how Micah and Hannah interacted at dinner?" Linda asked.

"Someone cut up her food so she could eat it," Cas said. "I assume that's what Micah did in your kitchen."

"He did," I said.

"What's wrong with her?" Linda asked. "Is it arthritis?"

"Possibly, or more likely a neurodegenerative disorder," Cas said.

"What are you guys talking about?" Molly asked. "Science wasn't one of my favorite subjects in high school before I dropped out to start modeling."

"Do you know much about Parkinson's disease or multiple sclerosis?" Cas asked. "Or amyotrophic lateral sclerosis?"

"Hey, I do," Molly said. "*The Good Wife*. The cute little lawyer guy has one of those diseases."

"And he's dying from it," I said. "I think Hannah has a problem like that and treating her is Micah's sole focus in life."

"I agree," Cas said.

"And maybe that's why he doesn't want to give you an interview," Linda said.

"I can't fathom what it must be like to have a disease that, as a physician, she knows has no cure," Cas said.

"Her feelings about that would make compelling reading," Linda said.

"How about I narrow my focus to Hannah?" I asked. "I could be wrong, but if we discover what's wrong with her, we might break this story. Everybody agree with that?"

Nods all around.

"Okay then, here are your assignments," I said. "Cas, I'll email you all the scientific papers Micah and the other doctors he works with have written over the past four years. Maybe you can figure out what disease Micah is working on."

"Great."

"Linda, you keep working on Micah's funding.

"Done."

"And Molly, you're the most important of all. You continue to contact Hannah daily and see how she's feeling, but without being obvious about it. We have to know about any worsening of her condition."

"And what are you going to do?" Molly asked.

"I'm going back to the dentist."

"Did he find a problem on Monday?" Cas asked.

"I don't know. He called this morning and said he wanted to go over my x-rays with me."

A little lie, but there was no reason to tell the girls that I had something else planned for Thursday morning. I was going to break into the dentist's house.

73

It was Thursday morning. I'd spent Wednesday perfecting my plan to break into Lorenz's house. I stood at Molly's front door with Kerry in her stroller.

"Thanks for doing this," I said. "Today was the only time Dr. Lorenz could work me in to go over my x-rays. It shouldn't take long. Is it okay if I stop at Whole Foods before I pick up Kerry?"

"Not a problem," Molly said.

I picked up my daughter and handed her off to Molly. As I folded up the stroller, there was a crash in the playroom. Molly took Kerry in one arm and the stroller in the other.

"Gotta go. Boys being boys."

A little before ten, I slow-jogged past Lorenz's office on the other side of the street. My plan was to make sure he had a 10 a.m. appointment. A black GMC Envoy drove up. It had tinted windows, and I couldn't see who was driving. But I recognized the passenger who climbed out; it was Donna the stripper.

Checking out your dental health?

Whatever Lorenz was going to do to her would give me plenty of time to break into his home. The Envoy left, and she entered his office.

I wanted to snap a picture of the license plate of the SUV as it moved away from me, but it would be too obvious and might attract the attention of the driver. Instead, I memorized the number and ran off to break into Lorenz's home.

74

When I reached our home, I sped into our alley, stopped at the trash cans, and entered the license plate number into my phone.

Earlier that morning, when I was out for my run, I'd hidden my backpack behind our trash can. I removed latex gloves from the pack and put them on. Holding the straps of the pack in my left hand, I lifted the latch on Lorenz's back gate and slipped into his yard.

My first task was to locate the phone line power box at the corner of his house. When I entered the house, the security system would go off. I didn't want a phone call going to the security company, so I had to disconnect that line. I unscrewed the two screws which held the panel in place. After putting it on the ground, I disconnected the phone line and replaced the panel but didn't tighten down the screws all the way.

I had been in Lyndell's home enough times that I knew her security control box was hidden in the front entry closet, the same place as ours. The box was about fifty feet from the back door. Once I opened that door, I would have exactly thirty seconds to run to the closet, pry open the face to the control box, and unscrew the power line to the system.

Hurrying up Lorenz's back patio stairs, I stopped at the outside box and punched in Lyndell's security code. It didn't work. I tried her key. It didn't work either.

I inserted the electric lock pick gun into the door lock and flipped it on. It whirred and shook in my hand for several seconds and stopped. A simple twist of the torque wrench and the lock clicked open.

As I stepped into Lorenz's kitchen, a loud explosion rocked the neighborhood. The kitchen windows shook from the blast's shock wave.

No! Not now!

75

My head began to throb. I knew what was coming, but the security system had started beeping.

Hurry!

I had less than thirty seconds before it began blaring.

Gritting my teeth, I ignored the impending PTSD attack and sprinted to the front closet. The jarring of my feet on the hardwood floors made stars burst behind my eyes.

After prying off the front plate with a screwdriver, I disconnected the power line with six seconds to spare. The beeping stopped. I closed my eyes and waited for the rest of the PTSD attack.

Relax. Breathe.

The light show in my brain was mercifully short. When it was over, I parted the front curtains, peeking out to make sure our house hadn't been damaged. It wasn't, but I could see smoke billowing up over the treetops to the north two or three blocks away.

I replaced the front plate of the security control box and pulled out my cell phone.

"Molly, I'm at Whole Foods," I said. "It sounded like a bomb just exploded. Did you hear it?"

"Sure did. I was afraid Chase had blown up the family room, but he didn't."

I waited. "And?"

"Oh, right. And I can see smoke about a block away. Maybe it's a gas main, or something."

"And Kerry's okay?"

"She's perfect. She's finger painting a picture for you."

"I'll help you wipe up the mess when I pick her up."

The explosion was going to attract the policemen and firemen in the area, keeping them from discovering my breaking and entering.

Good news for me.

I hadn't taken the time to lock the back door. I ran back to the kitchen and relocked it. I sniffed. The scent of bacon, eggs, toast, and coffee wafted over me. Considering Lorenz's plump body, his breakfast selection wasn't a surprise.

Hurrying down the hall, I rushed toward the room I assumed was Lorenz's office. My cell phone rang from my backpack. The unexpected noise made me jump. I'd forgotten to shut it off after I'd called Molly.

Dumb me.

"Tina, are you and Kerry okay?" Carter asked.

"We're fine," I said. "Why are you asking?"

"We received a report of a gas leak explosion near North Paulina and West Roscoe. I wanted to make sure both of you are safe."

"No problems here, but I can hear police cars and fire engines whizzing down Lincoln."

"Please stay home until I learn more."

That is so not happening, Honey.

76

I shut off my phone and dropped it into my backpack. My plan to steal Lorenz's information was based on a character flaw common to most men with a desk.

They clutter it with Post-it notes, stacks of computer printouts, and scribbled-on yellow legal pads. I would sift through the materials and copy what I needed by taking pictures with a special camera the *Post* had given me for a task like this. As a backup, I could use my cell phone to take more pictures.

Lorenz would never suspect I'd been there.

The smell of stale coffee and sweat wafted over me when I opened the door to Lyndell's office. I saw a computer sitting on her antique desk. My plan so far had worked perfectly, except for one problem: the desktop was spotless. There wasn't a single piece of paper, legal pad, or Post-it note anywhere. I slid open the desk drawers, but they were bare.

Lyndell's generic, gray-metal, three-drawer filing cabinet sat on the floor to the left of the desk. I peeked in it next. The insides were empty except for a few lonely dust bunnies. Lorenz was apparently too young to use outmoded technology.

Time for Plan B. I plugged in the flash drive I'd purchased in case this happened and booted up his computer.

Damn.

It was password protected. Hunting underneath the drawers of his desk, I hoped like me he couldn't remember his password and had written it down.

I was under the desk when the sound of footsteps on the back patio deck broke the silence in the house; that was followed by a key turning in the back door lock and the opening of the door.

I heard a cough.

No!

77

There was another cough.

Lorenz?

Yanking the flash drive out of his computer, I shoved it into my backpack.

Hide!

The door to the basement was across the hall from the office. There was no time to go anywhere else. I ran down the steps and paused at the foot of the stairs to listen. My pulse hammered in my ears, making it hard to hear.

A man spoke.

Uh-oh! Not English.

Another male voice answered him in the same language, one I'd heard in Afghanistan.

Arabic.

It wasn't Lorenz!

I opened the first door to my right. It was the bathroom. I hurried in and closed the door. I scanned the small space for somewhere to hide.

The linen closet.

My hands shook as I opened the door and stepped in.

Not big enough.

Jamming my backpack in the corner of the closet, I moved to my right and slid into the bathtub. I scooted down and pulled the opaque shower curtain closed.

A man said something in Arabic. It sounded like he was giving instructions.

Another cough.

It was followed by the pounding of different pairs of feet moving quickly around the house.

Call 911!

I reached for my cell phone to report a home invasion at Lorenz's, but the phone was in my backpack.

And it's in the linen closet.

Before I could climb out of the tub and grab it, the basement door opened and slammed against the wall. Someone ran down the stairs.

Sliding further down in the bathtub, I heard a door open. There was a pause. The door closed.

The process was repeated.

Someone is searching each room down here!

Then the bathroom door opened.

Help!

78

I sniffed.

Cigarette smoke.

The stench made me gag.

I swallowed the bile bubbling into my throat.

My heart hammered so hard against my sternum, I was sure he could hear it.

The intruder shouted a few words in Arabic.

A man.

He coughed.

The unexpected sound startled me, and I bucked against the tub.

No!

Had I nudged the shower curtain causing it to move?

Get ready!

I tightened up my muscles. I was not going down without the fight of my life.

A voice from upstairs answered him.

The man in the bathroom replied.

I heard him step toward the tub.

Anticipating the shower curtain being yanked back, I clenched my right hand into a fist.

Go for his eyes.

But he didn't touch the shower curtain. Instead, he coughed again, snarfed a loogie, and spit it into sink.

He walked out, and I heard his footsteps go up the stairs.

A new and different male voice yelled out from the front of the house. That was followed by footsteps running to the rear of the house.

The back door opened and closed. I listened, but the only sound was from my own rapid breathing.

I slid back the shower curtain and stepped over the edge of the tub. Grabbing several sheets of toilet paper, I swabbed the entire surface of the sink.

DNA.

If the lab could extract it from the blob, I had a way to identify the man. After retrieving my backpack, I put the wad of paper in an empty sandwich bag I had stashed in there.

Moving out of the bathroom, I heard a sound that was becoming all too familiar to my ears; it was a key turning in a lock, this time at the front door.

Dammit! Not again!

79

I stood in the hall outside of the bathroom and waited. The front door opened and then closed. Footsteps echoed off the wood floor in the hall.

Has to be Lorenz.

If he had Donna the stripper with him, she wasn't here for her dental health. If he took her to the third-floor master bedroom to do more than examine her teeth, I could easily escape. I tiptoed to the base of the stairs so I could hear his conversation with the stripper.

A man said something in English, but he didn't sound like Lorenz.

"I'm a little surprised the security system wasn't on," the man said.

"Like you told me on the way out here, Lorenz's assignment involved strippers," a different man said. "He probably wasn't as focused as he should have been."

Two men?

Footsteps went toward the back of the house and stopped.

"This the computer room?" the second man asked.

"Supposed to be. The SAC went over the house plans with me."

SAC?

I'd learned that acronym when I was in D.C.: Special Agent in Charge.

Oh. My. God!

The men upstairs were FBI agents!

"Where's the computer?"

"Not seeing it."

"Better search the rest of the house. Could be in a different room."

Hide again!

I grabbed my cell phone and screwdriver from my backpack in the linen closet. Climbing into the tub, I slid down and pulled the shower curtain closed.

I listened as one agent made a quick walk through the lower level. He didn't bother with the bathroom.

When he returned upstairs, I climbed out of the tub and tiptoed to the foot of the stairs.

"All clean down there," the man said. "What about the video and audio surveillance equipment? Don't want the locals to find our equipment."

Locals? Chicago cops?

"The boss told me the budget hadn't allowed for that. He didn't say it, but my initial impression was that he wasn't convinced this op was even necessary."

"With what just happened, I bet he wishes he'd taken this whole assignment more seriously."

"Got that right. Losing an agent is gonna look bad on his record."

WHAT?!

"What about the stripper? Did she make it?"

"No, she was killed in the explosion too."

OMG! Lorenz and Donna are dead!

80

Two people I know are dead! I have to do something!

The front door opened and closed.

The house was quiet again.

The agents are gone.

The explosion I'd heard had to have been Lorenz and Donna being blown up. And because of that, cops were going to process the dentist's entire house for clues. My hands began to shake.

Calm down.

I shut my eyes and took in several deep breaths. I had to be certain I didn't leave any clues behind that would connect me to being in Lorenz's house. I still had on my latex gloves, so my fingerprints wouldn't be a problem. And even if they were discovered, I'd been in Lyndell's home many times before.

But the bathtub was a different story. There would be fibers and debris from my clothing and running shoes that shouldn't be there. I found cleaning products on the floor of the linen closet next to my backpack and used them to scrub down all the surfaces I'd been in contact with.

I grabbed my backpack and rushed up the stairs to the office. The computer's hard drive was gone. Returning to the security control box in the entry closet, I reversed what I'd done before and reattached the power line.

Hurrying out the back door, I went to the phone box, unscrewed the two already loosened screws, and reconnected the phone line. I replaced the back and tightened the screws.

I halted in the alley and leaned against the fence to catch my breath. Tears began running down my cheeks.

Donna and Lorenz were dead.

And I'd almost been caught by the men speaking Arabic and then the FBI agents.

I wiped my nose.

This was way too close.

I began shivering even though the outside temperature hovered in the low 90s. I scanned Lorenz's back door and yard to make sure I hadn't left any of my equipment behind.

The security system!

The first intruders had come in that door. I'd assumed they'd picked the lock like I had. But why hadn't they been concerned about the security system? Did they have Lorenz's code? If they did, how did they get it? If they did take the computer, why did they do it? Were they associated with al-Turk?

I'm not going to figure this out standing in the alley.

Stripping off my sweaty latex gloves, I ran up my back stairs and rushed through the door into the kitchen. I ditched the gloves in the trash. From my backpack, I removed the sack with the intruder's DNA and hurried down to the laundry room, hiding it where I'd previously hidden al-Turk's trash.

I left my house and walked toward Molly's to pick up Kerry. On the way, I called Carter. "Any news on the gas explosion?" I asked.

An EMT truck blew by me.

"The blast occurred at a recently opened dentist's office. The police think a gas called nitrous oxide, which the dentist used for anesthesia, might have caused it. Two people are dead, presumably the dentist and one of his patients."

I had to be sure.

"Did you say dentist?"

"I did."

"Was his name Lorenz?"

He clicked his keyboard. "It was. Why do you want to know?"

My hands shook as I held the phone to my ear. Carter had confirmed what I'd heard the FBI agents say.

Lorenz and, most likely, Donna, are dead.

"Lorenz is, or I guess now was, our new neighbor."

"What?!"

"He'd moved into Lyndell Newens' house. She rented it to him."

"Have you met him?"

"I've seen him walking past our house."

I hadn't directly answered his question, a technique I'd learned when I was a talking head for the *Post* on CNBC. It wasn't a lie. But it wasn't the entire truth. He was upset by the news that Lorenz was our neighbor, and he didn't notice.

"Since I'm close, do you want me to work the story?" I asked.

"I've already assigned a reporter to the scene."

"Good luck. With Chicago traffic, your reporter might not get here until midnight."

"It's too dangerous for you to go there."

"Hey, I know what you can do. You can log onto Twitter and find out what's going on. It'll be quicker and save your reporter the drive out here."

"Tina, please do *not* go to the scene!"

I hung up.

A girl's gotta do what a girl's gotta do.

81

I called Molly and asked her to watch Kerry a little longer so I could work the scene of the tragedy. By the time I arrived at Lorenz's office, bystanders had already lined the far side of North Paulina Street. Two fire trucks, an EMT unit, and several police cars had parked haphazardly in both lanes with lights flashing and portable radios blaring.

As I watched, a Chicago CSI van arrived on the scene and screeched to a stop. I moved closer.

"What happened?" I asked the cop who appeared to be in charge of crowd control.

"Can't say, ma'am," he said. "It's an ongoing investigation."

The stink of soot and ashes mixed with the pleasant fragrance from shattered mouthwash and hand sanitizer bottles hung in the air.

Not again.

I closed my eyes and tried to prevent an attack.

There's no bomb here.

I tried to tell that to my PTSD-addled brain. It took several seconds, but I was able to gain control enough to open my eyes.

The front door had been blown out along with the shattered front office windows. The adjoining offices on each side had suffered minimal damage.

Several people around me took pictures with their cell phones and sent them into cyberspace. The rest looked like they tweeted what they were watching in real time.

This is why newspapers are dying.

Three TV vans had parked a block away. Cameramen shot videos, but there were no onsite TV reporters working on camera.

A brown Ford Crown Vic pulled up. Detective Tony Infantino popped out of the driver's side. A female cop jumped out of the passenger side. They put on latex gloves and green paper booties before they stepped over the blackened front door and entered the office.

Detectives?

Carter said the explosion was an accident. My brain whirled. Lorenz was an FBI agent. If the FBI hadn't alerted the Chicago police they were working a case right in the cops' own backyard, the locals would be extremely upset they hadn't been informed about what was going down.

And that was my bargaining chip to learn more details about the story that might resurrect my career.

82

Twenty minutes later, Tony stepped over the fragments of the blown-out door and out into the crowded street. He put on his sunglasses and gave the scene his once-over cop look, stopping when he caught me watching him. He stared back for a few seconds and then stomped over to me.

"A problem?" I asked sweetly.

"Don't start with the happy horseshit," he said. "I'm not in the mood."

I kept quiet.

"Dentist named Greg Lorenz lived next door to you, right?" he continued.

"Lived, as in the past tense?"

"You got it. He just died…" he jerked his thumb toward Lorenz's office, "…in there with a woman."

"Died? How?"

"Nitrous oxide blew up."

"Huh? An accident?"

"That's the story we're releasing."

"Then it's not an accident?"

He opened his mouth to answer but stopped. "Can't tell you about an ongoing investigation."

"Maybe I can help."

"How?"

"I live next door and watch what's going on."

"And?"

I held up my hand. "Only if you promise me an exclusive on the story."

He took off his sunglasses. "Okay, deal. Give it to me."

"Lorenz worked undercover for the FBI."

"You gotta be... How do you know that?"

"His FBI pals sterilized his house less than an hour after the explosion in this dental office."

Not about to tell you how I know this.

He twirled his sunglasses around in his hands. "It was the C4."

"That's what killed Lorenz and the girl?"

"No... I mean, yeah, C4 probably did kill them, but that's not why the FBI is working this. It was the C4 residue on your stolen trash that I gave to our lab guys."

Uh-oh.

83

My neck muscles began to tighten up. "Why didn't you tell me there was C4 on the trash samples I gave you?"

"You didn't specifically ask," Tony said.

Got me there.

"Okay, but why did you send it to the FBI?"

"Lab guys discovered traces of C4 the same day you gave me that trash. After 9/11, whenever our lab guys find any bomb residue, they have to ship the tested material to the FBI lab in D.C. They forwarded it the same night. Feds called me the next morning. I had to give you up as the source of the trash."

The memory of my encounter with C4 made my head begin to throb.

"I was blown up by a bomb made of C4."

"Heard about it from a reporter on the police desk. What, four, five years ago?"

"Five. I was almost killed."

"Dude said you got fired because of it."

Not going to respond to that.

"I don't remember getting a card or flowers from you while I was in the hospital."

"You survived. End of story."

How glad am I we broke up?

"Do you know much about C4?" I asked.

"Stable, but needs a detonator to set it off. You know, boom-BOOM!"

I shrugged my shoulders. "I don't understand what you mean."

"C4 can't blow up by itself. There has to be a detonator exploding next to it to set it off. Little boom followed by a big BOOM."

Now, I remember!

I was back standing in the hallway next to the men's bathroom in the Arlington Women's Clinic. I'd heard a thunderous explosion before I was knocked unconscious for several days. But milliseconds before the big blast, there had first been a smaller explosion, which, until this second, I'd ignored. Tony was right: small boom, big BOOM, the detonator and then the C4.

"It can be molded into about any shape," he continued. "And it can be traced like a fingerprint using a chemical substance called DMDNB."

"That detail might come in handy."

He yawned. "Might, might not."

We stood in silence.

"But anyway, thanks for promptly analyzing the trash," I said. "Your debt is paid."

"Better be. Had to call in a couple of favors to get it done."

"Did you give the feds al-Turk's name and the other three sets of fingerprints?"

"How dumb do you think I am? Not gonna let them steal my case."

"Did you run al-Turk's name?"

"Yep."

"But you didn't come up with much, right?"

"His record's clean."

"Your guys didn't find Lorenz's home computer's hard drive, did they?"

"Not yet."

"He had one in his office."

"What happened to it?"

"Meet me at my house in ten minutes. I have a clue that might give you the answer."

84

Ten minutes later, Tony double-parked on the street in front of Lorenz's house. His female partner went inside. He climbed up my front steps. I ushered him into the kitchen.

He glanced around. "Where's the kid?"

"At a friend's."

"Where's she usually sit?"

I pointed at the chair with her booster seat. "Right there. Why?"

"Don't wanna get glop on my pants."

He sat down in another chair. I handed him the sandwich bag containing the toilet paper I'd retrieved from its hiding place in the laundry room.

"This is from one of the men who took the hard drive from the dentist's computer," I said. "They entered Lorenz's house just before the FBI did. I swabbed this sample from the bathroom sink after they left and before the FBI arrived."

Tony glared at me. "You saw the perps? You freaking kidding me? These guys just blew two people up. They're not playing Ping-Pong here. You wanna live through this then tell me what's really goin' on."

At least he hadn't used the "D" word; I heard enough of it from Carter. And I hated to admit it, but Tony was right. I needed his help and protection.

"Mr. al-Turk, the man whose fingerprints you identified from the trash I stole, lives right there," I said pointing out our front window at his house across the street. "He moved in about a month ago."

Tony glanced at the house and held up the sandwich bag. "This DNA from him?"

"I don't know. I never saw that man's face. All I'm sure of is that he speaks Arabic. The other people with him in Lorenz's house did too. I don't know if al-Turk was even there."

He stretched back in the chair. "Sweets, all you have is one guy named al-Turk, who, by the way, has a clean record and C4 residue on his trash."

I held up my hands. "But..."

"...And an unknown number of perps who broke into Lorenz's house and speak Arabic. Not enough to build a case. If C4 residue is the only evidence you have, be hard to convince the captain to spend money on these DNA tests you want."

"There's a little more. A friend and I have been using GPS devices to track both of the vehicles al-Turk has in his garage."

He pondered that a few seconds. "Two cars? One driver."

"Yes."

"Both cars move around at the same time?"

"They do."

"Kinda hard for one guy to do that."

"I agree, but I can't prove who the other driver or drivers are. All I know is that there are four beds in al-Turk's house."

"Do four people live there?"

"I don't have any documented proof of that."

"Where do the vehicles go?"

"A mosque, the Twenties, Whole Foods, and a couple of Middle Eastern restaurants in the area."

"The Twenties? Strip joint near West Belmont and North Halsted?"

Why am I not surprised you know where it is?

"If you'd worked a little harder on your research on al-Turk, you would've discovered his name is on the liquor license for the Twenties."

Because you didn't do your job, buster.

85

I knew a lot about al-Turk, and Tony was waiting for me to tell him all of it.

"I ran a financial background analysis on al-Turk," I said.

Tony took out his small spiral notebook and a pen. "His money fronting all of this?"

"Probably not. I lost the money trail at a merchant bank in Luxembourg. And the female victim worked at the Twenties."

He arched an eyebrow. "She a stripper?"

"She is."

"What's her name?"

"Donna Allen."

He made a notation in his book. "How do you know this?"

"She worked out with us at XSport. I recognized her when I saw her stripping at the Twenties."

He raised his eyebrows and gave me a disdainful smirk. "You at a strip club? Don't see it."

"I do what I need to do to research a story."

He stared at me. I stared back.

"Two cars never go anywhere else?"

The sarcastic tone of his voice was starting to get on my nerves.

"As far as I can tell, they don't."

"Al-Turk Italian?"

"Hardly. Why?"

"Protection rackets. Mob uses C4 to convince storeowners they need protection by blowing up their stores. They're using it on the South Side by teaming up with a couple of the black gangs."

"A strange marriage."

"Scary one, too, but they have competitors. Any Mexicans involved?"

"Why do you want to know? All the evidence indicates that al-Turk is Muslim."

"Mexican cartels — especially from the Sinaloa district — are in the protection business along with selling drugs."

"The protection racket I understand, but why do they need C4 to sell drugs?"

"To blow up their competitors."

Blow up? C4?

I remembered my reporting days in Afghanistan and the bombings I had covered. My stomach began to churn.

"Tony, what if al-Turk is a terrorist?"

86

"Dude could be a terrorist, but he or his men would have to scout out potential locations to do surveillance of the targets," Tony said.

"I agree," I said.

His cop interrogation voice surfaced. "You said the two cars keep driving to the same places."

"I did."

"If he or his pals are terrorists, they would have to drive around to work their targets. And if they're in the protection business, they would spend a lot of time on the road to harass the vics."

"And they're not."

"So you say… And there's another thing. Why the hell is this al-Turk guy living in the middle of your peaceful Chicago neighborhood?"

"I've been wondering the same thing ever since I discovered he owns the Twenties."

"And?"

"I don't know, but let's say he's involved with drugs."

"Okay."

"A strip club is a perfect place to launder money."

He glanced at his watch and motioned for me to hurry up.

"He moves to our neighborhood where no one expects to find a bad guy."

He waved his hand again. And then yawned.

Jerk-off.

"He sets up an ongoing operation to sell a steady supply of product to local dealers."

"Where does he buy the raw product?"

"I was embedded in Afghanistan with the marines. One of the stories I wrote was about the pipeline of drugs from there to the U.S."

He threw his notebook on the table. "I know all that crap."

I need to convince you.

"In New York City, Al-Turk had partial ownership in an import/export company called Business Ventures. It did business in the Middle East. Not much of a stretch to assume that his imports could be raw heroin."

"How does he receive and deliver his drugs?"

At least you're now listening.

"He doesn't. I think the suppliers and buyers come to him."

He shrugged his shoulders.

"When he first moved in, I watched two men unloading boxes from a truck into his garage. Maybe he continues to use the alley for other deliveries."

"Not following."

"Suppose a supplier drives into al-Turk's alley and parks by his garage like the guys I saw unloading moving boxes. But instead of moving boxes, the guy brings raw drugs to al-Turk's garage."

"You think that's where he stores the product?"

"Yes, until he later takes it inside and cuts it down."

Tony yawned again.

"And when he's done, he moves it back to the garage for street sale. The buyer does the same thing as the supplier. He drives down the alley and stops. Al-Turk opens the garage door and puts the product in the buyer's car."

He made a notation in his notebook. "Deal wouldn't take more than thirty seconds."

"No neighbors would see it happen unless they were in the alley at exactly the same time."

"If you're right, then that's why Lorenz was offed."

What?

87

"When Lorenz began visiting the Twenties, al-Turk might have suspected the dentist was an undercover agent of some kind," Tony said. "When he found out for sure, he or his guys blew Lorenz up to stop the investigation and be an example to local dealers he isn't scared of a federal agent."

"Do you think the girl was collateral damage?"

"Only thing that makes sense."

"But if al-Turk's a drug dealer, why is the FBI running this and not the DEA?"

"Best guess is the FBI initiated the investigation because of the C4 on the trash, and they aren't about to give it up after spending money setting Lorenz up undercover."

"And then he gets killed."

"Bingo. Feds aren't happy when they lose an agent."

"What if the feds find out al-Turk is a drug dealer?"

"FBI will form an Organized Crime and Drug Enforcement Task Force with the DEA to take him down."

"What if he's a terrorist?"

"FBI will go it alone and hog all the headlines."

"We have to prove exactly what al-Turk is doing. I tried the GPS system. You need to tap his phone."

"A problem." He began counting on his fingers. "One, I would need a subpoena from a judge for the phone tap, and from what you have, no judge in Chicago would issue one. And two, without more evidence, captain won't go for it any more than he'll okay spending money on DNA tests."

"What'll you do?"

"Have to work it off the clock at the Twenties," he said, smirking at me. "It's a dirty, rotten, lonely job, but somebody's gotta do it."

"And you're the perfect man."

He shot his cuffs. "You got it, Sweets."

"What should I do?"

"You used to be a big shot reporter; get off your fat ass and begin investigating. If al-Turk's delivering his drug product and selling it from his garage, prove it."

"You're telling me you won't go to your captain to request the DNA test unless I give you evidence of that?"

"You got it."

"And my ass is NOT fat!"

"Just sayin'."

Now what?

88

Tony walked over to Lorenz's house to work the case. I went to Molly's to pick up Kerry.

"Did you have fun at Molly's?" I asked Kerry, as I pushed her stroller back to our house.

"I pwayed blocks."

"Did Elmo play too?"

"Uh-huh. We made big house."

We walked by Lorenz's house. Yellow crime scene tape surrounded the perimeter of the yard. I could smell the irritating odor of the cigarettes two Chicago uniformed policemen smoked on the sidewalk in front of his house.

"Hey guys, do you mind?" I asked them.

"Mind what?" one of the cops asked.

"The cigarettes." I pointed at Kerry in her stroller. "You're polluting the air in our neighborhood."

They stared at me.

"Maybe I should talk to the detective in charge," I continued.

One of them crushed out his cigarette with the heel of his shoe. The other one flipped his into the street and grumbled a word that sounded like bitch.

"Excuse me?" I asked.

They turned their backs to me. I continued pushing Kerry around the block to our back door. I didn't want them to know where I lived because I planned to watch the house through our windows.

When I walked into the kitchen, the landline rang.

"Are you okay?" Carter asked. "Is Kerry safe?"

Tell the truth, Honey. You called to make sure I'm not at the site of the explosion.

"We're fine. I'm making a snack for Kerry. Do you want to speak to her?"

"No, I'm busy."

But not too busy to check up on me.

"Any news about the accident?" I asked.

He hesitated, proof that his reporter was still stuck in traffic. "I'll let you know."

"No need. I'll go online and check it out."

He abruptly disconnected.

I played with Kerry and then put her down for her nap. It hit me as I watched Lorenz's house: *Lyndell.*

The feds required a house close to me, and Lyndell's arthritic knees needed total joint replacements. My guess was the feds talked to her two sons and offered to pay for the expensive surgery and rehab stay in exchange for the use of her house. There was one way to find out: ask Lyndell. She would tell me the truth.

I called her cell phone, but it went straight to voice mail. I dialed the Brookstone Center.

"Hello, this is Tina Thomas. I have a neighbor who recently moved into your facility. Her name is Lyndell Newens. I would like to come and see her. When are visiting hours?"

I heard clicking from a computer keyboard. "I'm sorry, but I cannot give out information about any of our patients unless you are an authorized family member," the lady said.

The FBI had probably flagged my name in case I called about Lyndell. The feds didn't want me to visit her and ask questions about the real estate transaction with Lorenz. Lyndell was too sharp not to have records proving what had happened. Money talked, and the feds had plenty of that. The sons would keep their mother content and away from me until this was over.

When I heard the familiar music of an ice cream truck in the street outside our home, I suddenly pictured how I could convince Tony and his captain that al-Turk was either a drug dealer or a terrorist.

But, first, I needed to get the playgroup sleuths together to brief them on the murders in our neighborhood.

89

Six hours after the bombing, the playgroup, minus Hannah and her children, sat in my kitchen. Through my front and side windows, we saw the crime scene tape wrapped around the perimeter of Lorenz's house. Our kids ran around, oblivious to the presence of police working the scene next door.

"I cancelled my kick boxing class and rushed over here," Cas said. "What's going on?"

"The dentist who rented Lyndell's home died in his office this morning along with Donna Allen, the girl we know from XSport Fitness," I began.

"Do you know what happened?" Linda asked.

"It was a terrible accident. The dentist and Donna were apparently using nitrous oxide for...fun."

"Not fun, you mean sex," Molly said.

"How do you know about that?" I asked.

"I learned a lot of stuff when I modeled."

"This is interesting and all that, and it's too bad about Donna, but what's that have to do with us?" Cas asked.

"More to the point, is al-Turk involved in this?" Linda asked.

"Donna worked at the Twenties, and that's all we know," I said.

"What do we do?" Linda asked.

"Carter and his reporters will cover this with all of their firepower. We can't compete with that. I don't want to miss my August deadline. I think we need to concentrate on Hannah and Micah."

And not risk you guys getting blown up.

"It's your call," Cas said. "They're your stories; we're just trying to help you."

"But do you want to give up on al-Turk and the Twenties?" Molly asked.

"It's taking an enormous amount of my time to follow those GPS trackers and chase the money trail," Linda said before I could answer. "I vote to let Carter and his reporters investigate al-Turk."

"Great," I said. "We can put that story on the backburner and plan to report what we've learned about Hannah and Micah at our next playgroup."

They didn't need to know I would never give up on al-Turk's story.

Part 4

90

Tony needed convincing evidence about what al-Turk was doing across the street. Friday morning, I reached out for help to prove it. While I ran, I called the Windy City Ice Cream Company.

"Elena, this is Tina Thomas. I hired one of your ice cream trucks to park outside our house during my husband's birthday last year."

"I remember," she said. "Did you have fun?"

"We did, and it's why I called. I know this is short notice, but I need one of the trucks as soon as I can get one."

"Let me see what I can do."

"And if Hugo's available, I would like to use him."

"Call you right back."

It took fifteen minutes for Elena to give the go ahead for my idea, but she couldn't arrange it until that afternoon.

While we waited for the truck, Kerry and I went downstairs to my office. The only new intel I hadn't addressed concerned the owner of the GMC truck that had delivered Donna to the dentist's office. I ran the plate on my computer.

The truck was registered to the Arun Corporation, which also owned al-Turk's home and his two vehicles. I needed to know where the truck parked and who drove it.

Time for another road trip.

"Kerry, Momma has to run an errand again."

She opened her mouth to protest, but I stopped her short.

"Why don't we buy donuts before we go?" I asked.

She blinked as she thought about this. "Elmo and Walph go too? They wuv donuts!"

Bribes always work.

Ten minutes later, after I had purchased a dozen Dinkel's donuts, we were headed to the Twenties. I drove around the block and saw the black GMC truck parked in the apartment complex behind the strip club. The driver was somehow involved in the story. But was the driver a man or woman? And was that person connected to al-Turk?

91

The pale-yellow ice cream truck arrived right after Kerry and I had finished lunch. The music reached my ears before I saw the truck, which was the major component of my plan.

Ice cream trucks are a daily part of summer life in Lakeview. They are in our neighborhood frequently, and most people ignore the music unless they intend to buy one of the goodies. The non-buyers don't "see" the trucks slowly moving up and down the street.

But not Kerry. When she heard the tunes, she jumped up and down. Pavlov would have been proud of her response. And my stomach began growling when the familiar songs drifted into our kitchen.

Following my instructions, Hugo parked in our driveway where al-Turk couldn't see the truck from his front windows. I carried my daughter down the back stairs to the driveway, and we stood by the truck's window.

"Thanks for coming," I said.

"My pleasure, Mrs. Thomas," Hugo said. "Elena said you have a special request."

"I sure do, and it's gonna be a little strange, but roll with me on it, okay?"

"Sure, but would your daughter like a treat first?"

"Kerry, would you like ice cream?" I asked.

"I wuv ice queam!"

"What's the magic word?"

"Pwease, Momma."

While Hugo prepared the order, Kerry and I climbed inside the truck. Kerry began eating her ice cream. I instructed Hugo to back out and drive to Belmont and turn right. We went three blocks and then turned back toward the alley behind al-Turk's house.

"Is this the right one?" Hugo asked.

"It is. When we get next to the target garage, you hold Kerry and I'll pop out and do what I have to do. It shouldn't take more than thirty seconds."

It didn't take that long. He stopped in front of al-Turk's garage. I threw open the passenger door and squatted down, using the truck's open door for partial cover. With tissues, I swabbed the garage door and the cement driveway leading into the garage.

I hopped back into the truck, and Hugo handed Kerry back to me. It went perfectly, the first easy thing I'd done on the story. He stepped on the gas and, at my suggestion, drove along three more alleys to make it look like he traveled that way all the time.

We returned to our driveway twenty minutes later. Back in our kitchen, I called Tony.

"I have what you need from al-Turk's house," I said. "Hopefully, it'll convince your captain to financially support this."

"On it," Tony said. "Gotta work the dentist's office. Be at your house this afternoon."

92

Friday night was difficult for me. After Carter arrived home, he wouldn't let Kerry and me out of his sight. The reason? His reporter had scooped the TV reporters and social media with the factual story from an "unnamed source in the police department" that the explosion had been caused by a small bomb made of C4. The article strongly implicated the sale of illegal drugs as being involved. There was no mention of terrorism.

Later that night, after I kept badgering him, Carter finally admitted the "unnamed source" had been Tony Infantino. Carter knew about my previous relationship with Tony and didn't like him. Tony felt the same way about Carter.

Carter couldn't figure out why Tony had helped him.

But I knew.

Tony was pissed that the FBI had not told the locals they were involved, and he wanted to make sure the public knew the murders were being investigated by the Chicago PD and not any other agency.

It was even worse on Saturday after Carter walked by the dentist's office and saw the bomb's destructive force. By Sunday, I couldn't take it any longer. I forced him to take Kerry and me to the Navy Pier.

When he left for work on Monday morning, he made me promise to stay around our house and not take Kerry anywhere. I did it, but only because I had mommy chores to do. By Monday afternoon I was stir crazy and couldn't take it any longer. I had to get out of the house.

And I needed to refocus my friends on Hannah and Micah. My August eleventh deadline was coming, and I still didn't have enough material to write an interesting first paragraph about Hannah and Micah. I called the playgroup to meet in Hamlin Park. I didn't include Hannah because we were going to talk about her.

It was the middle of the afternoon. We played with the kids and chatted. "How are you coming with your Hannah and Micah assignments?" I asked.

"I have the basics from his scientific papers," Cas said.

"But not what disease he's working on?" I asked.

"Not yet."

"Give us what you have."

"First, you need a little of the science background. I'll try to make it not too painful."

"Thanks," Molly said.

"Our assumption is that when Hannah got sick, Micah became interested in embryonic stem cell research."

Nods all around.

"There are two kinds of embryos used in embryonic stem cell research. One is left over from IVF. The other comes from a somatic human body cell."

"How does that second one work?" I asked.

"The nucleus is extracted from a patient's somatic cell and is inserted into a donor egg, which has had its nucleus previously removed. It's called a nuclear transfer, SCNT for short. The egg now contains the patient's genetic material and the reprogrammed cell develops into an embryo."

"Sounds like cloning," Linda said.

"It's called therapeutic cloning."

"If IVF embryos are destroyed to harvest embryonic stem cells, do they do the same thing with therapeutic cloned embryos?" Linda asked.

"They do. Micah's process has two steps: the creation of embryos solely for the purpose of stem cell derivation and then the destruction of those embryos."

"How does this donor egg stuff work?" Molly asked.

"Eggs harvested in excess of a doctor's need for IVF implantation are frequently used, but it's not the case in his lab."

"Huh?" I said. "I assume Micah uses IVF embryos."

"No, he doesn't."

"Why not?" Linda asked.

"He needs too many eggs."

"Where does he get the ones he needs?" Linda asked.

"Healthy young women are injected with hormones to create a hyperovulation state. Those women then sell their harvested eggs to him."

"How does he obtain the eggs?" Linda asked.

"He does a transvaginal ultrasound guided needle egg retrieval on the women to aspirate the eggs from their ovaries."

"Isn't selling body parts illegal?" I asked.

"Marketing and selling body parts is considered unethical and is banned in most countries," Linda said. "Human eggs are the notable exception to this rule."

"Then the only way Micah can get women to do this would be for them to volunteer their eggs or pay them." I said.

"Correct."

"Gosh, I need to talk to Micah," Molly said. "There's this killer pair of Louboutin pumps at Neiman's and Greg won't let me buy them. I can use the extra cash."

"You might want to hold off on this until we know for sure it's what Micah is doing," I said. "But the real question is what have we gotten into here?"

"Whatever it is, I think Micah is playing God by creating babies in the laboratory and then killing them," Cas said. "It's no different than an abortion as far as I'm concerned."

Abortion.

I needed to tell Cas and Molly what Linda already knew: that I was blown up in an abortion clinic.

93

"Linda knows about this, but I've never told either of you any of it before," I said. "Five years ago, I was injured in an abortion clinic bombing."

"No way!" Molly said.

"Oh, my God," Cas uttered.

Linda remained silent since she knew most of it.

"Do you have any residual damage?" Cas asked.

"I had an epidural hematoma, and a few people might say my brain's still a little scrambled."

Molly opened her mouth, but I anticipated her question. "The force of the blast ruptured an artery in my head. A neurosurgeon clipped the vessel to stop the bleeding. And to answer any other questions, I had a ruptured bladder and diaphragm, a collapsed lung, and a lacerated liver. I have a dandy scar on my abdomen because of the emergency operation."

"Gosh, when I saw it at the pool, I thought it was from a C-section," Molly said.

"Got one here too," I said pointing above my right ear. "But my hair covers up that one."

"You really got crunched," Cas said. "Do you still want to write Hannah and Micah's story?"

"I do."

"What if your bomber finds out what Micah is doing in his lab?" Cas asked.

"And that you're living here and working on his story," Linda continued.

I hesitated before I answered. "I don't want anyone to be injured or die because of the bomber's misguided way to protest abortion. If he's alive and free, I'll do whatever it takes to make certain he's caught."

"Maybe you can change the story a little," Molly said. "Kind of make it a personal interest story about Hannah and Micah and leave out the scientific stuff."

"I agree. I doubt the bomber, if he's even still alive, will read about it in a paper with a minuscule circulation like the *Lakeview Times*."

Hope I'm not wrong.

94

"Linda, do you have any new information on the spending from Hannah's trust?" I asked.

"I have been over it several times from several different angles," Linda said. "I've reached the same conclusion: her trust fund has contributed only twenty-five million dollars to the project."

"Did the Dallas bank account provide the rest of the money to fund the lab?" I asked.

"It did. Over one hundred fifty million dollars to date."

"Yikes," Molly said. "That's a lot of cash."

"It is. I broke down the spending by Loring. He's been a busy boy writing checks. He's even spent over four hundred seventy thousand dollars on mice."

"Wish I was a mouse farmer," Molly said. "Sounds like an easy way to make money."

"Do you know what kind of mice Micah is using in his lab?" Cas asked.

"Give me a minute here," Linda said. She took out her iPad. "Let me look it up."

"While we're waiting, Molly, what about Hannah?" I asked.

"We went to lunch at the Wishbone today."

I pictured Molly cutting up Hannah's food.

"And how did it go?" I asked.

"It was fun."

"How did you get to the Wishbone?"

"We walked."

"Did you have to help her?"

"No, why would I?"

"Because she limps and has to lean on her kids when she moves around at the park."

"Didn't happen today."

"No limp at all?"

"Nope."

"What about her eating?"

"She did better than I did."

I waited.

"I spilled my ice tea."

"It happens, but she had no problems?"

"None. I think it's from the new treatment Micah is giving her."

"For what?"

"For what, what?"

Talking to Molly was always fun. "Let's try it again. Is Hannah sick?"

"For sure."

"Did she say what's wrong with her?" Cas asked.

"Not exactly, but I figured it out."

"And?" I asked.

"It's a bad kind of arthritis."

"She said that?" Cas asked.

"Not exactly, but today on *The Doctors* TV show they had a woman on who acted exactly like Hannah, so I'm sure it's what she has."

Molly was doing her assignment but inserting conclusions instead of providing facts. I was convinced Micah was treating his wife for a crippling disease, but I didn't think it was arthritis.

"Oh, and one other thing," Molly said. "I talked Hannah into having playgroup at her house."

"Great," I said. "Firm up the date and text me when you have it."

Linda glanced up from her iPad. "Have the mouse data, Cas. Take a look."

She looked over Linda's shoulder and read what was on the screen. "Those are mouse models used to study multiple sclerosis."

"You think Hannah has MS?" I asked.

"If he's using those mice in his lab, I do."

"But we have no conclusive proof that's what Micah is doing his research on."

"Or if he's treating her for MS," Cas said.

"Molly, we really need to have playgroup at Hannah's house," I said.

95

On the way home from the park, I called Carter. "Honey, have a sec?"

"Sure," he said. "What's up?"

I told him the new information about Hannah.

"Based on the type of mice Micah is using in his lab, your conclusion is Hannah has multiple sclerosis and Micah is treating her for this disease, is that correct?"

He sounded skeptical.

"Yes, but I don't have objective evidence to prove it, which is why I called. Have any doctors or medical research labs in Chicago advertised for MS patients to enter a Phase I clinical trial?"

"Easy enough to find out."

He clicked on his keyboard.

"One week ago, Dr. Bruce Loring purchased an ad for that type of a trial. He needs twenty patients who have MS and are willing to come to his lab to be evaluated for an upcoming clinical trial. It is scheduled to run in next week's print and Sunday's online editions."

That can't be right.

"The clinical trial hasn't begun?"

"Not here in Chicago, but they might be doing it in another town. I'll flag the ad, which will allow me to follow it for you."

"Great, thanks. See you tonight. Love you."

The Phase I trial had not begun, but according to Molly, Hannah was better.

What is happening here?

96

All day Tuesday, I played with Kerry, ran errands, and did my mommy work around the house. When I had a chance, I researched multiple sclerosis online. My major conclusion? I was glad I didn't have it.

On Wednesday morning, Tony called me on my cell phone. "Need your help."

"Will it be risky?" I asked thinking Carter would freak out if it were.

"Probably not, but if it is, you got me to protect you."

Hard to argue with that.

Two hours later, while Linda babysat for Kerry, I rode with Tony in his white BMW to the Rosemont Park Cemetery. After a forensic autopsy, the police had released Donna's body, allowing her remains to be buried.

The interior of Tony's car still had the new car smell, an alien scent to me since our van always reeked of interesting odors from my daily activities with Kerry. His light brown leather seats were baby-skin soft. Before I climbed in, he asked me to take off my sandals because he didn't want me to track in any dirt or baby glop. I took advantage of it to rub my toes around on the plush, dark-brown carpet.

Heaven.

He parked his BMW about half a block from the funeral service. He kept the engine running and the air conditioner on full blast.

"Where's your partner?" I asked.

"I'm working off the clock. Our department doesn't have enough money in the budget for this." He stared out the front window. "Know any of these people?"

There were about thirty adults in attendance. The majority of them were young women. Al-Turk wasn't there, and I didn't recognize any of the men.

"The only ones I know are Sammy and Corky. They're the two standing in the front row. They work out at Xsport Fitness with us. They're also employees at the Twenties."

"Yeah, I've seen them there."

We watched the service for several minutes.

"I have an idea," I said.

Opening the passenger door, I stepped out into the humid Chicago morning. The wind from Lake Michigan blew the fragrance of the flowers and recently-mowed grass toward me. I slipped into my sandals and walked toward Sammy and Corky. An usher handed me the funeral program as the minister began the final prayer.

After he finished, the crowd stood in painful silence. The two girls turned around. Their eyes were red from crying, and neither wore any makeup. They were dressed in black, but the simple dresses could not disguise their fantastic figures.

I walked up to them. "I'm so sorry for your loss."

Corky put her arms around me and began sobbing. "It's so unfair. Donna was like our best friend in the whole world."

Patting her shoulder, I waited for her to speak. She didn't. All she did was cry. I glanced at Sammy. She cried too. I held out my other arm and led them to where the cars were parked.

"Did Donna have any family here?" I asked.

Corky stopped crying and wiped her nose with a tissue. Sammy did the same.

"I don't think she had anyone," Corky said.

"She might have had an aunt in Iowa, but that's all I know, Mrs. Thomas," Sammy said.

"Please, it's Tina."

We arrived at their car, a black GMC Envoy. I peeked at the license plate. It was the same one I'd seen Donna get out of at the dentist's office. And the one I'd found parked in the lot of an apartment building behind the Twenties.

Maybe that's where you girls live.

"Would you like to grab a cup of coffee? I've been through tragedies like this and have learned that talking with friends is one of the few ways to get through the grieving process."

"Thank you, so much," Sammy said. "Neither of us has ever had a friend who was murdered and it's..." She began crying again.

"...something no one should ever have to go through." I glanced back at Tony's car. "Tell you what. Meet me at Starbucks in Lakeview in ten minutes."

This is the part of investigative reporting I hate.

I was in a perfect position to comfort them and at the same time use their anguish to my advantage to hopefully break this story.

But I have to do it.

I felt the surge of the excitement I used to get when I was about to snag the information I needed. It was what I'd lived for as a reporter: to make a difference when lives might be at stake and, at the same time, write a terrific story.

I'm not back yet, but I'm getting closer.

97

I climbed into Tony's car. "I'm meeting them at the Starbucks in Lakeview."

He fired up the engine and pulled out. "I'll drop you there."

"Great. I need any new information on the Lorenz murders to help me question them."

"It started when he moved next door to you because of the C4 on the trash samples."

"Why me?"

"You were his only lead. His first move when he got here was to put a GPS transponder on your van and tail you."

"Hoisted with my own petard," I mused, more to myself than Tony.

He blinked but didn't respond. *Hamlet* wasn't one of his strengths.

"How did you figure it out?"

"Found it on your van, but the second device is well hidden."

Second?

"There are two?"

"First one is under the rear bumper. Second one is smaller than any of the ones we have. It's attached to the engine mount."

"Why two?"

"If you found the first one, would you search for a second one?"

"Probably not."

"Feds are smart. They expect you to find the standard device, but not check for the second one."

The feds had been following me since the day Lorenz arrived.

"It was last Wednesday," I said.

"What?"

"I drove to the Twenties to see if there was another new car parked there. It had to be how Lorenz made my connection with the strip club."

"Fits the time frame of what happened."

"What's your take on the Twenties?"

"Called the Chicago liquor license department. Club's under new ownership. They've been watching it."

"And?"

"It's clean. No drugs. No prostitution. No nothin'."

"Not surprising. Al-Turk seems to know exactly what he's doing."

"Agree, but got another problem. Al-Turk's listed as the owner of the Twenties but not his house. Can't find out why."

"I already know."

I told him about the Arun Corporation.

"I'm sure Lorenz knew about it too," I said.

"How?"

"He researched the Twenties and backtracked from there."

"Dude had the resources to find it."

"And because of that, the FBI knows Donna worked as a stripper at the Twenties."

"That's why the feds are here," he said.

"Here?"

"We're not the only ones watching this funeral. See the guy standing by the grave?"

"The cemetery worker?"

"Look at his shoes."

He wore thick-soled, black, cop shoes. "FBI?" I asked.

"Most likely, or the DEA, if they're going to work the case together. Probably has a friend sitting over there." He pointed at a white van about twenty yards away. "Taking pictures would be my guess. They're here because of Donna. They work funerals of murder victims and take pictures of the crowd."

"So they took my picture with you and they know we're involved."

"They do. You got a problem with it?"

"No. I want to find out as much as I can. I owe that much to Donna."

"What are you talking about?"

"If I hadn't gone back to the Twenties, Lorenz might never have discovered it and Donna wouldn't have been killed."

98

As Tony drove, I kept looking around trying to spot a tail.

"Are the feds following me? I asked.

"Could be, but they probably aren't — for the same reason I'm working this off the clock. Budget cuts. Takes a lot of manpower to physically follow one person twenty-four hours a day."

"So they won't see me with Corky and Sammy."

"Again, I doubt it. Probably no more than three people replaced Lorenz on the case, maybe only two. They're in a location where they can have cameras on your house and the house across the street. Might have one or two people on the Twenties, but more likely, they're using cameras there too. And they have access to the GPS devices Lorenz planted on your van."

"And I'm riding with you so they don't know where I am."

He pulled up and stopped. "You're clean. Now get to work and help me on this."

I stepped out into the humidity but couldn't control myself; I scanned the neighborhood trying to identify watchers. I didn't see any and walked into Starbucks.

Corky and Sammy were already there, sipping lattes and staring into space. I sniffed and savored the coffee aroma filling the room. I bought a skinny latte and gave them hugs before I sat down.

"Donna was such a sweet girl," I said. "Do you have any pictures to remember her?"

I needed to see who was in the photos with them.

They took out their iPhones and scrolled through their pictures of the trio touring Chicago landmarks. There were numerous selfies snapped with men in bars and restaurants. I didn't recognize any of them.

"Who would murder her?" Sammy asked after she clicked off the pictures. "She wouldn't hurt anyone."

"It could be the dentist was the target, and she just happened to be with him," I said.

"If you're right, then this sucks even more," Corky said. "He was a creep."

"I can't understand why she wanted to hang out with him," Sammy added. "He made me uncomfortable."

"Me too," Corky said.

"Uncomfortable?"

"He kept asking me and Corky about drugs and money and stuff like that."

Exactly what I would have done. "That's all he wanted to talk about?"

"He bugged us about Mr. al-Turk too," Corky said.

I pretended I didn't recognize his name. "And Mr. al-Turk is who?"

They stared at each other several seconds.

"He's our boss," Sammy said. "He gives each of us our own free apartment. And he paid for Donna's funeral."

"Plus, with our salary and tips, we make great money," Corky said.

"And we get free medical care," Sammy said.

"Does Mr. al-Turk ever chauffeur you around in a Mercedes or a Range Rover?"

Corky smiled. "Oh, no. Jamie drives us in his Envoy."

"Who is Jamie?"

Now Sammy smiled. "He's a cute guy who lives in our apartment building."

"What does he look like?"

"You should know," Corky said. "He works out at XSport Fitness and hits on all the women in there."

"Is he tan and muscular?"

"You got it," Sammy said.

"Does he do spinning?"

"He does all the classes he can, plus lifts weights," Corky said.

"Does he work for Mr. al-Turk?"

"I doubt it," she said. "Jamie never comes to the Twenties."

"He's just a guy in our apartment building who lets us use his Envoy when he's at work," Sammy said.

"And where is that?"

"Not sure it ever came up," she said.

"How does he get to work when you use his truck?"

"He has a Harley too," she said.

Was Jamie connected to the story, or was he a horny guy living in an apartment building with a bevy of strippers and driving a car registered to the Arun Corporation? Did the corporation pay him and give him free rent too?

Too many questions need to be answered.

I couldn't write this story without proven facts. I had to keep digging.

99

"Is Mr. al-Turk the owner of the Twenties?" I asked.

"He runs the club, but I'm not sure if he owns it," Corky said.

"And from what you said about all the benefits he gives you, he's a nice guy, right?" I asked.

Corky's face clouded over. "I wouldn't say that. He's like super strict. He won't let us near any drugs, and we can't drink alcohol at the club."

"What about, ah, being with the customers?"

Sammy glanced around and lowered her voice. "You mean prostitution?"

"I do."

"No way," she said. "One of the girls did it, and he canned her the next day."

"Was Donna having a thing with the dentist?"

"Maybe," Corky said.

She slowly spun her coffee cup around in her fingers. Sammy slouched in her chair. I waited.

No more questions. Let's see what happens.

"I was at work on the Sunday before Donna was killed," Corky finally blurted out. "Lorenz came in and, after he ordered a beer, he asked me about my breasts. I told him to get outta my face."

I glanced down at her chest. "I can't blame any man for noticing your breasts. They are impressive."

She blushed. "Thank you."

"Yours are too, Sammy."

"Do you really think so?" she asked.

"I do, and I'm sure you get asked about them all the time," I said. "Does the operation hurt much?"

"For me, the first operation killed, especially the menstrual cramps," she said. "The implants were 650 cc, and the surgeon put them under my chest muscle. But it wasn't as painful the second time."

"The second time?"

"Mr. al-Turk didn't like the way the first implants looked and felt. And he said they were too firm, not realistic enough. Molly said the same thing."

"Molly?"

"One day at the gym, she spotted them when we were working out. She let me feel hers, and she was right. Mine were like hard lumps of clay compared to hers. This pair is way better." She thrust out her chest. "And bigger, 875 cc. Do you want to feel them?"

I leaned back in my chair. "I'll leave that to Molly. Corky, what about you?"

"Donna and Sammy had theirs done first. I was scheduled for mine, but before I had it done, both of them had theirs redone. The second time, theirs were much better, so I did it. These implants feel totally natural."

"You seem to have complete confidence in your surgeon. Did Donna like him too?"

"She did," Corky said. "It's hard not to like him. He's so kind."

"And he's free," Sammy said.

Free?

"It's one of the advantages of working for Mr. al-Turk," Corky said.

Before I could ask them any more questions, Sammy glanced at her watch.

"I have to leave," she said. "I go on at three o'clock."

"Would you like to come to my house for lunch and to meet my daughter?" I said, hoping to keep the girl talk going. "Playing with a toddler will take your minds off of what happened to Donna. Kerry goes a million miles an hour."

"That would be great," Corky said. "I love kids."

We exchanged cell numbers, and I gave them a hug.

Free breast implant surgery? I need a consult.

100

From Starbucks, I walked to Linda's to pick up Kerry, but first made a quick detour and dropped by the home of my breast implant expert.

"What's up?" Molly asked, as she opened her front door. I heard her kids yelling at each other in the background.

"I need information about augmentation mammoplasties," I said.

She stared at me.

"Boob jobs," I continued.

"Oh, right. Are you thinking about having one?"

"No, but I'm kind of curious. Have you had one?"

"One? Honey, I've had four."

"Did it hurt?"

"God, it's hard to remember exactly, but I think the saline ones hurt more. The surgeon put them under the muscle."

"What about menstrual cramps after the operations?"

"None. The only time I've ever had bad ones was after the doctor harvested my eggs for my IVF. He said it was common after the egg retrieval."

"Did it hurt?"

"It sure did but not as much as my tummy-tuck."

"You had that done too?"

"Tina, having four kids ruined how I look in my bikini bottoms. With the last breast implants, the surgeon tightened up my stomach muscles and removed floppy skin." She blushed. "And he did me a little other work, you know, down there."

She pointed at her groin. I understood what she meant, but we were getting sidetracked.

"How are the implants inserted?"

"I had three through a nipple incision and the last one under the breast. But they can be implanted through a belly button incision or from the armpit. I haven't had that done because the surgeon said that would be painful."

"Have you ever heard about breast implant surgery being done for free?"

"Never. Greg calls them my million-dollar boobs, and he has the bills from the surgeons to prove it."

"If it costs that much, why have you had four?"

"I had my first operation when I started modeling. I did it to make my boobs pert and perky."

"How big were the implants?"

"250 cc."

"Kinda small."

"The designers didn't want them to distract from the lines of their clothes."

"I can see that. Why did you have them changed?"

"After Chase was born, my boobs drooped. Plus, they were saline implants, and they became all ripply. I couldn't have that."

"And you had them replaced."

"I did."

"And made bigger?"

"As long as I was going through the pain, why not?"

"Exactly. And Rex and then Stevie came along."

"A silicone pair for Rex, 650 cc, and a new silicone pair for Stevie, 800 cc."

"What about Cory?"

"Mastopexy. Same implant size, but the surgeon added a tuck-up of the skin to lift my boobs...again."

"Then technically, it wasn't an augmentation."

"Nope, and he did a tummy-tuck and vaginal rejuvenation at the same time."

"What do you think about Sammy and Donna's breast surgeries?"

"Let me tell you, the first ones felt weird, like the doctor had used an out-of-date batch of silicone. Way too firm. But the revisions are as good as mine, maybe better." She began to unbutton her blouse. "Wanna feel?"

What's with all this boob feeling?

I held up my hands. "I'll get back to you on that one."

"Whatever. Do you want to see the ones they took out?"

"You have them?"

"Yep. Greg said they'd cost so much he wanted them as a souvenir for all the money he spent. He keeps them on his desk."

Molly went into Greg's home office and came back with a box. She handed two implants to me.

"This is Rex's 650 cc silicone pair."

They were teardrop-shaped, and each one was about the size of a cantaloupe. I squeezed the implants. They felt like a baggie full of squishy jelly.

She held up two flat implants. "These are my saline ones, without the saline of course."

"What's this thing here?" I asked, pointing to what looked a valve. "Your other implants don't have it."

"It's where the doctor injects the saline after he inserts the implants."

Rolling the silicone implants around in my hands, I discovered six numbers on the back of each set.

"What's this?" I asked.

"All of the implants have a serial number."

"Why?"

"My doctor said it's so the company that makes them can follow the results of the surgery for complications. It began with the silicone scare a few years ago."

As I walked home, I had difficulty picturing a rippled breast. But I was thrilled she didn't want to show off her vaginal rejuvenation scars.

101

Thursday evening, Kerry played on the kitchen floor with Elmo and Ralph while I cooked sweet-and-sour chicken for dinner. As I stirred the sugar, vinegar, and pineapple juice together in a saucepan, my mind kept drifting to al-Turk's story.

The FBI agents have access to the two GPS devices Lorenz attached to my van. And they saw me at Donna's funeral.

Adding in the ketchup and soy sauce, I let the mixture simmer on low heat while I cut the chicken into bite-sized pieces.

Tony said two or three agents would be watching my house and al-Turk's.

I was going to have to be aware of new people in the neighborhood.

What else can they do to track me?

After rolling the chicken pieces into the flour-and-egg mixture, I cooked them in a pan with a smidge of oil.

I wiped my hands and focused on my landline phone. Picking up the receiver, I removed the screw and plastic covering to expose the guts of the apparatus. I poked and prodded, but if an electronic listening device were in place, I couldn't find it. I screwed the phone back together and put it down.

I studied the kitchen. The feds might put devices in places they didn't think I was sophisticated enough to find.

But they're wrong.

Removing the cooked chicken pieces from the pan, I put them on a paper towel and carried my daughter down to the laundry room. I retrieved my electronic scanning device, a rectangular black box about the size of a deck of playing cards. When I flipped the power switch, the green light came on. It immediately went out and the red light flashed on.

Uh-oh.

I walked around the lower level with Kerry in my arms and pointed the box in all directions. In each room the light remained red. I made two circuits while waving the box around. The result was the same until I went into the wine room. There, the light turned green.

Safe in here.

Stepping out of the wine room, I glanced at my computer. If they had gone to the trouble of bugging my home, it wasn't much of a stretch to assume they would monitor my computer too.

Gotta call Linda.

I would ask her to come over tomorrow and check my computer. But I had to buy a burner phone to do that. The feds would not only listen in on what I said in my home, but they would monitor my landline and cell phone.

"Kerry, let's go upstairs. I'll let you play with this black box. Let's see if you can make the light turn green."

It took fifteen minutes but she couldn't; with the exception of the wine room, our entire house was bugged.

102

Friday morning, I called Linda, and she dropped by with her daughter, Sandra. I took the girls out to play with me in the sandbox. Linda went down to the lower level to work on my computer.

It didn't take long.

Fifteen minutes later, she joined us in the heat and wind.

"Do you know what a keystroke logger is?" she asked.

"No, I've never heard of it," I said.

"It's a software package that captures what's written on a computer keyboard, allowing offsite personnel to spy on every keystroke that is typed on the keyboard."

"Please don't tell me I now have one on my computer."

"I'm sorry to say you do. Could anyone have broken in here and done this?"

"Doubtful. We have a security system. Is there any other way to install one?"

"There's a keystroke logging software called Magic Lantern that was developed by the FBI. It can be installed remotely via an email attachment."

"Then I wouldn't know my computer had been compromised."

"Why would the FBI do this to you?"

Gotta fess up.

"This is strictly confidential. Cas and Molly don't know any of this."

I told her about the new intel on al-Turk.

"Al-Turk is a drug dealer, and the FBI agents were after him?" she asked, when I finished.

"The FBI and possibly the DEA. But I'm curious. Hasn't anybody in the FBI read our Constitution?"

"Apparently not. The FBI denies Magic Lantern has ever been deployed."

"But it has?"

"Of course it has."

"Can the feds access the data on my hard drive?"

"No, they can't retrieve the files already in place, but they'll record all words and characters you type on your keyboard from now on."

I felt heat rise up my neck. "They can't do this to me."

"But they did, and you can't prove it. It's the beauty of their system. Does Carter use your computer?"

"Rarely. He carries his *Tribune* laptop home and uses it. I'm the only one who is screwed."

"Actually, you're not. You know it's there. Don't type any information on your computer you don't want them to have."

"Makes sense, but I still don't like it."

Linda and Sandra went home. Kerry and I returned to the kitchen. As I cleaned up the breakfast dishes, I stared at Lorenz's house.

Tony had given the FBI my name when they called him about the trash samples with the C4, and Lorenz was promptly dispatched to Chicago to investigate me. When I drove to the Twenties on Wednesday, Lorenz either followed me or used the GPS device to track where I drove during the day. On Thursday night, Molly saw Lorenz at the Twenties when he began expanding his investigation.

After Lorenz was blown up and his computer stolen, I was the only remaining lead the FBI had. Following me was the easiest way to find out what was going on. The keystroke logger was another way for them to continue their investigation.

I envisioned the trajectory of a fabulous story in my mind, but how was I going to work on it with the FBI monitoring all of my activities?

Buying a burner phone was now my top priority.

103

Saturday morning, Carter had gone in to work. Driving in my van without the FBI tracking where I went was impossible. I couldn't use my computer without them recording what I typed. And I needed a backup if they figured out a way to erase my files using another top secret cyberspace program. I went down to the computer room and downloaded the contents of my hard drive onto a flash drive.

Now, I need to hide it.

The wine room was a possibility, but I wasn't sure what the constant fifty-four degree temperature would do to the functioning of the flash drive. I settled on the laundry room, where I put it under a pile of rags.

That accomplished, my next task was to buy a burner phone. I took Kerry, Elmo, Ralph, and the stroller out on the front porch and glanced around the neighborhood.

The library!

"Let's visit the library and then buy Mommy a new phone."

"Okay, Momma. Elmo wuvs the wibrary."

The public library sits across North Paulina, directly east of our home. After I walked across the street, I looked at the building and then back toward our home.

A perfect sightline.

Tony said the FBI would select a location where they could watch al-Turk's house and ours. And the feds were on a limited budget. The library provided an ideal vantage point to do it without being spotted, and the cost was minimal: cameras and monitors with recording capabilities, and an agent to watch them.

From my many trips to the library, I knew the main room was about fifteen feet high. There were no standard windows facing the outside because bookshelves stood head-high in front of all the walls. To provide light, small rectangular windows had been built close to the ceiling, about fifteen feet from the floor. No one was tall enough to see in or out, but those windows would be the perfect place for video surveillance cameras.

I shielded my eyes from the sun and scanned the windows. *There it is.*

A video camera sat in the last window on the south side. It rotated back and forth scanning our home. A second camera was in the window above my head. It was pointed at al-Turk's home.

What about al-Turk's alley?

Pushing Kerry north on Paulina, I approached the alley. I checked the trees and the houses on each side for a camera.

There they are.

There were two cameras hidden high in the trees on each side of the alley. They were oriented toward al-Turk's garage.

There was one more thing I had to do. I pushed the stroller around the block and approached the library from the east side, away from the cameras watching our home.

I lingered in the entrance doorway. When I saw her, I congratulated myself on how smart I'd been to peek inside the library. One of Lorenz's probable replacements sat behind a desk to my right in the front corner of the library. She had her back turned to me and stared at three monitors that were a different brand than the rest of the computer equipment in the library.

Government issue?

The woman stood up and stepped into a glassed-in office located behind the desk with the three monitors. She had short blond hair and wore a white blouse and black slacks. I spotted her plain, black shoes. They screamed comfort, a necessity if you needed to follow a suspect on foot.

I leaned closer to her monitors. I could only see the one on the left but I recognized what was on the screen: our front porch.

Turning the stroller around, I walked away before the agent spotted me. Now, I had their cameras to worry about too.

The feds are boxing me in.

104

Sunday was a family day for us. Monday afternoon, Tony texted me to contact him about the swabs I'd given him. Kerry and I had been at the park, and now she napped in her room. I went to the wine room and called him on my new burner phone.

"Got the lab report from the swabs you took from the perp's garage," Tony said. "It's heroin. They didn't find any C4."

Finally, documented proof.

"Now what?" I asked.

"When the report came in, I went downstairs and drank a cup of coffee with the narcs. Couple of days ago, they busted a low-level dealer pushing a small amount of high-grade heroin."

"How high?"

"Too primo for a dude that far down on the drug distribution chain. Perp didn't want to give up his source because the product hadn't been stepped down. Wanted to keep it for himself."

"What did they do?"

"A little gentle coaxing. He finally admitted he bought it from a new guy on the street."

"Who was it?"

"Guy from the Middle East."

I let out the breath I'd been holding in. "Looks like Mr. al-Turk is a drug dealer."

"Or it's all a set-up."

Is that even possible?

"Why would he do that?"

"Wouldn't. Bad guys don't like working any harder than they have to."

"You vote drugs?"

"Unless I'm missing something, I do."

"At least I can narrow the focus of my investigation. What else?"

"Autopsy showed the vics were tied face-to-face. Bomb made of C4 was placed between them."

"Where was the detonator?"

"Bomb squad chief thinks it was small, probably about the size of a deck of cards because it had to be pretty close to the device."

"Did your guys find Lorenz's house key at his dental office?"

"Not sure they searched for it. Why?"

"The killers came into his house after they blew up the victims. I think they took the key from him before the device was detonated."

"I'll check the murder book."

"As long as you're at it, read the autopsy report and see if the ME could tell if Lorenz or the girl might have been tortured before the explosion."

"Why?"

"Even if the killers had Lorenz's key, they still needed the code to his home's security system and that would be the quickest way to get it. Plus, they stole his computer and they needed his password to access his files."

"I'll check on it too."

"What about the DNA I gave you from Lorenz's bathroom? Did your captain okay the money for the test?"

"Only after he read the report about the heroin. But the lab didn't get any hits."

"Darn it. I was positive they would."

"Don't want you to be surprised, but I had to send the C4 residue from the dentist's office to the feds. Asked them to compare it to the C4 our lab found on the trash you stole."

"Good idea."

"But the report might not come to me."

"Why?"

"Captain wants to move the murder investigation to Narcotics."

Crap.

"Because of the heroin?"

"You got it."

"Are you off the case?"

"Kind of, but no way I'm givin' up a double homicide. I'll keep workin' the girls at the Twenties, but off the clock."

"Good. I need your help."

"But hangin' out with all those strippers is wearing me out."

"I have a suggestion. Maybe you need a couple of those blue pills for all of your 'hard work.' "

"*Hard* work! That's a good one. Gotta remember that."

It shouldn't be difficult. What else do you think about?

105

Tuesday morning, Kerry and I were playing outside in her sandbox when my cell phone rang.

"Tina, this is Corky Gibson. I wanted to call and tell you goodbye."

"Goodbye?"

"Uh-huh. You were super nice talking to us about Donna and all, and I wanted you to know we're leaving."

"Where are you going?"

"I'm going to San Francisco, and Sammy's moving to L.A."

"Wow. That seems sudden. Why?"

"Mr. al-Turk promised to make us featured performers in his new clubs there."

"Congratulations. Are you excited?"

"We all are, for sure."

"All?"

"A bunch of us from the Twenties are going to new locations he is opening all over the country."

"I would love to say goodbye to you face-to-face before you leave. Why don't we meet at Hamlin Park after my daughter's morning nap? Say around eleven?"

"You don't have to do that."

"Please. I want to."

Because I need one last interview.

"Okay, see you there."

At eleven o'clock, Corky and Sammy arrived in the black GMC Envoy. Sammy drove. I pushed Kerry on the swings. In their tight-fitting exercise outfits, they would draw more attention than I would in my mommy uniform of blue shorts and a white top.

Corky stooped down to greet Kerry. "Who is this cutie?"

"My daughter, Kerry," I said. "Kerry, this is Corky and Sammy.

Kerry held up Elmo and Ralph.

"I'm sorry, Honey." I pointed at her two companions. "These are Kerry's friends, Elmo and Ralph."

"Is it okay if I pick Kerry up?" Corky asked.

"Sure, but don't forget Elmo and Ralph."

"Let's go play on the jungle gym with your friends," she said.

She took Kerry out of the swing and slowly twirled her over her head. Kerry giggled. She walked to the jungle gym with my daughter and her two friends.

Sammy and I sat down on my favorite bench. I reached into my backpack and took out my knitting. I needed to relax and really focus because it was my last time to interview them.

"Are you excited about leaving?" I asked.

"Kind of," Sammy said. "We'll miss Chicago, but we've worked the dancing circuit in other clubs around the Midwest. Moving is part of the business. Making new friends is too."

"Are you going to miss your doctor?"

"Doctor?"

"The one who did your breast surgery."

Her voice became hard. "I'm not supposed to talk about it."

Easy. Don't lose her.

"I realize that. I'm asking because I have a friend on the police force who is working the case to find out who killed Donna."

"Is the cop named Tony?"

"You know him?"

"He's been hanging around the club and has questioned all of us dancers."

"Did he ask about the doctor?"

"He did, but I blew him off."

"He's trying to pick up any loose ends on the case, and since there's a dentist involved, he's investigating the doctor too."

"I get that."

Ask her right now.

"What's the doctor's name?"

"It's like Dr. Middleton or whatever."

I stopped knitting. "What did you say?"

"Middleton or Mittelman." She furrowed her brow. "That's it, Mittelman."

106

"What did you say?" I repeated, hoping I'd misunderstood her.

"His name is Dr. Mittelman," Sammy said.

You have to be wrong!

Micah could not be the surgeon working with al-Turk. I began to sweat, and it wasn't from the humid Chicago weather. "Where does Dr. Mittelman do the surgery?"

"At his office."

"Where's it located?"

"It's in a brand new surgery center around the corner from the Twenties."

Is it the building I saw when I drove past the Twenties?

"How do you know the surgery center is new?"

"The first time I went in, there were plastic covers on a couple of the chairs."

"Is it a busy place?"

"Don't think so. The girls from the club are the only people I've ever seen there. And our apartment building is on the corner across the street from it. We can have our surgery and go right home."

It is that building.

Why was Micah doing breast augmentation surgery? He definitely didn't need the money.

"Did Lorenz ever ask you about your breast surgery?"

"Yeah. He did at the Twenties on the Saturday night before Donna died. I remember because Corky said he questioned her about her boobs on Sunday."

"She mentioned that to me too. She told him to get out of her face."

"I did too."

"Why do you think Lorenz asked you about the surgery?"

She stared down at her hands. "See, ah, Donna got drunk on Friday night and told him about her surgery. She was terrified Mr. al-Turk would find out, and she begged us not to bust her out to him."

Friday was when I'd seen Donna go into the dentist's house. "When did she tell you about it?"

"On Saturday morning, when she finally got back to our apartment building. She was super hung over, and she didn't want Mr. al-Turk to know about that, either, because we aren't supposed to drink."

"Did al-Turk ever find out that Donna told Lorenz about the breast surgeries?"

Sammy's face turned red. "We didn't mean to, but Mr. al-Turk called me and Corky into his office on Monday morning. He started screaming and threatened to fire us if we didn't tell him about Donna and Lorenz."

"And did you?"

She nodded but remained silent.

Corky brought Kerry and her two companions back to me. I gazed at the empty swings, digesting what I'd just heard.

"Tina?" Sammy asked. "Are you okay?"

"What? Right... Sorry, I was having a moment."

Corky and Sammy were my only witnesses to whatever was going on, and they were moving.

107

Keep pushing!

I had to take the risk they would catch on that I was asking way too many questions.

"When are you guys leaving?" I asked.

"We were scheduled to move in late September, but that's all changed," Sammy said.

"Changed?"

"We're leaving Thursday, which is why I called to say goodbye," Corky said.

The lump in my stomach felt like it would explode. "Thursday? Like two days from now?"

"It is," Sammy confirmed. "My plane leaves O'Hare first at five o'clock in the afternoon. Corky and the other girls leave after that. But Mr. al-Turk said we should all be there by two at the latest."

"Other girls?"

"There are nine of us going to different cities," Corky said. "Mr. al-Turk gave us our tickets this morning."

"Are you all flying out of O'Hare?"

Sammy nodded. "We are."

"Is Jamie driving you to there?"

"Nope," Corky said. "All of us can't fit into Jamie's SUV with our luggage. Mr. al-Turk gave us cab fare."

"By the way, what's Jamie's last name?"

"Gosh, I don't think he ever said, and I sure never asked," Sammy said. "Do you know, Corky?"

She shook her head. "No."

Kerry began playing in the wood chips with Elmo. Ralph watched. I put down my knitting and watched too. I didn't want another wood chip catastrophe with Kerry's airway.

"Al-Turk is being nice to you," I said.

"He sure is," Corky said. "We're supposed to meet at the United Room South on the B concourse, and one of his guys will give us extra expense money."

"What about your furniture and personal items?"

"We don't have to worry about that. Our apartments are furnished, and our new ones will be too. We can take two suitcases, and Mr. al-Turk will have Jamie send the rest to us."

"Seems well organized."

"I guess, but there's like this big rush for all of us to leave Chicago," Sammy said. "And nobody is telling us why."

"But don't forget the bonus," Corky said.

"Bonus?" I asked.

"After a couple girls bitched about moving so fast, Mr. al-Turk gave us each five thousand dollars cash for extra expenses."

And to keep your and your friends' mouths shut.

108

They drove away. I secured Kerry in the stroller and pushed her home from Hamlin Park. On the way, I called Linda on my burner phone and told her what I'd learned from Corky and Sammy.

"Wow," Linda said. "I don't know what to say."

"I need documented proof of the breast surgeries. Do you think Micah kept records of the operations?"

"I have no idea, but as a physician and scientist, I'm sure he's used to keeping files about all of his work."

"Do you think it's in his computer?"

"It's where I would keep it, but I wouldn't do it at my lab. I would store it on my computer at home."

"And if the information is there, can you hack into his hard drive without his password?"

"All I need is physical access to his computer."

"Last Monday, Molly mentioned Hannah might have all of us over the middle of this week. I'll text Molly and see if she can set up the play date for tomorrow morning."

"And while the moms and kids are playing, I'll download the data from Micah's hard drive."

"Without going room to room, how are you going to be sure where the computer is?"

"I'll hack into the power grid to their house," she said. "It'll show me where his computer is being used."

"Great. I'll text Molly and set it up."

109

When Kerry and I returned home, we had a snack and went downstairs to my computer. I texted Molly about having a play date at Hannah's house the next day. My daughter began yawning. I put her in the portable bed and she fell asleep.

I stepped into the wine room and called Linda on my burner phone.

"I'm going to text you the pictures of the apartment building behind the Twenties and the non-descript building around the corner from it. I need to run the addresses, but I can't use my computer keyboard."

"Got it. I'll text you back on your new cell phone when I have the information."

Twenty minutes later, Linda texted. The apartment building had been purchased on April first, the same day al-Turk closed on the sale of the Twenties. The Arun Corporation owned it. The other building had been purchased the same day, but the Chicago Surgery Center, LLC was listed as the owner. It was a shell company which was also owned by the Arun Corporation.

She found building permits registered to an Illinois company that did build-outs for outpatient surgery centers. The certificate for the operation of that center had been filed with the state medical association on April fifteenth and the permits to open for business had been issued on June twenty-second.

The two purchases and the certification to operate a surgery center were building blocks for my story. If the breast surgeries were done there, I had to know when those procedures began to prove my story.

Hopefully, it would be on Micah's computer.

Part 5

110

Molly had come through with her assignment. On Wednesday morning, I walked into Hannah's home to help Linda break into Micah's computer. Kerry and Elmo were in my arms. Ralph was in my backpack.

"Hannah, your home is stunning," I said, as I walked into her family room. "I love your art."

"They are original pieces I inherited from my parents."

My interest in Hannah's home had more to do with checking for internal security cameras than with the original Renoir painting of a yellow flower hanging over her couch. There were the external cameras I'd seen before, but I didn't spy any inside.

The house itself was at least twice as large as ours. Linda's home had been professionally and tastefully decorated. Hannah's interior was a huge step up from that. The furniture and *objets d'art* could have come straight out of *Architectural Digest*.

Linda and Sandra arrived right behind me. As an accomplished hostess, Hannah switched her attention to Linda.

"Welcome to our home," she said, effortlessly placing her right hand on Linda's shoulder.

Wow! She IS better.

"Thank you for inviting us," Linda said. "Where is your kitchen? I need to plate up the treats I brought."

"Just there, down the hall and to your left."

Linda never brought food for playgroup, but Hannah had no way of knowing that. Linda would have plenty of time to hack into Micah's computer while the rest of us played with our kids.

Linda went to the kitchen. I took Sandra with Kerry and me. Hannah led us down to the lower level. She walked without a limp.

I glanced around. "Hannah, where is your manny? Molly told me all about him."

"He is presently not staying with us because I'm feeling much better."

No kidding.

The playroom looked like a branch of Toys "R" Us. "Your kids are fortunate to have all these toys to play with," I said.

"I am a little embarrassed, but Micah cannot say 'no' to our children. If they ask him for a toy, he buys it."

The doorbell rang, announcing the arrival of the remaining playgroup members. Hannah went back upstairs and brought them down. A few minutes later, Linda rushed downstairs. There were droplets of sweat on her forehead.

"The food will be ready shortly, but I need a little help," Linda said. "Tina, could you lend me a hand?"

Linda remained silent until we stepped into the kitchen. She whipped around to face me. "The door to Micah's study is locked."

"No problem," I said. "Be right back."

I retrieved my backpack from the foyer, carried it into the kitchen, and showed her my electric lock pick and torque wrench.

"What is that?" she asked.

"A little device that is going to get us into his office."

"I don't know how to work it."

"But I do. I'll let you in and you can do the hack."

"Okay, but Hannah might wonder what's taking so long with the food," she said.

"We can tag-team it," I said. "I'll let you in, and you start the download. You leave and relock the door."

"And you go back in about fifteen minutes and shut down his computer."

"Tell me how to do it."

Linda wrote the instructions on a piece of paper and showed me a flash drive. "Follow the instructions and remove this when the download is complete."

"Where's his office?"

"Follow me."

I grabbed my backpack, and we went down the hall, stopping at the second door. It was locked. All I had to do was insert the gun's picking needles into the lock and go to work. It took less than thirty seconds, and I opened the door.

"I'll start the hack and lock the door when I leave," she said.

"Great." I said, as I turned around and went back to the rest of the group.

111

Eight minutes later, Linda walked into the playroom with a tray of dishes piled high with sandwiches, chips, and fruit. I sniffed and spied a stack of chocolate chip cookies.

I stood up to help her serve and grabbed a cookie. "Did you make this?" I whispered.

"You know me better than that," Linda whispered back. "I called John Benker, my mother's caterer, and he prepared everything. All I did was put it on Hannah's plates." She glanced around. "You better get going."

Once I was back upstairs, I used my equipment to unlock the door again to let myself into Micah's study. On the opposite side of the room sat an antique French desk with a computer on the top. The hard drive hummed, and it appeared the download was finished. I stepped into the room, closed and locked the door, and dropped the tools into my backpack.

Sitting down at Micah's computer, I followed Linda's instructions to shut it down. Before I could remove the flash drive, I heard a key in the lock and then the door opening behind me. That was followed by a sound I recognized — a bullet being chambered into a gun's barrel.

I turned around. A bearded young man stood in the doorway. He pointed a gun at my chest.

Oh, my, God!

It was Hannah's driver/manny. He wasn't smiling. "I want that flash drive from Dr. Mittelman's computer." He had an English accent.

I have to distract him.

My voice croaked. "Do we know each other?"

My heart pounded so hard I thought he could see it banging against my sternum.

"No."

I cleared my throat. "But I'm sure I've seen you in the neighborhood."

He gestured toward the computer with the gun. "Enough! Give me the flash drive."

"Flash drive?" I asked. "I have no idea what you're talking about."

"I think you do," he said, stepping into the room. The odor of cigarettes drifted in with him.

My backpack!

Maybe I could fool him with what I had in it. I stood up and used it to block his view of the computer.

Unexpectedly, Hannah appeared in the doorway. "Tina, your daughter began whimpering, and I came looking for you," she announced. "What is going on?"

The man turned around to face her. He lowered the gun to his side, hiding it from her view. I reached into a side pocket of my backpack and palmed the flash drive I'd shoved in there after my failure to access Lorenz's hard drive.

"I was touring your fabulous home," I said. "It's exactly what Carter and I have been hunting for, and honestly, I was stealing a few of your decorating ideas."

Along with the contents from your husband's hard drive.

"In Micah's office?" she asked.

As my lie took on a life of its own, I began to do a mini Tina-two-step. I continued to clutch my backpack in front of me to conceal what I was about to do.

"Carter and I are into offices. You know how writers are."

My right hand touched the computer as Hannah turned to the man.

"Farhad, Tina is a guest in my home. You do not have to worry about her. She is no threat to me or the children."

He glared at her. "My job is to help you if there is a problem, and this is what I am doing." The gun remained at his side hidden from Hannah's sightline.

While they talked, I switched Linda's flash drive for mine. I stepped forward and took Hannah by the arm. I guided her into the hallway and ignored Farhad.

"I love how you've displayed your family pictures," I gushed.

She turned back toward the office. "Let me show you how Mr. Berry, our interior designer, did it."

I glanced over her shoulder as Farhad reached out to remove my empty flash drive. I clamped my hand on her arm and rotated her toward me, hoping she wouldn't see what he was doing.

"No, it's okay," I said. "Let's join the kids."

As we stepped further into the hallway, Hannah glanced at the office door. "This is strange. Micah always locks the door to his office. It is off limits to the children. Was it unlocked when you came in?"

"It was. It's possible he didn't lock it because he has so much on his mind." I turned around. "I'm sure Farhad can lock up for you."

"I will." He flipped the empty flash drive up and caught it. "I have what I need."

112

"Did you get the flash drive?" Linda asked, as we walked out of Hannah's front door.

"Have it in my backpack, but now what do I do with it?" I asked.

"Meaning the keystroke logger on your computer."

"I do. I don't want the feds to know what we're doing."

"Let's go to my house and use my computers."

"I hoped you would say that."

Twenty minutes later, we walked into Linda's computer room. Her nanny took over and played with our daughters. I shivered after going from the mid-nineties outside heat to the frigid room, which was no more than sixty-five degrees. The air smelled artificial. And there was a low hum from the servers. Three computer screens sat on her desk. On the far wall were six more wall-mounted units.

"I feel like I'm on the flight deck of the Starship Enterprise," I said. "How long did it take you to build this?"

"When I gave up on music in college and switched to computer science, my parents went a trifle overboard one Hanukkah. It was my first expensive computer. They kept adding to it."

I handed the flash drive to her. "Let's do it."

She inserted it into her main computer. I pulled up a chair and watched over her shoulder. There were three sections.

"The first one is titled 'the Hamlin Park Irregulars,' " she said.

"I recognize this," I said, pointing at the screen. "It's background information about me, Carter, and Kerry."

"But not your names."

"And you're in there with your family."

"But we're not named either."

"Cas is in here, too, with her family."

"And Molly with hers but, again, without any of their names."

"Wonder what the 'Hamlin Park Irregulars' means?" I asked.

"Micah spent a lot of time in England," she said. "I bet he became a fan of Sherlock Holmes and his Baker Street Irregulars. He might have used this as a code name for all of us."

"Why?"

"I'm not sure. Maybe he worried that a keystroke logger had been installed on his computer."

But who would do that?

113

The second section had a spreadsheet with five vertical columns. There were twenty-two rows in the first column, each row beginning with two capitalized letters. It took half an hour to analyze the data.

"The first column has to be initials of the breast surgery patients," Linda said.

"But I don't know a stripper with the initials SK," I said. "Or the next two, TT and HG."

Using my burner phone, I called my stripper expert and put him on speaker. Linda leaned close to listen.

"Tony, do you know any of the stripper's names from the Twenties?"

"Know 'em all."

"Do any of them have the initials SK, TT, or HG?"

"That would be their stage names."

"Which are...?"

"Donna Allen's stage name was SK for Special K. Sammy Simmons is TT for Topsy Turvy. And Corky Gibson is HG for Hoot Gibson and her 45's."

I checked the second column of the spreadsheet. There were two different six-digit numbers next to SK. I saw the same thing by TT. Each of the next eight initials only had one six-digit number. I remembered the identification numbers on Molly's implants.

"Do you have access to Donna's autopsy report from the murder book?"

"Got it right here."

"What does the medical examiner report about her breast implants?"

I heard him flip through the pages of the murder book. "ME wrote there were a couple of numbers on the pieces of the implants recovered at the scene. He followed that lead and discovered the implants came from the Nagor Company in the UK. He talked to their head man who said that the implants had to be specially ordered because of their large size."

I pictured Molly's saline implants. "Did the man from Nagor mention a valve of some kind?"

"Implants were ordered with a valve for the filler to be injected during surgery."

"Did he say what the filler was?"

"Nothing in here about that."

"What were the numbers the medical examiner recovered?"

"He found an eight and two. According to the company, there should have been six. ME indicates he was lucky to find any numbers considering the force of the blast."

"Did the Nagor guy say when the first ones were delivered and where they were sent?"

"June twenty-first, but apparently he wouldn't give the ME any more information without a court order. Why all the questions?"

"Working the story. Like you said, I used to be a big shot reporter. I'll let you know what I find." I paused. "And I do not have a fat ass!"

114

"Okay, we have the name problem solved," I said.

"And we have the serial numbers of the implants, the dates of the first surgeries, the two revision surgeries, and the sizes of the implants that were inserted," Linda said.

"Plus, the schedule for the twelve implants to be done on the other strippers later in August," I said. "Do you think the strippers are mules carrying drugs in their new breasts?"

"Nine girls couldn't carry enough drugs to make this whole operation profitable. What are we missing?"

We went back to the spreadsheet.

"The fifth column is the only one we haven't figured out," she said, pointing at the computer screen.

"It lists CTDSP along with 70 cc of SAE 10 non-detergent motor oil twice on June twenty-third, with 70 cc and 135 cc in all the other entries."

"What's CTDSP?"

"Haven't a clue."

"Until we figure it out, we can't go much further."

"Let's check the last section."

It was written in an encryption code.

"Can you crack this?" I asked.

Her fingers raced over the keyboard. "This was done by an expert. I'm having trouble opening it."

"What now?"

"The solution might be in Micah's computer."

"This is from Micah's computer."

She raised her eyebrows. "Oh, right. I mean the one in his lab."

"What do we do?"

"You play with those letters. Use that computer on your left. I'll work on this."

I took out my knitting and began a new row as I went over the entire saga in my head. Twenty rows later, I had it.

"Oh my God!" I said. "I figured it out."

"What?"

"CTDSP stands for the chemical formula cyclotrimethylene trinitramine; dioctyl sebacate; and polyisobutelene."

"Which is?"

"C4."

115

"I am such a dummy!" I said. "Tony told me the police lab found heroin residue on al-Turk's garage door, which convinced me that he was a drug dealer using the Twenties to launder money."

"But he's not?" Linda asked.

"He still could be, but it looks like he's a terrorist having Micah inject C4 as the filler for the breast implants."

"Do you think he purchased the strip club to give him an endless supply of young women to unwittingly carry the bombs?"

"It makes sense. Tony said C4 can be molded into any shape. From my research on the abortion clinic bombings, I discovered the viscosity of C4 can be varied by making it into a slurry using SAE 10 non-detergent motor oil as a solvent to dissolve the chemical binder of the C4."

SAE?

"I think I can prove it. Can you access the files from my computer?"

"You're kidding, right?"

In two minutes, she put up the pictures I snapped while the two men unloaded the boxes into al-Turk's garage. On one box were the letters "SA". She enlarged the letters. We could now see part of an "E," proving motor oil had been delivered to his garage.

"The SAE is listed in the fifth column of the spread sheet along with the CTDSP," she said.

"The implants were ordered with valves, allowing the C4 to be injected into them without the patients knowing what was in the chemical makeup of the mixture."

"Do you think Micah harvested eggs from the strippers during the surgery?"

"Great question. I'll call Corky."

I put her on speaker. I needed a simple question first. "I'm still helping Detective Infantino with the investigation. He needs your address here in Chicago."

Corky told me, and I entered it on the computer. I pointed at my files, which Linda still had up on one of her screens. It was the same address for the apartment building behind the Twenties. I mouthed "more proof" to Linda.

"Got time for one more question?" I asked.

"Sure, if it helps catch the creep who did this to Donna."

"Didn't you say you had menstrual cramps after your breast surgery?"

"Did I ever. That pain was almost worse than my chest."

"Did you have any vaginal bleeding with it?"

"Yeah, I did, and it's kinda weird, you know? That part of me is a long way from my boobs."

"Did Mittelman say why it happened?"

"He said it was the way he did the operation and, since it was free, we should stop complaining. We were afraid he would tell al-Turk, and we shut up." She paused. "Oh, and he gave us gigantic shots in our butts a month before he did our boobs. It killed. Sammy got a bruise so big she had to put makeup on it."

Gotcha, Micah.

I hung up. "He used those strippers to provide his supply of human female eggs."

116

"Looks like we were wrong about Micah being such a nice guy," Linda said.

"No kidding," I said.

"As an officer of the court, I have to advise you that we need to tell those girls they might be walking bombs."

"But what if we're wrong and their implants are full of silicone and not C4?"

She pulled out a yellow legal pad from her desk. "Let's list what you have."

"Don't you want to use your computer?"

"I'm a lawyer. This is the way I always do it." She paused. "Just like you do with your knitting when you need to relax and think."

"Ten girls received breast implants, all done by Micah in an outpatient surgery center owned by a shell corporation, which is controlled by the Arun Corporation," I began.

She wrote it down.

"The Arun Corporation also owns al-Turk's home, two vehicles he uses, a GMC, and the apartment building the girls live in rent-free."

She shrugged. "You haven't shown me any concrete facts."

"The money came from JDL and Associates in Luxembourg."

"And?"

"And what do we know about them?" I asked.

"I still haven't been able to crack into their computers," she said. "Sorry."

"Okay, how about this? Sammy's breasts were redone because Mr. al-Turk didn't like them."

"What does that prove?"

"Maybe he needs them to be as natural as possible to pass a manual inspection at the airport, if it comes to that."

"Or he simply wants his strippers to have more realistic breasts to please his customers."

"What about the human female eggs?"

"Good. What do you have other than what Corky just said?"

"Micah injected the strippers with chemicals one month before their surgery," I said. "The drug forced a hyperovulation cycle. He harvested the eggs when he did their breast surgery, all without their permission or without them knowing about what he did to them."

"Or was it a vitamin, or an antibiotic as part of his pre-op protocol?"

"What about Lorenz? Did al-Turk get rid of him because he was a fed and on to him? Did that give him an opportunity to see whether Donna's breast implant bombs worked?"

"If her implants were bombs."

"Is al-Turk going to detonate the boob bombs again tomorrow, but this time with the girls sitting next to unsuspecting passengers flying in nine planes all over the country?"

"But that's a stretch," she said. "Are the breast implant bombs powerful enough to bring down nine modern planes? How can al-Turk be certain the bombs would accomplish his goal?"

"I have an idea." I called Corky again.

"Got time for one more question?" I asked.

"Sure," she said.

"Where is your ticket?"

"In my purse."

"No, I mean where are you sitting?"

"Let me look." I heard her moving around. "Here it is: 22A."

"Is it an exit row?"

"Uh-huh. Mr. al-Turk did it to give us extra leg room."

"Thoughtful of him. Thanks for your help." I turned to Linda. "An explosion next to the emergency exit door could blow it out and the plane would crash."

Linda put her pen down. "You still don't have enough."

"I'll call Tony."

"Will he shut down O'Hare with no documented evidence of a possible terrorist attack?" she asked.

"I don't know."

But writing this story will put me on the front page of every paper in the country.

"If you attempt to stop the nine planes from flying and are completely wrong about this, you'll be laughed out of the newspaper industry forever," she said.

She's right. What should I do?

Part 6

117

When Kerry and I returned home from Linda's, I put her down for a nap.

If Tony wouldn't stop the strippers from flying, I would. I couldn't take the risk that the breast implants were C4 bombs, and thousands of people might be blown up in the worst airline disaster in history. If I was wrong, so be it. I would have to take the heat.

I took out my knitting and began another row. I had to figure it out. It took thirty rows this time.

I don't have an option.

No one had believed me about the bomber five years ago in Arlington, but as I went into the kitchen to call the TSA at O'Hare, I prayed this time the trained employees at the airport would.

The front doorbell rang. I hoped it was Tony. Face-to-face, I might be able to convince him to stop those planes. I put my knitting on the kitchen counter and went into the entry hall.

When I opened the door, it was a man I recognized — but it wasn't Tony.

Slam the door in his face!

Anticipating my move, the man jammed his foot against the door before I could react.

"Mr. al-Turk," I said.

"Mrs. Thomas." His voice was raspy from too many cigarettes. "May I call you Tina?"

"No, you may not."

I'm not giving you a damn thing.

"As you wish."

His right hand held an object in his black warm-up jacket pocket. I was certain it wasn't a cell phone. He motioned with that hand. "I think it might be better if we have this conversation inside, don't you think? It would be much easier to hear your daughter if she cries."

Having no option, I let him come in. As he stepped next to me, I suppressed a gag from the harsh stench of tobacco drifting off of his clothes.

He glanced around. "Tastefully decorated."

I remained silent. My throat was too dry to even swallow. The only other time I'd been this scared was when the bomber dialed his cell phone to detonate the bomb in the Arlington clinic.

But this time, the killer was in my home and my daughter slept upstairs.

Al-Turk nudged me into the kitchen.

"Sit down," he demanded.

I was determined not to show how terrified I was, but my legs trembled, giving me no option but to follow his instructions. I sat down at the kitchen nook table.

He sat down next to me. "You are probably wondering why I am here."

I glared at him but kept my mouth shut. He slid a handgun out of the right-hand pocket of his warm-up and placed it on the table. It was a Glock 19, a weapon I was familiar with.

"I intend to sit here with you until our plans today are completed," he declared.

No! Not today! It's supposed to happen tomorrow!

"Why would I let that happen?" I tried not to show any emotion.

"There are many reasons." He spun the gun around on the table. The end of the barrel now pointed directly at me. "But I can think of one that presently supersedes the rest."

Why is he talking so much? There has to be a reason.

The FBI agent at the library had to have seen him come into my home. She could activate her listening devices and hear him talking and then swoop in to rescue Kerry and me.

Keep him talking.

"Micah's an Israeli," I said. "Why is he helping you? He should be your enemy."

"We keep track of Jews like Mittelman, who we can force to help us."

"Force?"

"Indeed. After his family moved into his condo in April, I met with him at his lab and told him to do our bidding or we would torture, and eventually kill, his precious family."

"Why would he believe that?"

"Two of my associates visited his condo under the pretext that they were his friends visiting from Israel. Hannah let them in, and all it took to convince him to cooperate was for me to show him a real time cell phone photo of them with his wife and children. In effect, we abducted them in their own condo."

"Have you done this before?"

"Many times." He fingered the gun to validate his point. "It is an extremely effective technique."

118

He's doing the same thing to Kerry and me.

"I had one of my men move in with them on a full-time basis," al-Turk continued.

"Farhad," I said.

He nodded.

Keep him talking. The FBI has to be on the way.

"And he doubled as Hannah's driver," I continued.

Al-Turk shifted in his chair. "We added security cameras at his home to further monitor them."

"And you told Micah about them."

"Of course we did."

"Did you have them inside too?"

"Yes. Those cameras caught your friend Linda inserting the flash drive into Micah's hard drive and you retrieving it. We realized you would figure out our end-game, and we had to accelerate our plan."

He sat back and crossed his legs, shifting in his seat again, moving a little further away from his gun. "I am amazed you did not deduce why we moved into your neighborhood."

"Obviously, I wondered about it."

"The practical truth is we needed the proximity to their house. The video cameras in their home have a fairly long range, but the audio transmitters will not work beyond a few hundred yards. To overcome this, we moved here, two streets away."

I should have figured this out.

"When Lorenz and, after him, two other FBI agents, began spying on us, we could no longer have Farhad live in their house. Except for when you were there, we have not had any physical contact with them."

"But you still monitored them."

He smiled, his teeth a disgusting yellow-brown color.

"How did you discover I was interested in you?"

"You are the reporter. You tell me."

I pictured Micah's computer. "You installed a keystroke logger on his computer and read the section he typed in about me."

"Micah did all the research for us. He discovered that you are a reporter. We realized you might be a problem and focused on you."

My aggressive pursuit of his story got me into this.

Use that aggression to save you and Kerry. But I need a weapon!

"Who are the Hamlin Park Irregulars?" I asked.

"Micah gave your group a code name. When he discussed you and your group with Hannah, he assumed we would not know who he was talking about. Of course, he did not know about the keystroke logger. But we had another way to follow what you and your friends were doing."

I remembered Molly flirting with the hunk at the gym who was the driver for Corky, Sammy, and Donna.

"Jamie?"

"Very good. Molly and Jamie became great friends and she provided him with all the other details we might have missed."

Can this get any worse?

His eyes narrowed. "Is it safe?" he asked.

"What?"

"I am disappointed that you do not recognize the question. After all, it is from one of your favorite films."

He was wrong. I knew it well; it was the chilling line from *Marathon Man,* one of our favorite classic movies.

"How do you know about that?" I asked.

"Turn on your little black box," he said.

A shiver went down my spine.

"What box?"

"The one that alerts you when the listening devices in your home are active."

The box sat on the counter next to me. I did as he requested. The red light came on. He took out his cell phone and hit speed dial. He spoke in Arabic. He smiled as the light turned green.

No! The bugs didn't belong to the FBI. They were his.

119

"How did you get in our home to plant them?" I asked.

Al-Turk smirked, and I had the answer before he said another word.

"It's when I run and forget to set the alarm," I continued. "But how could you or Farhad walk up our front steps without being seen by Mrs. Newens?"

"Jamie did more for us than talk to Molly and drive the girls around."

The Cox Cable man!

"And Jamie didn't only install listening devices, did he?"

"No, he is an expert with computers. The keystroke logger on your home computer is ours, not the FBI's."

"You listened to Tony and me talking about you being drug dealers, and you planted the heroin residue around your garage for me to discover."

"We did, but we were fearful you would think discovering the heroin residue was too easy. But you did not."

Damn!

"You had Farhad sell the heroin to low-level street distributors."

"It was one of my other men, but we wanted to throw off your focus to give us more time to continue with our mission." He smiled. "A nice touch, don't you think?"

I didn't respond.

"When we initiate a scheme like this, we assume the FBI will become involved at some point," he continued. "Lorenz moved in next door to you. We thought he might be an undercover agent put in place because of the C4 on our trash. We were sure of it when he immediately began coming to the Twenties and questioning the girls."

"Weren't you afraid killing him would bring the U.S. government crashing down on you?"

"You live in a democracy and the wheels of justice turn slowly. Your court system and your laws protect us. In our country, we would have immediately been arrested and put in jail. But here they need irrefutable evidence to even obtain a search warrant for our home."

Which I didn't have.

"Why not just leave?"

"The competition between your federal agencies works in our favor to slow their communications down, allowing us sufficient time to initiate our plan." He cleared his throat. "Although we did have to speed our timeline up a bit — thanks to you."

I kept my mouth shut, refusing to respond to the insinuation I was responsible for the upcoming carnage he was orchestrating.

"You knew I tracked you because I downloaded the GPS software on my computer."

"We did, and we temporarily removed the devices any time we needed to drive to locations we did not want you to know about."

"What about the trip to O'Hare?"

"A regrettable mistake; Farah drove Jamie to work in the Mercedes, and he forgot about the GPS transponder."

Jamie works at O'Hare.

"And you listened to us watching movies."

"Not just any movies — classics. I assumed you would recognize the line since you recently watched that film."

"Okay, I'll play. Is what safe?"

"Our plan."

"Why should I tell you?"

He tapped the handle of the gun. "You tell me what I need to know, or..."

"...Or you'll kill me."

"*Au contraire.* This is the last thing I want to do. As for your daughter, this depends on what you tell me."

His meaning was clear. He might not kill me, but my daughter was another matter. I had to do whatever it took to make sure that didn't happen.

You're keeping me talking? Why?

"I will make my question more specific. Did you use your recently acquired burner phone to call the rest of the Hamlin Park Irregulars? How much do your friends know?"

"My friends?" I croaked.

There's the answer.

He'd been working on me, getting me to relax for this moment. All he wanted from me was how many people he had to kill.

"How much have you told them about Dr. Mittelman and the breast implants?"

"Nothing," I lied, even though Linda already knew about the breast bombs. "Not a damn thing."

He stared into my eyes. "Are you telling me the truth?"

I stared back. "I am. You arrived before I could call any of them."

"Fortunately for your friends, I believe you."

"What happens next?"

"We sit here and chat until the last plane takes off. We have nine girls ready to go. Tonight, nine planes will be blown out of the sky. You and Micah will know how it happened, but you will never tell anyone."

"Why not?"

"Let me put it to you this way: If you had to choose between saving the life of your daughter or the lives of the hundreds of strangers flying on those nine planes, which would you choose?"

120

"I would save my daughter," I said without hesitation.

"In April, when I asked Micah that question, he made the identical choice about his wife and children," al-Turk said. "But Micah is not the 'White Knight' you think he is."

"You forced him to do what you wanted, but he obtained human eggs which were vital to his research."

"He did, and thanks to his surgical expertise, here is what will happen. After the planes and all the passengers are destroyed, we will continue with more girls until the FBI finally catches on, and then we will disappear."

No!

"You will tell the FBI nothing, or we will torture and kill your daughter, as we will with Micah's family. We might also kill your husband, but I would prefer to keep him alive. He can then grieve over the horrendous and tragic death of little Kerry."

I pictured my daughter's angelic face and wanted to smash his face in.

"I don't suppose you have a spot of English tea? It is a taste I acquired while residing in London."

This asshole was going to make me brew tea for him. I used the kitchen counter to push myself up. My right hand grazed the knitting needles.

Yes!

I had a weapon, and he didn't notice.

Unexpectedly, Kerry woke up and began to talk to Elmo and Ralph.

Al-Turk turned his head toward the voice coming from the baby monitor sitting on the kitchen counter behind him.

Do it!

Grabbing one steel knitting needle, I rammed it into the top of his right hand. I used all my strength to shove the metal tip through the dark skin.

I pushed down with every ounce of my strength and twisted the handle of the needle. The full length of the needle crunched through the small bones and jabbed into the muscles and tendons.

It took only a few seconds for the metal tip to jam into the wood kitchen tabletop.

He screamed and clawed at the needle in his hand.

The gun!

I grabbed the barrel.

He swung his left hand backward toward my face.

I ducked.

Air whooshed past my face.

I bashed him in the face with the butt of the Glock. There was a loud thump, and blood squirted out of a gash on his forehead.

He grunted as he yanked his right hand free from the tabletop and ripped out the knitting needle.

I turned the Glock around and grabbed the butt in both hands. He lunged at me, knocking me backward.

We hit the kitchen floor with a thud.

The force of his weight landing on top of me drove the air out of my lungs. I gasped for oxygen.

He grabbed my hair and pounded the back of my head into the floor. I saw stars with each blow. He wrapped his bloody hands around my neck and choked me.

Do it! Save Kerry!

I wedged the Glock against his chest and pulled the trigger.

121

The bullet struck al-Turk's center mass. His chest muffled the blast of the gunshot.

His fingers were still around my throat, but his grip no longer had any strength.

I shook my head free from his hands and gasped for air.

Blood began to ooze out of his chest wound. As it did, the copper smell of fresh blood enveloped me.

The sticky fluid flowed onto the floor from both sides of our entwined bodies and then slowed to a trickle.

I struggled to push his dead weight off of me. As I did, his head dropped down and I found myself face-to-face with him. His black eyes were open, the pupils already beginning to dilate.

You wanted to kill my daughter!

Enraged, I found the strength to shove him to the side and rolled out from under his lifeless body. And then I did what any mother would do in the same situation: I put the Glock to the back of his head. I was going to make sure he was dead.

But I couldn't pull the trigger. I wasn't a killer. I was trying to save my baby, and the gun had discharged during my struggle to survive.

I nudged his body with my toe. He didn't move.

He's dead.

Staring at his body, I was overwhelmed by dizziness and threw up in the sink.

Call Tony!

But I had a big problem with that. To prove to me the listening devices were his, al-Turk had speed-dialed one of his men to turn them off.

That man is across the street.

I grabbed the black box off the counter and switched it on. The green light came on and didn't turn red; the listening devices were still off.

I rinsed my mouth out with tap water and attempted to call Tony on my burner cell phone. But my hands and fingers shook, and I misdialed his number three times before I got it right.

He answered. "Detective Infantino."

I opened my mouth to scream, "I just killed al-Turk!" But I disconnected before I did.

Dummy!

If I told him al-Turk was dead on my kitchen floor, Tony would dispatch a black-and-white, and my home would become a crime scene. After all the other cops arrived, I would spend the next several hours being processed for committing a possible murder.

And Hannah and her kids would be killed by the man across the street…

And nine planes would be blown out of the sky because I didn't have one shred of evidence to prove to the cops what was going to happen…

Go get Kerry.

But al-Turk's blood had splashed on me. Rushing to the entry hall, I opened the front closet that held our winter coats and grabbed Carter's trench coat. Wrapping it around me, I sprinted up the stairs to be with my baby and hold her safely in my arms.

"Why Momma qwying?" Kerry asked when I picked her up.

Until that moment, I hadn't realized tears were streaming down my cheeks. Hugging her tightly to my chest, I nuzzled her hair. "It's okay. Momma got scared, and it made me cry, but it's all better now."

Potty training would have to wait. I placed her on the table and changed her diapers. When I finished, it hit me.

If I had to choose between saving the life of my daughter, or the lives of strangers flying on those nine planes, which would I choose?

That had been the question al-Turk asked me, but now I had to make a decision. Do I help Hannah and her kids, or the people at O'Hare? I couldn't be in two places at once.

I had to save Hannah and her children before that guy realized al-Turk's plans for me and Kerry had gone haywire.

With Kerry in my arms, I went down to the family room.

"Sweet girl, Momma's going to put you down in here with Elmo and Ralph for a little bit, is that okay?"

"Uh-huh. Momma smell funny."

Did I ever. I had to fix that pronto.

"I'll be right back with apple juice."

When I ran into the kitchen, the overpowering stench of feces, urine, and dried blood made me begin to gag, and this time I threw up on al-Turk's legs. My uninvited dead guest had pooped his pants and peed all over the floor as his parting shot to me.

122

I ran up to our master bedroom with Kerry's apple juice in my hand, put it on the counter, and hopped into the shower. Then, I took the fastest shower in history, rinsed my mouth out again, and left the blood-soaked clothes on the shower floor. I grabbed the brown shorts I'd worn at XSport the day before and threw them on, along with an old yellow golf shirt and a pair of running shoes. I pulled my wet hair into a ponytail and took the apple juice to Kerry in the family room.

Now what?

Leaving Kerry with her two friends, I ran back into the kitchen to call Tony on my regular cell phone.

"I have new intel," I said.

"Give it to me," Tony said.

"Dr. Micah Mittelman is a world famous medical researcher." My frustration bubbled to the surface, and I began talking faster. "He has developed a process to create embryonic stem cells in the laboratory and is using them to treat multiple sclerosis."

The line went silent. Science was never Tony's strong suit.

"And?"

"He's been forced by al-Turk and his crew to do surgery on unsuspecting women to implant C4."

"Where'd the doctor put the C4?"

"Nine of the strippers at the Twenties had augmentation mammoplasties done by him."

He didn't react.

"Breast implants."

He still didn't react.

"The C4 is in their boob jobs."

"Exploding boobs? No way. You got proof of that?"

"Al-Turk confessed to me."

"He around so I can question him?"

"He's in my kitchen right now."

Sort of the truth.

"How long is he gonna stay there?"

I wanted to say "forever," but I had to focus Tony on the nine strippers at O'Hare.

"He'll be here as long as you want him to be. Our bigger problem is at O'Hare. The nine strippers are already there."

"Are you sure about this?"

"Yes, I'm *freaking* sure! You need to go out there and stop this!" I took in a breath. "The girls will be in the United Room South on the B concourse. Go there, and don't let them near any airplanes."

"I can be there by 1420."

"Okay. It'll be at least forty minutes before I can get there. I'll meet you in the United Room South on the B Concourse."

Hannah and her kids come first.

123

But I can't call Hannah.

Al-Turk's man had to be monitoring her phones too. If he heard and recognized my voice, he would know his boss was in trouble and would kill Hannah and her kids immediately.

If I called 911, the Chicago PD might send out a patrol unit. But when the man saw the cops drive up to Hannah's home, he would rush in the back door of her house and kill all of them before the cops had turned off the engine.

I was Hannah's only chance to survive, and to do it, I needed a weapon. I reached down and picked up al-Turk's Glock 19. Ejecting the magazine, I counted the bullets. A full clip contained fifteen 9mm rounds. I'd fired the gun one time and now there were fourteen left. I reinserted the clip and jacked one bullet into the barrel.

Carter would go ballistic if he discovered al-Turk dead in our kitchen. But my hubby would go completely nuts if he knew I planned to save Hannah and her kids. Hopefully, the terrorists had a manpower issue, and there was only one man in al-Turk's house. But if there were two or three of them across the street, I was in real trouble.

I need help.

The only people I could count on were my playgroup friends.

Cas.

She wouldn't back down from anyone, especially a man, and if there were injuries, her ER experience might save lives.

I didn't want to leave Kerry, but I had no choice. As she sipped her apple juice, I called Mrs. Sanchez. She agreed to watch Kerry and Cas's two kids.

Next, I called Cas. "I need you to meet me at al-Turk's house. It's gotta be right now and no questions."

"What?"

"Just listen. Park in my driveway. You know Mrs. Sanchez. Drop off your kids with her. I'll sneak down the alley to the back of al-Turk's house and wait for you there."

"Then what?"

"When you're in position in front of al-Turk's house, call me and then ring the doorbell. I'll sneak in the back door."

"Tina, what is going on?"

"There's a man inside al-Turk's house who might seriously harm Hannah and her kids."

"What if there are more guys in there?"

"Bring your Taser and your first aid kit, and we'll figure it out."

124

I grabbed my backpack, put the gun inside, and dropped off
Kerry at Mrs. Sanchez's house. After sprinting down the alley, I
squatted next to the gate where I'd tried to hide the night I'd stolen
the trash. If the gate from al-Turk's house opened, I wanted to have
a clear shot at whoever came out.

My cell phone vibrated.

"At the foot of the front steps," Cas stage-whispered. "The
drapes are closed."

"Hang on."

I rushed to al-Turk's gate and opened it a crack. The drapes
in the back of the house were closed. I pushed through the gate
enough to enter the backyard and ran to the back steps.

"Heading to the back door," I whispered, as I tip-toed up
the stairs.

"Going to the front."

I took out my lock pick gun and torque wrench. I put the
Glock in my left armpit.

"Count three. Ring the doorbell and pound on the door.
Make as much noise as you can."

Thrusting the phone into my backpack, I waited until I heard the doorbell ring. Using my tools, I opened the door and slipped into the kitchen.

I shoved the equipment into my backpack and put it on the counter. I grabbed the gun and assumed a shooter's stance. Standing still, I listened for any human sounds while sweeping the gun back and forth in front of me, anticipating the sudden appearance of the terrorist. The only noise came from the ringing front doorbell and Cas pounding on the door.

I sniffed. The pungent smell of spicy food permeated the kitchen air and turned my stomach. I sniffed again.

Cigarette smoke.

Taking a deep breath, I swallowed the bile that had erupted into the back of my throat. I inched forward and slowly moved the gun back and forth in front of me. I opened the door for Cas. She stood on the front stoop and lurched backward when she saw the Glock in my hand. She held her first aid kit in her left hand.

"I didn't know you owned a gun," she whispered.

I pictured the late Mr. al-Turk on my kitchen floor. "Just picked it up," I whispered back.

"Can you shoot it?"

"I'm from Nebraska: we all know how to fire guns."

"Good to know, I guess."

"Check the first floor. I'm going upstairs."

There were four bedrooms. Three of the beds had been slept in, and those rooms smelled of sweat and cigarettes. The fourth had a mattress with no sheets. Dirty towels were haphazardly strewn around three of the bathrooms. I retraced my steps and rejoined Cas on the first floor.

"I'm going to the lower level," I said. "You stay here and yell at me if one of them returns."

I descended the basement stairs with the gun in front of me and entered a brightly lit room. Stacked on one wall were containers labeled with chemical names. Boxes of SAE motor oil were lined up on the adjacent wall. A large metal desk covered with mixing bowls sat in the middle of the room. The odor of recently smoked cigarettes hung in the air.

I finally have proof.

To my right was another larger room with a bank of ten monitors. On one of the ten screens I could see Hannah in her kitchen. On another screen, Jason, their oldest son, was working on a computer in his bedroom. The other kids were visible on a third monitor; they were on the lower level playing with their toys. The rest of the screens showed views of the exterior of the house and other empty rooms, one of which was Micah's study.

I noticed a knob on the desk. I put down the gun and turned the knob to the right. I heard Hannah loudly singing to herself, unaware I was eavesdropping.

A hard object poked my low back.

Gun barrel?

"Where is Mr. al-Turk?" a man's voice behind me asked.

NO!

125

"What?" I asked.

"Mr. al-Turk," the man behind me repeated. "He is supposed to be at your house."

He jabbed me with the object, harder this time.

It is a gun!

I slid my hand toward the Glock lying on the desk.

The man poked me again. I stopped moving.

"Move away from the desk," he said.

I did. He coughed, and I recognized his voice.

"I know you," I said, as I slowly turned around to face him.

"I do not think so."

"You cough a lot and like to hack and spit into sinks." I stated this as loudly as I could without being obvious.

Cas is my only hope.

"I am going to call Mr. al-Turk. If he does not answer, I am going to kill you and then the Jews."

He held the gun in his right hand and speed-dialed al-Turk's cell phone. The phone rang several times before it went to voice mail.

Turning off the phone, he raised his gun to my forehead. Cas hadn't heard me talking. She wasn't coming to save me.

"Please don't do this," I begged, tears cascading down my cheeks. "I have a baby girl."

He slapped my face with the back of his left hand. "Shut up!" he screamed.

The force of the blow caused a shower of lights behind my eyes. My head began to spin, and I bent over and vomited on his shoes.

126

The terrorist jumped back and screamed at me in Arabic. I continued to dry-heave. Shaking the vomit off his shoes, he pushed me up and pointed his gun at my face.

"Pendejo!" Cas yelled from the doorway.

The man shoved me down and whipped around. She pointed a spray can at him and fired a long stream at his face. When the liquid hit his eyes, his groans filled the room. Dropping his gun, he fell to his knees, clawing at his face. She dropped the can, ran to him, and put the Taser on his neck. Instantly, he began flopping around on his back like an oxygen-deprived carp.

Reaching into her first aid kit, she took out a zip tie, knelt down, secured his hands together behind his back, and then did the same thing with his legs. She forced him into an arched-back position and bound his feet and hands together with another zip tie.

Cas stood up and gave me a hug. "You okay?"

My throat was too tight to speak. I hugged her back and began sobbing. The man started to wiggle. She leaned down and zapped him again with the Taser.

I wiped my tear-stained cheeks with my hand. "I was terrified you didn't hear me, and he was going to shoot me."

"I heard Hannah singing, and I came down to see what was going on."

"I'm really, really glad you did."

"Why didn't this guy come to the front door when I rang the bell?"

Huh?

"Maybe he was in the bathroom. I didn't look in there."

I noticed the can she'd thrown down on the floor. It was Raid Wasp and Hornet Spray. I didn't have time to ask her why she'd used it instead of pepper spray.

"What do you want me to do now?" she asked.

"Pick up your kids and Kerry and go to Hannah's. Gather all of them up and hide out at Molly's house."

"Done. Where are you going?"

"To O'Hare. This story is coming apart. I have to be there. I promise I'll explain later."

She nodded toward the man. "What about him?"

"Leave him here. Tony can have one of his guys pick him up after he finishes up at the airport. I'll call you when it's over."

127

As I sped to O'Hare in the mommy van, I couldn't forget al-Turk's dead eyes and the bullet hole in his chest.

I killed him!

Nausea enveloped me once again. Powering down the window, I let the hot Chicago wind blow on my face.

At least Tony should have the girls corralled either in the United Room or, more likely, a detention area in the TSA offices. I'd missed it, but I didn't have a choice. Hannah and her kids had come first.

Story? O'Hare?

Dang it!

I didn't have a ticket to get into the terminal. I reached in my backpack for my burner phone, but I'd left it in my kitchen. I did have my old cell phone. I used it to call Linda.

"Make a plane reservation for me to fly one-way out of Chicago this afternoon on any United flight, and it doesn't matter where."

"What? Are you...?"

"Please, just make it. We'll discuss it later."

"Oh, I get it. You don't want to use your own computer because of the Magic Lantern installation."

"I'm in my van. I'll give you the money tomorrow."

"I'm on it."

"Wait. Where are the two vehicles?"

She typed on her keyboard. "That's weird. The tracker on the Mercedes is off. So is the one on the Range Rover."

Al-Turk had removed them before he came to my home.

He was going to kill me and my daughter.

128

I saw no extra police activity when I parked in the garage at O'Hare, proof that Tony had done his job and the nine women were being held far away from any airplanes and the press.

Missed it, but I saved Hannah and her kids.

Linda had done her job. When I arrived at the United check-in desk, my ticket was online in the United computer, ready for me to retrieve it. I printed it up and ran to the security line, which wasn't too long. Again, there was no extra TSA activity. I made it to the first desk in less than five minutes.

"Ticket and photo ID please," the male TSA agent requested.

I reached for my backpack, which I didn't have.

"It's in my van."

He stared at me. "And?"

"And it's in my backpack, and that's where my driver's license is."

"Can't let you through without a photo ID."

The action was over, but I would still have to run back to the van and stand in line again, and it would take too long.

"Do you have any other photo ID?" he asked.

Searching through my shorts pockets, I found my ID for XSport Fitness, which I'd used the day before. It had my picture and name and address on it. I handed it to him.

"How about this?"

"Works for me, but I'm not sure it will if you book a return from Omaha," he said, as he stamped and initialed my ticket.

"Omaha?" I asked.

"Isn't that where you're going?"

I hadn't looked at my ticket. I did a mini Tina-two-step. "Right, right, Omaha."

Moving forward, I faced another hurdle I hadn't anticipated: the long line of people waiting to go through the full-body scanners. I called Tony to save me, but he didn't pick up.

I waved at a female TSA agent. "Can I skip this line? I'm late and need to get to my gate."

"Oh, really? We hear that a lot. Let me see your ticket."

Because I didn't give a damn about the ticket, I had no idea what time my flight left. The TSA agent held the ticket in front of me.

"You leave in four hours," she said. "Don't look like much of a rush to me."

129

When I walked through security to the B Concourse, it was business as usual. There were flight announcements over the loud speakers. Passengers walked to their planes. A few ran. People talked. Kids cried.

Perfect!

Tony had taken care of the threat, and no one would be blown up.

I looked at the clock on the Arrival/Departure board. It was 3:45 p.m. The first plane was scheduled to fly out in an hour and fifteen minutes. Thank God Tony had arrested the strippers. Otherwise, there might not be enough time to stop them from boarding the planes.

As I turned to walk to the United Room South, I heard someone yell my name. I turned around. Tony walked toward me from the security line. He was alone.

No!

"Did you just get here?" I demanded.

"Got hung up at work. Looks like you're late too. Where are the strippers you were talking about?"

My head began to pound. "Where is the SWAT team, the TSA, maybe even the FBI and DHS?"

"Didn't contact them. I need proof before I call in reinforcements."

You jerk! You never believed me!

I'd put way too much trust in Tony. I should have called the TSA myself.

My big mistake.

I reached in my back pocket for my cell phone to do that. He blocked my arm before I could.

"Whaddya doing?" he asked.

"Calling the TSA to tell them what's going on."

"Not happening, Sweets. No reason to screw up all these passengers' travel plans. Give me proof and I'll shut down this whole airport."

"Then let's get to the United Room."

130

Thirty feet to our right, directly across from the entrance to the United Room, I spotted a Montblanc store. I stopped. Tony did too.

"Remember when I gave you the trash I stole?" I asked.

He nodded.

"Do you recall what was in it?"

"A couple of cartons for plastic dishes and pen and pencil boxes."

"The boxes were from Montblanc."

"And?"

"The location of this store across from the United Room has to be more than a coincidence."

He pondered my statement. "Lorenz."

"What about him?"

"Our bomb crew chief said the detonator was about the size of a deck of cards."

"Or a pen and pencil set."

"You got it."

I saw Jamie behind the counter inside the store. "See the young blond man working on the computer behind the counter?"

"Buffed guy with the tan?"

"Yes," I said. "Al-Turk told me Farhad, one of his men, drove that guy out here to go to work. His name is Jamie."

"Looks like an American."

"He is, and no one notices him."

"So?"

"I think that when Jamie comes to work at O'Hare, he brings in tiny parts of the bomb detonator's components, and security doesn't pick it up on the scanners."

"Okay, let's say you're right. Dude doesn't need much C4 packed into a pen or pencil to act as a detonator, but he still needs some. How does he get the C4 past security?"

"In toothpaste tubes."

"*Toothpaste tubes?*"

"There were also empty Crest toothpaste boxes in the trash I stole. I think al-Turk and his guys sucked out the toothpaste and injected tiny amounts of the C4 into the empty toothpaste tubes."

"Where do they make the detonators?"

"In the backroom of this Montblanc store and then they add the C4."

He rubbed his chin. "A compact discharge next to the C4 on the person's body would trigger the C4, causing a bigger blast. Gotta get to the United Room and find those strippers, right now!"

131

Crossing the concourse, we entered the United Room and rode the escalator up to the main floor. Tony's badge would gain us admittance without any hassle.

He stepped up to the two women behind the front desk and showed them his gold detective shield. I couldn't hear what he said, but he must not have mentioned the breast bombs because the two women didn't show any signs of concern.

We walked into the seating area. The room's décor reminded me of a library without the books. There were several rows of upholstered club chairs, desks with lamps, and plugs for computers and cell phones.

I didn't see any of the young women. I also didn't see anyone who looked Middle Eastern.

"Are you sure this is the right joint?" he asked. "The lady at the desk said there are four clubs in two different terminals."

"I'm sure this is the club Sammy mentioned."

We walked around the club twice but still didn't find them.

"This has been fun and all that, but I gotta get back to work," he said when we finished.

There were several clocks on the wall indicating different time zones around the world. The first plane was supposed to take off in sixty-two minutes. My hands began to sweat. There were carry-on bags scattered throughout the room. Several of them were unattended, and none of the employees were concerned.

Bags!

That was why al-Turk had picked the United Room. It was the least secure area in the entire airport. When I had been there before, I'd dropped my bags by my chair, or in the bag storage room, while I walked around or worked at one of the computer stations. Anyone could have put an object in my carry-on before I boarded my plane, and I never would have spotted it.

Worse, since the airlines didn't do a secondary bag check once a passenger passed though security, the bags were never searched again. The terrorists were going to put the pens and pencil detonators into the girls' carry-on bags making them walking bombs.

And none of them would know it.

132

"Tony, follow me to the bag storage closet," I said. "I can prove I'm telling you the truth."

"Gotta better idea," Tony said. "I'll meet you in there."

He went left toward the front desk. I turned to the right and rushed into the bag storage room. Several bags were stacked in open lockers. No personnel guarded them, and there were no security cameras.

The Montblanc sets have to already be in their bags.

I pawed through three carry-on bags before I found one that belonged to a woman who listed her address as the apartment building by the Twenties. Opening it, I pulled out a Montblanc pen and pencil set.

Yes!

Lifting the lid of the case, I found a pen and pencil inside attached to a blue cardboard backing. Both appeared normal.

Tony walked into the storage closet. He had a piece of paper in his hand.

"What's that?" I asked.

"Asked the women at the front desk if they check all the passengers in."

"I forgot they used to do that with me."

"They also check the passenger's flights for them. Strippers are here." He held up the paper. "And I have their gates and the times they take off."

"Let me see."

He handed me the paper. I scanned it. Each girl was listed with her gate, time of departure, and destination.

He took the paper back and put it in his pocket. "Shoulda believed you, but I need those detonators."

I handed him the pen and pencil box. "I might have one."

He opened it and studied the contents. "Look at the tops of each pen and pencil." He pointed to two slender, blue wires attached to each top. I'd missed them because they blended into the blue color of the cardboard.

"Other ends of the wires disappear behind the cardboard into the back of the case." He weighed the set in his hands. "Too heavy to contain only a pen and pencil."

"Is it a detonator?"

"Looks like. Pen and pencil probably have batteries inside to power the device."

"Why don't you take it apart and make sure you're right?"

"And risk getting blown up?" He held up his hand. "Might be booby-trapped. Bomb squad guys get paid to do that."

But I finally had his full attention.

133

Tony checked his watch. "First stripper is leaving on the five o'clock flight for L.A. With this…" he said, while holding up the detonator, "…I have enough evidence to shut down the airport and arrest the strippers."

"You call the TSA, and I'll look for the strippers."

He pondered that. "Good idea. Let's do this."

He turned to leave. I grabbed his arm.

"I need a gun."

He pulled away. "Not happening."

"I need a weapon, and you know I'm capable of using it." I pointed at his lower leg. "I know you have another one on you."

"But I can't give it to you. You aren't a cop, and as a civilian, you aren't authorized to carry a weapon in here. I'll lose my job if I do this."

"Listen to me, big guy. I called you and told you about this attack. You haven't done one damn thing to prevent it. The front-page story in tomorrow's *Chicago Tribune* will be about a detective who ignored my warning and let nine strippers get on different planes, resulting in the deaths of hundreds — or maybe even thousands — of people. You won't be able to get a job guarding a sandbox. And I will write that story, unless you give me a gun."

"Okay, okay, I shoulda believed you." He pulled his ankle gun out. "Take my Smith and Wesson."

I hefted it and gave it back. "I've never fired a revolver like this. I know how to handle a Glock."

He put the gun back in his ankle holster and handed his Glock to me. "Do *not* show this to anyone unless you have to."

"If you don't get me a lot of help in a heck of a hurry, it may be the only option I have."

I dropped the magazine to make sure it was full and there was one in the chamber. I put the gun in the back of my shorts and covered it with my top.

"Check the bags and grab the rest of the detonators," he said. "Try and find the strippers. If you don't, meet me at the gate for the United flight to L.A."

He ran down the escalator steps with the detonator in his hand.

134

I began going through the remaining carry-on bags, searching for ID tags that listed the owners as living in the apartment building by the Twenties. I found one and opened it. Inside was a Montblanc pen and pencil set identical to the one Tony had taken with him.

"What the hell are you doin'?" a tall, ruddy-faced man asked. He had a deep, raspy southern accent.

He stomped toward me from the doorway. He wore a cowboy hat and smelled like he'd had too many Jack and Cokes.

I held up the box. "I was putting these United complimentary gifts of Montblanc pen and pencil into all the passengers' carry-ons."

"Bullshit. United's too cheap to do somethin' like that." He stepped toward me. "What's goin' on here?"

I can't let you stop me, cowboy.

Sliding my right hand behind my back, I wrapped my fingers around the butt of Tony's gun. "My job is to put these…" I waved the pen and pencil box at him with my left hand, "…in each passenger's carry-on."

I slid my finger to the gun's trigger guard.

"Tell United I don't want their goddamn gift." He yanked his bag off the shelf and staggered off, bumping into the doorframe as he left.

It took eleven minutes to find six more of the bags with the detonators and another four before I discovered the last carry-on. It belonged to Sammy. I went through it but didn't find a detonator. I turned it upside down and dumped the contents on the floor; nothing but clothes and toiletries. Counting my stack of pens and pencil sets again, I still came up with seven. Tony had one, which made eight. That took me another three minutes.

Sammy has to have the ninth detonator with her.

I went to call Tony. My cell phone showed "no service." The TSA was shutting down the airport, which included jamming all phone transmissions. I couldn't call Tony and warn him he was walking into a trap.

135

I grabbed the Montblanc boxes and searched for a place to stash them until this was over. I saw the sign for the bathroom.

Arlington.

The bomber had hidden his bomb in the bathroom in Arlington, and it would have to work for me. I ran to the bathroom and entered. It hit me as I approached the trash can.

No!

My head began to throb. Until that second, the possibility of a PTSD attack hadn't entered my mind. I shut my eyes and tried to control my breathing.

Maybe it was remembering Arlington and having explosive devices in my hands. Maybe it was stress. Or the combination. Whatever it was, I couldn't let it take over. I had to fight it.

Concentrate.

I kept my eyes shut.

When I opened my eyes, my vision was blurry, but it cleared with a few blinks.

I have to stop the devices from working.

Could a manual signal from a trigger on the concourse one floor below me not only set off Sammy's Montblanc detonator and her boob bombs but have range enough to ignite the seven detonators in the bathroom too? If it could, the explosion would most certainly cause major destruction and injuries in the United Room.

Tony said the detonators might be booby-trapped. If I yanked out the wires from each pen and pencil, I might be blown up.

Hurry!

I heard a toilet flush in the stall to my left.

Batteries? Water!

I pushed open the door of the other stall and stepped in. My idea was to put the detonators into the toilet, hoping the water would soak the batteries in the triggers and render them useless and thus unable to explode.

But there isn't any back to the toilet!

The plumbing went into the wall.

Now what?!

I threw the detonators in the toilet and watched them sink to the bottom.

Flush them or not?

I decided not to risk having them plug up the toilet, which might cause a mini flood in the bathroom. Instead, I locked the stall door and crawled out underneath it.

I sprinted down the escalator and ran out the door of the United Room.

Sammy leaves for L.A. in forty-two minutes.

136

I remembered Sammy's gate number from the sheet Tony had shown to me. I began to speed-walk toward her gate to find Tony and his troops to warn them about the one missing detonator. The bustling activity and noise from the passengers had not changed since I first arrived on Concourse B, but I saw several people staring at their phones, probably wondering why they no longer worked.

You'll know soon enough.

As I pushed through the mass of passengers, I abruptly stopped when I saw the nine strippers strolling out of a bar. Farhad, the terrorist who had accosted me in Micah's study, walked next to Sammy. They were at the front of the group. Behind them were Corky and Micah and the rest of the strippers. They were closely bunched up and chatting, oblivious to what might happen.

The last detonator could be in Sammy's purse, making her a walking C4 bomb. But if Farhad had a manual trigger for her bomb implants, that could be a disaster.

Oh my God! What if Farhad has a trigger that will detonate not only Sammy's C4 breast bombs but all the other bombs at the same time too?

My head began pounding.

Breathe.

If the manual trigger was a cell phone, we might be okay. Tony had the TSA shut down all the cell phone service, and Farhad might not know that.

But al-Turk might have anticipated such a move by the TSA and given Farhad had another way to detonate the C4. He might be carrying a trigger device capable of manually blowing up Sammy's C4. And maybe all the other bombs too.

If her boobs blew up, would it cause a chain reaction with the other boob bombs, even if Farhad's device couldn't individually detonate their bombs? I had to do something before the whole area was vaporized and thousands of people were injured or killed.

Where is Tony?

When I needed him the most, he wasn't around.

It's up to me.

137

I pulled Tony's gun out of the back of my pants and assumed a shooter's stance. I slid my finger onto the trigger guard.

They haven't seen me yet.

"Stop!" I yelled. "I have a gun!"

When the word "gun" left my lips, the world around me went crazy. Many of the passengers on Concourse B heard me. Others saw the gun. Instantly, it seemed like all of them began screaming, "Gun!" and running and shoving each other toward both ends of the long corridor. The noise from their feet hitting the floor and the screaming about the gun was deafening. Several passengers were knocked down, but they hopped up and began running again.

I ignored the chaos and focused on Farhad. Though other passengers flew past me, all the girls had stopped moving when they saw my gun pointed in their direction.

Farhad grabbed Sammy and wrapped his left arm around her neck. He turned her toward me, using her as a human shield.

Just like Arlington.

Micah stood next to Corky who began sobbing.

"Tina, Sammy has a Montblanc box in her purse," he said, confirming my fears. "Farhad put it in there."

As he said this, Farhad started to put his right hand into the pocket of his blue blazer.

"Stop, Farhad!" I shouted. "Don't you dare move your hand!"

His right hand stopped moving, but it hovered above his pocket.

If he shoves his hand into his pocket, shoot him!

But could I? On the gun range, it was easy to hit a stationary target, but it didn't have a heartbeat.

I slid my finger to the trigger.

Can I do this?

138

Footfalls echoed on the floor behind me, but I didn't turn around, afraid of losing my focus on Farhad.

Please be Tony.

I braced for a TSA guard trying to tackle me. Tony skidded to a halt next to me and pulled out his ankle revolver. He was alone. The remaining running passengers saw the second gun and began screaming louder, making it hard to hear.

He trained his revolver on Farhad.

"What's going on?" he said over the noise.

"Farhad's making a play for a second trigger in his pocket. Where are the cops and the TSA?"

"They're coming up with a plan."

"They'll be too late!"

"Relax. Dude is scared shitless of me. Check his eye."

I could only see Farhad's right eye because he kept ducking behind Sammy's head. But that pupil was widely dilated, and from what little I could see of his forehead, he sweated profusely.

We inched toward him.

Sweat dripped off of Farhad's forehead. "Do not move any closer!"

We stopped moving.

"Let me go, or I will detonate all the bombs!" he continued.

"Tony!" I screamed. "He can blow up all the boob bombs!"

boom-BOOM!

139

My head began to throb. My vision became fuzzy.

No! Not now!

I took in a deep breath and blinked my eyes. "Let's try and reason with him."

"No way. Let me handle it."

Tony's gold detective shield hung from a chain around his neck. He held it up in his left hand. "I'm Detective Infantino with the Chicago PD. Do not put your hand in your pocket!"

Sammy blinked back tears and looked like she was going to faint. I made eye contact with her.

Hold on, girl.

I slightly jerked my head to the right as a signal to move so I would have a shot.

She nodded back.

Focusing on Farhad, I stayed in a shooter's stance. My right hand was sweating on the butt of the gun.

Breathe slowly. Stay in control.

"Farhad, let Sammy go," I said. "We can talk about this."

Was he ready to die? I had no way of knowing, but I wasn't going to let him kill me.

"Do not reach for that trigger!" Tony said, taking his own aggressive approach.

No, Tony! Give him a way out.

Farhad's right eyelid narrowed, and his pupil became a black dot.

Ah, man, don't do this.

I focused on what I could see of his face. His right arm was partially obscured by Sammy's body. If he moved his hand toward his pocket, I had to shoot him.

Remember Arlington.

Farhad moved his hand toward his pocket.

"Sammy, now!" I screamed.

She slugged him in his side with her right elbow and pulled down and away from him.

"*Allahu Akbar!*" he screamed as he staggered back from Sammy's blow. He jammed his hand into his pocket and yanked out a black box.

I didn't hesitate.

I fired twice.

A micro-second later, Tony did too.

140

My first shot hit Farhad's right shoulder. The second bullet entered his right upper chest. Farhad's torso jerked from the impact of my two bullets, causing both of Tony's shots to miss high and right.

The black box flipped out of Farhad's hand and flew behind him. He hit the floor with a thud and landed on his right side. He groaned and rolled to his back. As he writhed around, blood flowed from the wound in his shoulder and shot straight up from the other one in his chest, like a bright red Old Faithful stream. That crimson stream pulsated with his heart beat.

The copper odor of fresh blood and gunpowder enveloped us.

Sammy began crawling on all fours away from Farhad.

My ears rang from my gunshots and Tony's, which had gone off next to my right ear.

Sammy jumped up and slipped on the rapidly expanding puddle of Farhad's blood. She lurched and skidded but was able to sprint away from the madness next to her.

I waved at the rest of the strippers. "Get out of here! Follow Sammy."

They did. Micah didn't.

Micah's a doctor!

"Micah!" I screamed. "You're a doctor! Help him!"

Micah crossed his arms across his chest and didn't move.

Farhad's bleeding to death!

"Dammit, Micah, do something!" I screamed again.

Micah uttered several words in Yiddish, but he made no effort to do anything.

Farhad's thrashing slowed down. The geyser of blood pumping from his chest wound transformed to a dark red-black color and no longer pulsated.

The fingers of his right hand clenched and re-clenched in an attempt to activate the device that was behind him.

We have to help him! He's too young to die!

I took a step forward to save him, but Tony stopped me with his left arm. "I'll do this."

He kept his gun trained on Farhad as he slowly walked toward the terrorist.

Micah stared at Farhad but remained standing still with his arms crossed over his chest.

Farhad's movements were minimal. The flow of blood from the two wounds slowed to a trickle. The puddles of blood on his chest began to clot and looked like chunks of liver.

Farhad stopped moving.

Tony squatted down and, taking no chances, jammed his gun against the terrorist's head and searched Farhad's body for another trigger. He didn't find one.

He picked up the black box and put it in his pocket. It looked like a garage door opener.

He walked over to me. "Give that to me."

"What?" I asked. My ears were still ringing.

"Give me my fucking gun!" he muttered, nodding at the gun in my hand.

I handed the Glock to him. He slipped his ankle revolver into the palm of my hand.

"Take this and tell them this is the gun you fired."

141

Before I could ask why he wanted me to switch guns with him, there was a commotion behind us. Swarms of Chicago policemen and policewomen, TSA agents, and a SWAT team ran toward us. Sammy and the other strippers sprinted toward them. A small group of TSA agents broke off from the main group and stopped the girls. The larger core group continued moving toward us.

When they reached us, they screened off the passengers who were still fleeing in both directions. The result was that Tony, Micah, and I were isolated from the chaos around us. When the group saw our guns, they trained their weapons on us.

Immediately behind them, men and women wearing blue FBI windbreakers with yellow lettering approached us. They had their weapons drawn and pushed between the law enforcement personnel.

Micah hadn't moved. He stood still, staring at the young man. I did too. Farhad's body lay at our feet.

I killed him.

I raised my arms, holding the revolver in my right hand. Micah lifted his empty hands.

Tony held up his gold badge and his Glock. "I'm Detective Anthony Infantino. I have this situation under control."

"I don't think so, Detective," said one of the FBI agents, as he stepped forward. "This is a matter of national security. We're taking everyone into custody."

"Hold it," an athletic young man in a cheap, blue blazer said. He grabbed Micah's arm. "I have a Presidential Order," he said, waving around a piece of paper. "Dr. Mittelman is going with me."

The FBI agent and the man began arguing. Tony joined in. A TSA agent added his voice to the heated discussion. The late Mr. al-Turk had been right; none of our agencies cooperated with each other.

142

Al-Turk!

His lifeless, black eyes flashed into my memory.

Farhad's body lay in front of me.

Al-Turk.

Farhad.

I'd killed both of them!

I started breathing rapidly, and my hands began to tingle. Black dots clouded my vision. Tony's revolver slipped from my grasp and clattered to the floor. Tears streamed down my cheeks.

A female wearing a blue FBI windbreaker quietly ushered me away from the mass of law enforcement personnel around Tony, Micah, and Farhad's body. As we walked, I continued to sob and lost awareness of my surroundings.

She led me to a small windowless room in the basement of the airport. She stepped inside with me and shut the door. There was one metal chair and a metal table in the middle of the room. A white blouse, green shorts, and ASICS running shoes sat on the table.

She grabbed the clothes and shoes from the top of the table and handed them to me. "Please remove what you're wearing and put these on," she instructed.

"What?"

I had trouble focusing. Only the blank glare of dead eyes filled my mind.

"Put these clothes on."

I killed al-Turk.

I killed Farhad.

With no will of my own, I did what she said.

She stood there while I undressed and put on the clothes.

Whoa. Everything fits, including the shoes.

I stopped crying and began to pay attention.

"Please give me your cell phone," she requested. Her voice was flat.

I handed it to her.

She took it and gathered up my clothes and shoes, left with my belongings, and closed the door behind her. I heard a click. I tried the doorknob. The door was locked.

Am I in trouble here?

I sat down in the metal chair and waited.

What time is it?

There was no clock in the room. Without my cell phone or a watch, I had no way of knowing what time it was. The only noise came from the hum of the florescent lights and the air conditioner fan clicking off and on. The room's walls and ceiling were stark white. The floor was gray cement. The air was stale. I smelled sweat and sensed fear. Some of it came from previous inhabitants of the room. Some came from me.

Do I need a lawyer?

If I did, how was I going to contact one without a phone?

I just wanted to go home and write my story.

Standing up, I tried the door again. It was still locked. I walked around the perimeter of the room, searching for another way out. I didn't find one.

I made another circuit around the room and looked for security cameras and listening devices. I didn't see any.

The third time around the room, I paced it off.

Eight feet by ten feet.

I sat down again and put my elbows on the top of the table.

Come on, guys.

Finally, the agent came back into the room.

"Mrs. Thomas, you are free to go," she said.

"*What?*"

"You can leave."

"But..."

She opened the door. I walked out of the room. She escorted me outside into the sunlight and turned to leave.

"What about my cell phone?" I asked.

She handed it to me.

"And my clothes and shoes?" I continued.

She glared at me and left me standing on the airport's curb.

143

My cell phone wouldn't work. I ran to my van and roared away from O'Hare. When I turned onto the Kennedy, I tried my cell phone again. This time the transmission wasn't blocked.

I called Carter and took a deep breath before I spoke. I wanted to sound calm and keep from sobbing. But it was hard.

Because I killed Farhad. And al-Turk.

"Honey, there's been a little dustup at O'Hare," I said.

"We received a report that the airport has been shut down, but there is a total communication blackout." He hesitated before he spoke again. "How did you find out about it?"

"I'm, um, kind of here."

"Here? Where is 'here'?"

"At O'Hare."

"*What?!*" He yelled into his phone. "Why are you there? Where is Kerry? Is she safe?"

"Relax, Carter. Kerry's fine; she's with Molly and Cas."

"And?"

I took in another deep breath. "And I was working on Micah's story when it went to hell, and I rushed out here."

"Are you sure you're okay?"

I dabbed tears from my eyes as I pictured Farhad's lifeless body. "I'm fine."

But I could tell from his voice he knew I was lying.

"I'm coming out there."

"Better bring reporters and photographers with you. This is the story of the year."

I told him where to go in the airport.

"And I'll meet you at home," I said when I finished.

"Home? You can't be serious?"

"I'm tired of this, and I want to be with Kerry."

"Isn't this the story you wanted to write?"

"I've had all the excitement I can stand for one day. You take care of this, and I'll pick up Kerry."

And figure out what to do with al-Turk's body.

144

I called Molly. My hands continued to shake as I dialed.

"Molly, is Kerry okay?"

"She's fine," Molly said. "She's running around the house with my kids."

"Where is Cas?"

"She took her kids home when those men came here."

A lump formed in my throat as I pictured more terrorists I hadn't accounted for. "What men?"

"Three cute government guys. They talked to Hannah and then took her and her kids home."

"Could you keep Kerry a little longer? There are a few more details I need to work out."

"No problem."

Carter and his reporters would begin to work on the story as soon as they arrived at O'Hare, but I was positive that account would be heavily sanitized by all of the federal agencies involved. The reporter who possessed the whole story hadn't written it yet, but I was ready to begin.

If I ever stopped crying.

145

Walking into our home, I sniffed, anticipating the stench of death.

Uh-oh.

The air smelled artificially clean. I sniffed again. Same result.

Go back and get al-Turk's gun out of the van.

Instead, I went into the kitchen. Mr. al-Turk's body was missing. A lady sat at our kitchen table. She watched me stare at my spotless kitchen floor.

What the heck is going on?

She wore a black power suit with a high-neck, white blouse. She had a round face and man-short gray hair. She didn't have on any jewelry, but there was a bulge under the right side of her coat.

Gun?

"We need to talk, Mrs. Thomas," the lady said. "I've been waiting for you, and I don't have much time."

"Who are you?" I asked, looking back up at her.

She reached into her jacket and pulled out a leather wallet. Flipping it open, she displayed an FBI badge.

"I am Georganne Roth, Deputy Director of the FBI."

A Deputy Director? Big dog here.

I glanced at the clean kitchen floor again.

"That problem has been taken care of," she said, as she watched me do it. "We've also cleaned up your upstairs bathroom, washed your bloody clothes and your husband's trench coat. And sanitized the house across the street and removed the man your friend Cas tied up."

"Efficient."

She nodded. I glanced toward our lower level stairs. She saw me do it.

"There is no reason to search in the laundry room for your flash drive or in the garage for the rest of the trash you stole. We have it all."

"Am I to assume the files about the terrorists have been deleted from my computer's hard drive too?"

"We pride ourselves on being thorough." She handed a sack to me. "I brought this for you."

I glanced inside. It contained the brown shorts, yellow golf shirt, and ASICS running shoes I'd worn to the airport.

"Do you want these back?" I asked, pointing to the clothes and shoes I'd been given at the airport.

"I think not, but I suggest you put on your own clothes after I leave. That way your husband won't know what we've done."

"And what exactly have 'we' done?"

"For starters, we removed al-Turk's body."

"Obviously. What happened to it?"

She stared at me. "This is *none* of your concern."

"It most certainly is. I need that information for my story."

"Ah, yes, about that. We've made a few changes to solve your problem with the shooting. At this moment, the NSA is planting a background story on the Internet, where your husband and his reporters will discover incontrovertible proof that one of the men who lived across the street from you was at the airport attempting to force Dr. Mittelman to give up his secret medical formula. This information will identify the other two men — who worked for and lived with al-Turk — as agents for a prominent foreign pharmaceutical company whose home office is in Iran."

"But what about the gun I fired? I didn't have a license for it."

"That has been taken care of."

"But not by you."

Her jaw muscles twitched, but she remained silent.

"It was the guy at the airport with the presidential pardon, right?"

"Let's just say if that problem had been left up to us, you would still be in that room at O'Hare."

146

"But Carter will go crazy when he watches the security footage and sees me shoot Farhad," I said.

"Those videos now show a female FBI agent firing the second gun," Deputy Director Roth said. "The agent was chosen for this assignment because she resembles you. She met with the press with her hair in a ponytail and…" She pointed at the sack she'd handed to me. "Those clothes you had on at O'Hare… Dressed like that, she gave an interview with our version of the events. As corroboration of what happened, the press has been provided copies of the altered recordings showing the female agent's head Photoshopped on your body as she fires the second gun."

"The gun that missed."

"Well, we needed a hero, and it couldn't be you."

"Tony."

"Exactly. He certainly loves all the attention. He may never stop talking."

"What happens to the strippers?"

"In one week, they will have revision surgery with normal implants."

"Paid for by the government?"

She glanced at her watch and scooted back her chair.

"What about the terrorists in the Montblanc store at O'Hare?" I asked.

"He will be formally charged as a terrorist, and I am certain will be given a suitable prison term."

He? Didn't you forget someone?

"There were two terrorists in that store. One is an American whose first name is Jamie. I don't know his last name."

"There was only one suspect in the store, and he was Middle Eastern. He was arrested."

"You let Jamie go? Why did you do that?"

As she smiled, her lips compressed into a thin line. "No comment."

The answer is written on your smug face.

"You're going to follow him to see if he leads you to other terrorist cells in this area, right?" I asked.

Roth stood up.

"Hold it," I said. "What about me? Jamie knows I shot al-Turk and one of his buddies. I brought down their entire plot. He'll blame me for that."

She walked into our entrance hall. "You might consider keeping al-Turk's gun handy, in case you need it."

"You bitch!"

She smiled widely. "I've been called much worse, but there's a lesson here for you. I urge you to stick to writing your local column. The last time you did an investigative story, you ignored specific orders from an FBI agent not to enter the clinic, and you were blown up."

"And letting Jamie go is payback, right?"

Roth opened our front door. "It's a risk we will take to catch other terrorists. If unfortunate events occur because of it, we will consider that to be collateral damage."

She walked out without closing the door.

147

It was midnight. Carter was still at O'Hare, and Kerry was in bed. I'd let her stay up way past her normal bedtime. Even though she had a fun time at Molly's, I felt engulfed by guilt at having left her for several hours.

We'd cuddled up on the couch with Elmo and Ralph, and she had her favorite strawberry ice cream for a treat. I read two Dr. Seuss books to her, but she nodded off before I was halfway through the second one, and I put her to bed.

Checking my cell phone, I scanned my messages. Two were from Cas, one from Molly, and three from Linda. I would call them tomorrow, especially Linda. She knew about the C4 and the boob bombs. Since she was my lawyer, those discussions and discoveries had been privileged communications, and she couldn't tell anyone unless I gave her permission.

And I was never going to do that.

The front door opened, and Carter slumped in. He kissed me on the cheek. I stood up and hugged him for a long time.

He kissed me on the lips and looked into my eyes. "I'm glad you're safe."

My response caught in my throat, and I remained silent, as I held back the tears. I didn't want him to know why I was crying.

We sat down on the couch. "It's a compelling story, but unfortunately, the available details at this point are sketchy," he said, switching to his reporter voice.

"What did you find out?"

I didn't want to be caught in a lie.

"The only thing we have for certain is this is a case of industrial espionage. Apparently, a man attempted to force a scientist to give up his secret formula. The man was shot by a female FBI agent and a Chicago PD detective."

Roth did tell me the truth.

"Did they give you the name of the scientist?"

"It was Dr. Micah Mittelman."

"Which was why I was at the airport. Hannah called in a panic worried Micah might be harmed before he flew out of O'Hare to a medical meeting. She didn't know what to do and asked for my help."

"And you called Detective Infantino?"

"Carter, I appreciate how you feel about him, but he is the only policeman I know."

He stared at me.

I'm not lying about that.

"He and the female FBI agent were made available to us for a detailed interview. They showed security video footage of the shooting. The FBI agent looked like you and wore clothes and ASICS running shoes exactly like yours."

I pointed at my brown shorts, yellow golf shirt, and ASICS running shoes that had been handed to me by FBI Deputy Director Roth.

"Obviously, it can't be mine because I'm wearing them." I handed three sheets of paper to him. "Read this."

Before Carter had arrived home, I'd gone online and printed up the background story about the neighbors that the NSA had planted. It was good. All the details were included except one: what Micah did in his lab. His research was discussed in general terms, but no specifics were included.

Carter would have to believe it. Heck, I believed it, and I knew it was phony.

He went through the material.

"Then the story is factual, but it isn't an investigative piece," he said. "Do you want to write it?"

"I do. It's not the in-depth story I've been looking for, but it's way better than my monthly column."

I didn't add that writing it would help take my mind off of the two men I'd killed.

"What's my time frame?" I continued.

"It's local news. I need it for our morning print and online editions."

"May I have your notes from what you learned at O'Hare?"

He reached into his wrinkled blue blazer's pocket, pulled out his reporter's spiral notebook, and handed it to me.

"Sorry there isn't more."

"Whatever you have will save me a lot of time." I pictured Linda's face. "What does this assignment pay?"

He smiled. "I'll find money in the budget for this one."

"I better get to work."

He held up the fictitious research. "You already have."

Part 7

148

That night, I wrote my fake story. Doing an investigative piece might take weeks or even months to write, edit, rewrite, and re-edit. It was a local news story, and I could easily type it on Carter's work laptop in a couple of hours. I included the details from the airport shooting, excluding the true female shooter's identity and the specifics of Micah's research.

The article made the Thursday morning print and online editions. Several former newspaper friends called to congratulate me on my return to writing. That the story was bogus troubled the ethical portion of my brain, but there was no other option.

Friday was the deadline for my column for the *Lakeview Times*, and I was going to miss it because I didn't have a story for Gayle. I decided to resign, but I didn't want to do it by email.

I called her as I stretched before my morning run. "Gayle, I'm sorry, but I'm going to miss my deadline."

"It is totally understandable after what I read in yesterday's *Tribune*," Gayle said. "It was a terrific article. You're a wonderfully talented reporter."

Who you wanted to fire.

"I sincerely hope you'll find time to continue with your column. I might even find extra money in my minuscule budget to give you a raise. But please remember I was the one who helped revitalize your career by hiring you to write for the *Lakeview Times*."

Guilt trip. I called to resign.

"I promise I'll try and find a juicy story for you," I said.

"I am so happy. Don't forget me."

Crap. Now I would have to try to cobble together a story for her.

I hung up and began running. After going only two blocks, I was soaked in sweat from the muggy early morning heat. After three more blocks, I couldn't shake the feeling I was being watched.

Thanks to the FBI.

Because of them, Jamie was still out there. Was I safe from him? And what about the Hamlin Park Irregulars? Was he a danger to them?

Or was my brain reminding me about the man who blew me up in Arlington? Did he know about Micah's research? What if the bomber tried to destroy Micah's lab?

Too many unanswered questions.

Stopping my run, I reached into my backpack and pulled out al-Turk's handgun. I racked a bullet into the chamber. From now on, the Glock was going to be as much a part of my life as Elmo and Ralph were of Kerry's. I wouldn't tell Carter about the gun until I had to. I prayed I would never need to use it.

149

As I continued to run, I listened to Wilco's songs through my ear buds. Before I realized it, I ran past Hannah's home on West Henderson.

Stopping in the middle of the block, I jogged in place and watched the outside security cameras rotate back and forth. Other than Jamie, those cameras were the only remaining evidence al-Turk and his crew had been terrorists.

Whirling around, I intended to sprint away before the NSA or FBI agents monitoring the security cameras recorded my presence. I detected movement out of my peripheral vision, and before I could react, I crashed into a fellow runner, knocking him flat on his back.

"Oh my God, it's you," I said, when I saw who it was.

"Me?" he asked.

I wanted to tell him he was Lyndell's leprechaun, but he might take it as an insult, even though with his green eyes, red hair, and freckles, he did look like one.

He picked up his New York Yankee baseball cap and black horn rim glasses, both of which had been knocked off, and put them back on.

"Are you hurt?" I asked.

"I'm okay. How about you?"

"I'm fine." I reached down toward him. "Let me help you up."

The man waved my hand away. "No need." Rolling to his knees, he stood up.

I held out my hand. "Tina Thomas."

"David John." He had a firm grip, but not overly aggressive. His voice was soft without a trace of an Irish accent.

"Maybe we'll see each other again," I said, thinking about Gayle and my promise to her.

"Looking forward to it." He ran toward Belmont.

Once I began running again, my brain shifted to reporter mode. When I found time, I would do an online background analysis on David John, and if I discovered facts which were remotely interesting, I would ask him for an interview.

I shivered as I ran.

Someone is watching me.

Look for Book 2 in the *Hamlin Park Irregulars* series

— *Déjà Boom!* —

and learn the answers to Tina's questions.

And this is what started it all.

Lonely Stay-at-Home Mothers Are Now Wooing Each Other

By CHRISTINA DUFF

Special to *The Wall Street Journal,* Nov. 17, 2000

(Reprinted with permission from the author.)

CHICAGO -- Lipstick on and baby in tow, Sarah Jane Marshall cruises the streets here trying to pick somebody up.

She plants herself and her 11-month-old, Noah, at a table in a bagel shop known for attracting good prospects. "I feel like such a loser," says Ms. Marshall, 35 years old, smoothing her hair and eyeing the door.

A single mother? Actually, Ms. Marshall has been married for four years. But she is one of today's more overlooked lonely hearts. Mothers who leave careers to stay home with new babies are trying to do what men have attempted for ages: Meet, seduce, date, then settle into a lasting relationship with a desirable woman. "There has to be someone out there for me," says Ms. Marshall, a former technology-group manager, gazing longingly at two mothers sharing a Barry bagel.

With so many books and Internet sites now devoted to caring for newborns, professional mothers-to-be expect few surprises. They buy the baby backpack and the designer diaper bag. They've read up on infant sleep patterns and the advantages of breast-feeding. Yet rarely do they anticipate loneliness. Their own mothers didn't prepare them. Back then, plenty of women were having kids at the same young age; most hadn't already spent time in the work force. But many of today's at-home mothers, having worked for a while, are used to having colleagues around for gossip or lunch -- and they miss that at home. Without bosses to provide the atta-girls they learned to crave, they look to other women. The question is, how to find them?

Organized mothers' groups work something like singles clubs. At a 20-member group in Fort Collins, Colo., Nancy Ebby says she began to "panic when the whole room started hooking up." Two mothers were arranging lunch. Two more made plans to see a mall Santa Claus. "It hurts," says Ms. Ebby, 33, who left a career as a physician's assistant to care for her daughter. But she vows -- sometime -- to invite over one mother who lives nearby. "I don't want to be too forward," she says.

Other groups provide more cover, maintaining that they are really for the babies, not the mothers. At Chicago's Adams Playground, a line forms at 7 a.m. to sign up for under-age-two classes that feature art projects and tumbling. "It's worse than getting concert tickets," says Maureen Belling, the playground supervisor.

Never mind that the babies can barely walk. Indeed, Marc Weissbluth, a pediatrician and clinical-pediatrics professor at Northwestern University Medical School, says that until the child is closer to two years, organized preschool activities have "no direct benefit either in terms of social development or instructional education." For the mother, however, they can keep her from being "worried, anxious or isolated," he says.

And so what if a potential mate doesn't cook or like the same movies. Moms on the make can't be bothered about "hobbies or shared interests," says Vicki Iovine, mother of four and author of *The Girlfriends' Guide to Surviving the First Year of Motherhood.* "That woman who picks up a Kleenex when your daughter's nose is running? You love her. You don't care if she's a Martian."

Choosing the pick-up joint isn't hard. There's the park, the zoo, the mall. It's the execution that's tricky. Here are several rules Dr. Spock doesn't divulge. One, flatter the mother, but really pile it on her baby. Two, never walk away without a phone number. Three, if you chat someone up, make sure you could have a future together.

Gosia Dolinski, a nanny in northwest Chicago, is a daily tease. Pushing 13-month-old charge Sam Stevens around a Whole Foods store, the fashionable brunette -- who looks a lot like Sam --

first gets some stares from a mother across the vegetables. Then some smiles. The mother giggles when Sam grabs a green pepper.

Ms. Dolinski shoots her down: "His mother says he'll eat anything." (Read: I'm the nanny.) The mother nods, wilts, then moves on to dairy.

Mothers are "always friendly, until they hear I'm a nanny," says Ms. Dolinski, 31. She tries to break it to them "before they get too interested. It's sad."

But try busting into the world of women-chasing-women -- as a father. David Ginsburg, a former high-school teacher with a one-year-old, Victor, is the only stay-at-home father he knows. At Chicago's Hamlin Park, the mothers sing to and flirt with each other's babies in falsetto. Mr. Ginsburg, after 40 years of acting only one way around women -- manly -- simply can't join in. "I'm so inhibited at the swings," he says.

Yet even he finds cause for hope. One day at the park, he spots the ideal companion. Young. Attractive. Great conversation about nap times. But he doesn't get her number. Each day, at his wife's urging, he looks for her. She doesn't come. Finally, she's there -- talking to other mothers. Mr. Ginsburg keeps on walking. "I'm not worthy of getting involved with," he tells himself. "She's got other people." He rounds the corner, stops, and says, "D--- it! Be a good role model to Victor!" He turns back.

She spots him and calls to him -- by name. They talk a bit. But still, he doesn't get her number. That requires his wife,

Corkyne, an accounting manager, on a later park visit: "I need your phone number for my husband," Ms. Ginsburg tells her.

"It's more acceptable for me to be on the make than David," Ms. Ginsburg says.

Try telling that to Katie Weissler. Ms. Weissler, 32, plunked down $196 for 14 weeks of Sing 'n Dance classes for her daughter, Emma -- not because the six-month-old can carry a tune, but because Ms. Weissler's friends either work or live far away, and she needs to hook up.

The former emergency-room nurse sits with Emma in a circle of mothers on their first day. With a grin, she approaches the woman next to her -- by talking to her kid.

"Look how strong you are!" Ms. Weissler says, eyes wide. She is surrounded by other couples. Rachel and Barb, whose babies are a week apart, met in prenatal class. Susan and Liz live in the same neighborhood.

Two more women, a physician and a stockbroker, hit it off and talk over the music. Ms. Weissler continues her one-way conversation with the baby to her left: "That's a good toy, your toes." No reaction from the mom.

"It's hard to find someone to have a permanent relationship with," Ms. Weissler says. Across the circle, Melissa Kane, age 30, is just beginning to realize this. She spends most of the class rocking a fussy Anna. After quitting her public-relations job, "I'm just starting to branch out," Ms. Kane says.

After class, in the snack room, Ms. Weissler and Ms. Kane discover they live near one another. "We should get together sometime," Ms. Kane says. Two weeks later, the two plop down next to each other in the circle, talking about travel plans.

But they still haven't taken it to the next stage: meeting outside of class. Ms. Weissler had better hustle; Ms. Kane is already planning lunch with a couple of women from one of Anna's other classes. ~

Acknowledgements

One of the several published authors who read this first book of the Hamlin Park Irregulars series was kind enough to email me: writing a novel is HARD! Man, she nailed it. Thanks to Shannon Baker for this and the suggestions.

Nancy Taylor Rosenberg began like I did, with no formal training, only a burning desire to tell a story. And because of her enormous talent, she went on to being a *New York Times* best-selling author. Without her encouragement and advice, I probably wouldn't have continued writing.

The unrelated Taylor girls: S.J. and Katherine. Both of you have advanced literary degrees, and I was terrified when you read this book. Your comments and suggestions were enormously helpful, and you never laughed at my effort.

And finally, Rich Krevolin. He has been everything for me in writing this book, and I couldn't have finished it without him.

Now, quickly, on to friends and patients who have read the book. TNTC — too numerous to count — thanks to all of you.

And, family. Thanks to: Jeffrey Taylor; James E. Duff; Julia Morrison; Brittany Haynie; and Luke Haynie.

A special shout out to Christina Duff Taylor. Thanks for being "Tina" in the book. Without you, there is no book.

And to the three women in my life who have contributed more than they will ever know: Ann, Suzy, and Mindy.

And to Nancy Cohen who corrected the grammar in this book: you are the best. But I gotta tell you, I hate all the freaking commas!

Let me know what you think about this book. Contact me at www.HamlinParkIrregulars.com.

The next book, *Déjà Boom!*, continues with the Hannah and Micah story, but there is that mysterious leprechaun guy too. After that, I jump into medical issues in the next two novels. Then, a little change to a love story/thriller involving baseball and medicine. And in the last one, check out the last name on the wall: Air Force 2nd Lt. Richard Van De Geer. It's my first venture into a piece of history of the Vietnam War researched by the Hamlin Park Irregulars.

And finally… Here's a free sneak peek at the first two chapters of *Déjà Boom!*, the next book in the Hamlin Park Irregulars series:

Déjà Boom!

1

"When were you going to tell me?" I asked.

I was furious, and I'd held my anger in as long as I could.

My husband, Carter Thomas, had consumed way more than his share of wine at the Saturday night dinner party we'd just left, so I drove our mommy van home. We had traveled one block before I'd lost it.

"Tell you what?" Carter asked.

"About the bombing of an abortion clinic in our freaking neighborhood!"

"It was not in our, as you call it, 'freaking neighborhood.' "

That stopped me. "It wasn't?"

"No, it wasn't."

Something's not right.

"Then why were you and Jason discussing it?"

Carter is an assistant managing editor for local news at the *Chicago Tribune*. Jason Buss is a reporter under Carter's command. We had been at their home for dinner.

"It's late, and I'm tired. We can talk about this in the morning."

I slammed on the brakes. "Where was the clinic located?"

Cars behind us began honking, but I wasn't moving until he told me what I wanted to know.

"In Deerfield."

"Deerfield? You didn't think I would be interested in hearing about a bombing..." I took a deep breath, "...thirty minutes from our front door?"

"Tina, please, the people stuck behind us aren't part of this."

The car horns blared, but I didn't care. "Do the police know who did it?"

He shook his head.

"Was it the same M.O.?"

"Yes, it was. The bomb was in the men's bathroom."

I powered down the driver's window and threw up.

Déjà Boom!

2

Carter and I live with our two-year old daughter Kerry in West Lakeview, an upscale North Chicago neighborhood. Our home is a three-story, all floors above the ground home at 1702 West Melrose. Our two-car, detached garage faces the cross street, North Paulina.

When I pulled into the garage, I was still pissed off. I didn't speak to Carter until I'd put Kerry down for the night and he'd returned from walking the babysitter to her home across the street.

We were in bed and the lights were out.

"You should have told me," I said.

"I knew how you would react, and I didn't want to ruin a perfectly enjoyable evening with our friends."

"So, now you can read my mind? Couldn't you at least have had the common decency to let me voice my own opinion without doing it for me?"

"But you still would have acted the same way."

"Maybe, maybe not."

He took me into his arms. I could smell the faint odor of the Tom Ford black orchid cologne I'd given him for his birthday.

"I'm afraid you'll want to pursue this story," he whispered. "I love you so much. I can't stand the thought of you being involved with a bombing again."

Bomb!

In the darkness of our bedroom, that word thrust me back into the hallway of the Arlington clinic. I knew what was coming next: a PTSD attack.

First, there would be a blinding flash of light behind my eyes, followed by the sound of an explosion and the smell of broken medical bottles, cleaning solvents, and burned hair and skin.

And then, a pounding headache.

I took in a deep breath to center myself and let the headache pass. It was over in less than a minute.

"Okay, I might have overreacted a little," I said. "Honestly, I'm petrified that this is the same guy who blew me up."

"And if it is? That fear should be enough to convince you not to work on this."

"Carter, that monster almost killed me. I will never forget that."

"I understand, but why not let another reporter assume the risk?"

"It's my story. That will never happen."

"Tina, please. It's too dangerous."

The "D" word, again.

My husband is consistent when we have arguments like this. My response is always the same.

"I was the one who was blown up. This will be my decision and my decision alone."

"Even if I totally disagree?"

I desperately wanted to snuggle into his arms. I needed the man I love to hold me and help me forget that terrible night five years ago when I almost died.

"This discussion is over," I said. "Goodnight."

I rolled away from him.

No one is going to finish that story but me.

Made in the USA
Monee, IL
10 March 2022

92565068R00243